PENNY SAVING

PENNY SAVING

Susan Moody

MICHAEL JOSEPH

London

For Benedick

MICHAEL JOSEPH LTD

Published by the Penguin Group
27 Wrights Lane, London W8 5TZ, England
Viking Penguin Inc., 375 Hudson Street, New York, New York 10014, USA
Penguin Books Australia Ltd, Ringwood, Victoria, Australia
Penguin Books Canada Ltd, 2801 John Street, Markham, Ontario, Canada L3R 1B4
Penguin Books (NZ) Ltd, 182–190 Wairau Road, Auckland 10, New Zealand

Penguin Books Ltd, Registered Offices: Harmondsworth, Middlesex, England

First published in Great Britain 1990

Set in Monophoto 10/12 pt Sabon
Filmset, printed and bound in Great Britain by
Butler & Tanner Ltd, Frome, Somerset

A CIP catalogue record for this book is available from the British Library

ISBN 0 7181 3385 4

The quotation on page 67 from 'This be the Verse' from *High Windows* by Philip Larkin
is reproduced by kind permission of Faber and Faber Ltd and Farrar, Straus and Giroux,
Inc.

Spring, the sweet spring. Then blooms each thing. Then, according to the poet, maids dance in a ring. Not that there was a lot of that sort of thing going on in Chelsea. Probably couldn't find enough maids.

Penny Wanawake closed the doors out into the garden and poured herself a double bourbon. Phew. If it came to a choice between dancing maids and courting frogs, she'd have taken the former any time. At least they'd have packed up and gone home at the end of the Military Two-Step or whatever. Frogs not only stuck around, they multiplied. It wouldn't have been so bad if they'd gone forth and done it. This lot stayed home. And when a frog decided to multiply, everyone knew it. Not an inhibition among the lot. Tiny screams of ecstasy made the evenings hideous. Grunts of lust perpetually split the night. Every night.

Barnaby's fault. Last winter he'd gone Green as Fairy Liquid and decided to rehabilitate the lily pond which lurked under a *Ficus* in the garden. A pair of designer wellies later, the garden was knee-high in gag-making mud and the pond was down to its concrete skin. After that, he'd filled it up again. Not just with water and plants but with newts and goldfish. Every frog in the district had made a beeline for the place. Now it was a kind of amphibian Blackpool. There was all-night carousing. Drunken choruses. Aristophanes would have loved it.

She switched on some music. A Beethoven string quartet began to shoulder its way round the high, extravagantly corniced room. Complex music that eased a complex life. Also drowned out the batrachians singing each to each. She sipped her drink, feeling her guts untangle. Music and bourbon: it was a helluva combination to relax with. And boy, did she need to relax. Since hitting her twenty-seventh birthday, she seemed to have shed a skin or two. Three, even. The top layer might still be black, but inside she was growing increasingly yellow. The world outside was a scary place, full of gut-twisting wretchedness, and her camera didn't miss a trick. She'd spent the afternoon developing film. She'd earned the booze.

With Barnaby away, she was alone. Sometimes alone was what a person wanted to be. *Needed* to be. Being alone gave a person time to get on with a person's own life, her singular as opposed to half-of-a-couple life. Not that they were a couple in the legal sense. Marital status: strictly unmarried. Which was the way she liked it. And intended to keep it. She stretched. Being alone also gave her time to attend to some of the zillion details connected with her part in the BlackAid Gala which was being held at Wembley next month. It'd started out with her being asked to set up an exhibition of photographs in the entrance foyer. It had gone on to include duties ranging from the secretarial to the entrepreneurial with a certain amount of devil's advocacy in between. Some of the organisers had the wildest notions.

When the doorbell rang, she looked at her watch. Whaaat? Midnight plus ten? Not exactly normal visiting hours. For a moment or two she debated remaining where she was. You could bet the rent that a post-midnight visit didn't mean someone wanting to socialise. Whoever the caller was, it spelled trouble. With a capital T. Question was: did she want trouble?

No one in their right mind would answer yes.

She got up. Still holding her glass she walked barefoot into the hall. She squinted through the spyhole. A man stood outside, staring straight into her eye. He smiled slightly, as though he knew she was watching him. He puckered his lips up into a silent kiss. There was a top hat on his head and a red-lined opera cloak about his shoulders.

She opened the door. 'Let me guess,' she said. 'You're the Phantom of the Opera.'

'Wrong.'

'Count Dracula?'

'Two down and one to go.' He stepped into the house, still smiling. There was a scar high on his left cheek. As he walked down the hall, Penny moved backwards before him towards the drawing-room.

'In that case, you must be Ludovic Fairfax,' she said.

'Right.'

'I thought that kind of rig' – Penny waved a hand that was as close to quizzical as a hand could get at the white tie and tails her visitor was wearing – 'went out in the last desperate days before the war. At least, for the ordinary man.'

'You obviously don't move in the right circles. Besides, you ought to know that I'm a far from ordinary man.' He opened his arms. 'Come here, Penny. I feel like kissing something and it's you or the hat-stand.'

'Ludo, it's been *years*.'

'Five, actually. I counted them on the way here. You taste of extremely good bourbon.'

'Have some, then you will too.'

He followed her into the drawing-room. She poured him a glass and held it while he removed his cloak and the top half of his tails. He wore braces with a tapestry pattern. A monocle on a black silk ribbon lolled against his stiff shirtfront. 'Does the outfit disappear at midnight?' she asked.

'Not unless I lose my glass slippers.'

'Isn't it uncomfortable, dressed like that?'

'It's worth it.'

Penny sprawled back against the sofa cushions. 'How?'

'The young lady on your arm never fails to be impressed by tails.'

'Hey, Ludo, I got news for you. She didn't fall for it.'

'How do you mean?'

'Otherwise you wouldn't be here at' – Penny checked her watch again – 'quarter after midnight. Alone.'

Ludo took his glass over to the french windows leading into the garden. He stood here, looking out. 'She was impressed, all right,' he said, without turning round. 'But not with me. It's the story of my life.'

'How is your life, anyway?' said Penny.

Ludo turned. He was no longer smiling. Round the stem of the glass his fingers were tense. 'Not the way I want it to be.'

'And you, Ludo. How are you?'

'A different man from the one who escorted you to May Balls,' he said. 'Do you remember?'

'I loved to dance, but oh, your feet,' said Penny. She sat up straight, pressing her knees together. 'I see you sometimes in gossip columns. Not that I often read the kind of papers that write about your kind of person.'

Ludo stretched his neck behind the white bow-tie. 'What kind is that?' He inspected his glass as though he'd just caught sight of Neptune taming a seahorse in it.

Uh-oh. Penny waited. Something was bothering Ludo Fairfax and, unless she could stop him, he was about to tell her why. For some reason she didn't want him to do that. Didn't want to get involved. The last couple of months had been gruelling. There'd been three harrowing weeks in the Sudan, three weeks filled with the sounds of death: the moans, the tears, the rasping drag of breath and the sudden ceasing silences. By-passing the agencies, she'd travelled across country, dodging roving bands of mercenaries and guerrillas, to distribute the supplies she'd brought with her from London: medicines, blankets, sacks of beans and rice, gasolene to power the jeeps. And watching men with nothing left but dignity wrap their families in grey rags and scratch them into the dry ungiving earth, she felt hopeless, cast-down, despairing. You could save ten lives, twenty, a hundred, even. But thousands died for every one saved. It was the death of children she couldn't handle.

The problems of the super-rich seemed irrelevant. 'You're still winning Oscars for the Bertie Wooster impression,' she said, éclair-light.

'I am?'

'Right. Filthy rich golden-spoon playboy, heir to a vast pile in Cornwall or somewhere, a real let-them-eat-caker, without a thought for the downtrodden masses.'

He snapped his upper and lower jaws together. Some muscle bulged under his ear. 'What the hell do the downtrodden masses care about me? If any such creatures still exist.'

'They do, believe me.'

'I don't think I do. I see them all trooping off on their holidays to Benidorm or Morocco, stuffing their supermarket trolleys full of food, crowding the High Streets on Saturdays ... it's the downtrodden masses who've made shopping into a leisure activity. Spend, spend, spend.' He made a sound of disgust. 'Sod the lot of them.'

'Hey, Ludo. Lighten up, will you.' Penny was alarmed. In his Cambridge days, Ludo had aimed at suavity and scored a bull's-eye. He was way off target now.

And realised it.

'Sorry,' he said. 'It's just, I find it so ironic. I grew up without ever giving a second's thought to money. Now it's all I ever think about. Money. How to get it. How to keep it. What I'd be prepared to do for it. Hating those who seem to have more of the damn stuff than I have.' His face had darkened with blood and anger. 'I never realised how many things you can't do when you haven't got it.'

'Who said you could never be too rich or too thin?' You had to say something when one of your childhood friends acted like he was about to burst a vein. Penny thought about adding a tension-easing laugh and decided against it.

'Somebody very rich and very thin,' Ludovic said. 'And Wrestebury's in Norfolk, darling. Not Cornwall.' He'd forced himself into a lighter tone of voice. 'Besides which, the pile is Amabel's, not mine. At least, not yet. When it is, I suppose I'll be forced to do the usual Stately Home stuff – helicopter pads, or haute B and B in the west wing. But while she's still alive . . .' He paused. 'It's her home, after all.'

'Of course.'

Ludovic perched on the edge of one of the big chesterfield sofas. 'You've no idea – at least, *you* probably have, but most people haven't – how difficult it is to keep things going. We were caught for nearly seven million pounds in death duties when Father died so soon after Grandfather. And we found he'd made some frightful investments, lost a packet. It took absolutely every penny we could scrape together to hang on to the place. Just about all the pictures went.'

'Not the Rembrandt,' said Penny. It had always been a particular favourite of hers.

'Not yet. But it's only a matter of time. It's the upkeep that's the killer.'

'What about going commercial?'

His laugh was unpleasant. 'Of course we've thought about it. We seem to talk about nothing else. But Amabel would hate it so much. And as I said, it's where we *live*. We don't *want* strangers with gold chains round their necks or crimplene cardigans wandering round gawping at our lavatory seats and fingering the curtains in the bedrooms.'

'Now, now,' Penny said. 'Do you mean you wouldn't mind so much if they wore hand-made brogues and Savile Row suits?'

'One is trying to preserve a little bit of the national heritage,' Ludo said. 'It sounds pompous, but it's the truth. I didn't opt for the responsibility: it was thrust on me by birth. Given that, I see it as my duty to do my best to pass it on intact to the next generation.'

'One way is to open the doors to the hordes.'

'I have, finally. On a strictly temporary basis. It was the only way we could pay off some of the more pressing bills, actually.'

'What kind of horde did you let in?'

'Some kind of language school.' He looked disgusted. 'One of those places that offer intensive teaching of English to rich foreigners is taking the place for two months this summer.'

'Do I congratulate you or order a wreath?'

'The wreath would be more appropriate. Frankly, I didn't think it was an offer we could refuse. They're paying an enormous rent. The fact is, between us Amabel and I aren't bringing in enough money to keep things going. Farming the estate works only to a limited degree. And things like dry rot in the attic or a bill for partial replumbing can bring you out in a muck sweat.'

'What about English Heritage?'

'They're swamped with people like us.'

'This language school sounds like economic sense. You've got an asset. They're prepared to pay for it. The two of you are doing business. What's wrong with that?'

'Nothing,' Ludo said. There was a touch of the catacombs about his voice. 'But even with what they're paying us, it's not enough to keep the place going. There's still the winter to get through. Burst pipes. Frost damage. God. I never dreamed when I was at Cambridge that this was what it would all come to. Worrying about death-watch beetle.'

'And I suppose you can't sell the place.'

'Not even if we wanted to.' His mouth tightened at one corner. 'What I've done instead is sell myself.'

Penny swallowed the bourbon she had been holding in her mouth. 'My God, Ludo. Who bought you?'

'The Bank of England.'

'What for? A mess of pottage? Twenty-nine pieces of silver?'

'Rather more than that, Pen. I did get a First.'

'In that case, they haven't stuck you behind a grille, cashing cheques. So what *are* you doing?'

'Basically, I'm working as an investigator, looking into suspected cases of large-scale fraud. There's an awful lot of it about, especially now that computers are so widespread.' He looked away from her in a manner that made her suspect that for some reason he was being fairly economical with the truth. Why would he want to do that?

She made her eyes go big. 'Kind of a latter-day Peter Wimsey, do you mean?'

He inserted his monocle and lifted insouciant eyebrows. 'More like Sir Percy Blakeney.'

'You're kidding.'

'I'm not.'

No. He wasn't. Kidding had never been part of his game-plan. She had forgotten how heavy his habitual *gravitas* weighed. Or was it that it hadn't, last time they met? Not this heavy. Looking at him now, she saw how the old man he would be hovered behind his thirty-year-old face.

'Scion of nobility, pure-hearted, high-minded, setting out alone to pit himself against the evil forces of Mammon,' she said. She tried for carefree. Didn't altogether make it. Carefree didn't come easy when something was gnawing your vitals. Call it premonition. Call it foreboding.

'*Handsome* scion,' Ludo said.

'It's the stuff celluloid dreams are made of.'

'Or nightmares.' Ludo turned down the corners of his mouth.

She stretched out on the sofa again. Carefully. P. Wanawake in a white halterneck – in *any* colour halterneck – was a sight calculated to have the average man's libido sitting up and begging to be noticed. And as Ludo had pointed out, he was not an average man. She recalled a night-time session or two in a punt, that had set half the ducks in Cambridgeshire quacking indignantly in their sleep. Why had he never married? There'd been some mention of it, surely, in one of the gossips.

'Ludo,' she said. 'It's really neat of you to drop by like this, fill me in on your CV, chat about things. Why don't you get down to the nitty?'

'All right.' Ludovic set his glass down and stood up. 'It's very simple. Your papa is hosting a dinner party next week, down at Hurley, before old Charlesworth's ball, right?'

'Right.'

'I want an invitation.' Ludo picked the Jack Daniels bottle up by the neck and refilled both glasses.

'Simple as that?'

'Yes.'

'Can I ask why?'

'You can ask.'

'I have to have a reason before I'm gonna put myself out.'

'Do you?'

'Bet your sweet ass.'

'I suppose you do.' He turned again to the open windows and

gazed into the garden. He thought about it. He said: 'For your ears only: there's a man on the guest list I want to see.'

'Called?'

'Zachary Osman.'

'See, meaning talk to?'

'See, meaning . . .' he lifted shoulders, waved hands from side to side '. . . observe. Meet. Whatever.'

'I wasn't planning to be there myself.'

'Then plan.'

'Taking you as my escort? People might talk.'

'Since when did that bother you?' He stood up, brisk, pre-occupied with whatever it was that was eating him. 'I'll leave the details to you, Pen. I have infinite faith in your capacity to make things happen.'

'And if I get you asked to this dinner party, that's all there is to it?'

'Promise.'

'No sweat. No strings. No comebacks.'

'Without prejudice of any kind, Pen.'

'Just the simple invite. Nothing more.'

'I swear it.'

The dining-room at Hurley Court had last been redecorated somewhere around 1870. The incumbent Hurley had got out of slavery just in time and used the fortune he'd made to make several more. This rococo riot of plaster and gilt was one of the results of a visit he'd made to the Great Exhibition in Paris. The other was a severe case of gonorrhoea. Since he was seventy-seven at the time, this had been seen as an occasion for rejoicing rather than lamentation. In among the plaster there was a lot of mirror.

Penny sat halfway down the long table. She could see herself reflected in the mildewed glass on the opposite wall. White jersey silk did a lot for a girl. Especially when Bruce Oldfield had a hand in it. Pearls chokered her neck. Three rows of them, perfectly matched, united by a diamond clasp. At the head of the table sat her mother. Lady Helena was in green silk and the Hurley emeralds. Stunning. When I'm fifty, Penny thought – if ever – I hope I'll look as good.

It was an exceptionally fine evening. All the windows facing the gardens were open, letting in the sweet scent of lilac. Somewhere in there was the bitterness of early geraniums, too. Smell-wise, Penny always went for stimulating rather than for cloying. The air was still and sultry so that the candles set in their silver holders all down the mahogany shine of the table scarcely blinked. Fresh flowers smirked pinkly between the glass and cutlery. Lovely. You grew up in a place, you tended to take it for granted. Coming back, she now saw how lucky she had been, how ordered this way of life was, how carefully it preserved a standard and a tradition.

She knew most of the forty guests. Zachary Osman and his American wife were among the handful she didn't. Introduced by her father, Osman had bent over her hand. At five foot four, give or take a millimetre, her hand was about all he could manage to bend over. Apart from her knee-cap. She told herself that he was merely being polite. Definitely not estimating the carat of her gold ring or anything like that. So why did she feel that for two pins he'd have whipped it off her finger and bitten it? He was small and round, his scalp bare and mottled. He had gold-rimmed glasses and a pair of exuberant dimples. Every now and then he giggled endearingly.

The week before, over what was left in the bottle of bourbon, Ludo had filled her in on him. Origins obscure but with an eastern cast. Slum landlordism. Property-developing. Diversification into pharmaceutical supplies and travel agencies. Finally, in middle age, the slow march towards acceptance and respectability via a country house, a pretty wife, a series of flamboyantly philanthropic gestures, a string of thoroughbreds and a soon-to-be child.

For the pretty wife – known to millions as Chrissie Cooke – was massively pregnant. Also instantly recognisable. And somewhat older than she appeared on screen. Penny rarely watched TV and *never* watched game-shows, but it seemed as though whenever she switched on, there was Chrissie, going into her Bo Peep act, all breathless little-girl voice and cascading red hair. Most of the time she behaved like a dog with fleas, jiggling and wriggling and throwing her hands up with irritatingly cutesy-poo excitement whenever she scored a point. Nothing made a person reach faster for the OFF button.

Close to, it was obvious that Bo Peep had decided she was never going to find her sheep and had settled for the wolf instead. She held her husband's arm and gasped a lot. Every now and then she opened her eyes to the size of manhole covers, clutched her stomach and said, 'Ooh, Junior, be quiet, can't you?' You had to be made of stern stuff not to ask when Junior was due. Penny was. Most other people weren't. Junior turned out to be due like, would you believe, about five minutes ago?

Ludo asked if she was going to look after the baby herself.

'Of *course*,' she said. 'Though obviously we'll have to have a nanny to help out.'

'Got anyone lined up yet?' said Ludo.

'Not yet.'

'Try the R. H. Domestic Agency,' Penny said quickly, before anyone else could get in. Might as well give Antonia Ivory a plug, she thought.

'Where's that?' Ludo asked her.

'In the basement of my house. One of my sitting tenants runs it and I'm telling you, it's supposed to be the tops.'

'Oh yes,' gasped Chrissie. 'I'd heard of it. Junior, take it *easy*.' She saucered her eyes at Ludo. 'Obviously I'm not too keen on the idea of some other woman taking over the care of my child, but Zachary likes me to be there for him.'

'You mean instead of being there for some other man?' Penny said. She was really interested in the answer.

'Penelope,' her mother said sharply. 'There's someone over here I'd like you to meet.'

Penny held her wine glass to the table with two fingers on the foot and watched the wine level rise as her mother's temporary butler refilled it. Montrachet 1972. One of her father's choicer white burgundies. Did he just feel like drinking something really good, or was there someone here he wished to impress?

She looked up and down the table. What did it represent, this dinner-jacketed, bejewelled company? All that was best of England? A heartening fusion of new money and old? Privilege based on class and wealth? Or none of the above? There were farming neighbours, a sprinkling of diplomats, some millionaires, several people prominent in the world of the arts. Some, like her mother, Lady Helena Hurley, had been members of the English aristocracy for over six hundred years. Others, like Zachary Osman, were self-made men. The flamboyant man with the wolfish smile had been recently appointed to the London Embassy of one of the Central American countries. The dessicated lady with the mad eyes and grubby earrings was a novelist famous for the intricacies of her plots. The small man with the shock of white hair was one of the new breed of petit-pointing bishops.

10

She told herself she was being too analytical. You couldn't generalise from such a small sampling. Anyway, why look for trends in a dinner party? Instead, she looked for Ludo. He was further up the table, being charming. Penny had forgotten just how Anglo-Saxonly good-looking he was. Blondish hair, attractively thick. Blue eyes, appropriately sincere. Tall, but not too thin. One thing Penny couldn't abide was a scrawn. He gave an impression of bone-and-muscle hardness which had not been there in his Cambridge days. His eyes never strayed towards Osman, who was seated opposite him.

Why had he needed to observe Osman at such close quarters? He'd said that the Bank suspected Osman of large-scale financial fraud. Of money-laundering. Of transferring vast sums through his travel agencies, which specialised in holidays in the East. A hundred million pounds per annum, *minimum*, Ludo had said. It had to be stopped. The leaks plugged. The task of plugging and stopping had been entrusted to him.

Penny turned to the man on her left. A well-known travel-writer. A man whose *Boys' Own* adventures, serialised in the Sunday papers, left every couch potato in the western hemisphere yawning with lazy excitement. Man-eating orchids. Rabid yaks. Frost-bitten balls. You name it, this guy had been there. He started to tell her about the dismal failure of his attempts to find sponsorship for his latest excursion. Tracing the footsteps of Nanook of the North or Eskimo Nell. Something like that.

'Trouble is, there's no pioneering spirit left,' he said. 'The masses are far too busy these days stuffing themselves with junk food and gawping at the box. Getting to grips with elementals, pitting oneself against the worst that Nature can contrive, finding the survivor instinct that's buried in every man beneath the veneer of effete civilisation – nobody's interested any more.'

There it was again. 'The masses.' A word which meant nothing more than a collection of individuals. 'Surely pioneering spirit in the masses is the last thing you want,' Penny said.

He squinted at her. One of his eyes seemed to be habitually closed. Possibly against sudden attack. 'How do you mean?'

'Otherwise they'd all want to come along on the trip, wouldn't they?'

'Would they?'

'Stands to reason. Trouble with the call of the wild, it only works as long as no one else answers it, right?'

11

'Well, obviously one doesn't want to turn the untamed quarters of the globe into Piccadilly Circus . . .'

'I mean, the hell with pioneering spirit. Basically all you want from the masses is their money, isn't it?' She gave him the fish-eye.

He stared at her. 'Put like that, I suppose you're . . .'

'But when it gets right down to it, why *should* anyone be interested? Why should they fork out so that you can go on having a whale of a time at their expense, and then come home and make a fortune out of books and television appearances and lecture circuits?'

He shrugged self-deprecatingly. 'Some of us get out there. Others just read about it. It all boils down to a man having to do what a man has to do.'

'Why does a man have to expect that others will pay for his fun?'

He was about to make a reply that Penny would have hated, when there was a girlish scream. A commotion was taking place around Chrissie Cooke Osman. She had risen to her feet and was running her hands through her thick red hair. When everyone was watching, she clutched her belly and shrieked: 'Heavens to Betsey! My waters have just broken.'

How to break up a dinner party in one easy move.

2

That was then. This was now. It had been one of those long summer days that only happen in England. Since dawn, the garden had swarmed with leafy heat. Innumerable bees had murmured. A dove or two had moaned. She had deadheaded a rose. Noticed greenfly. Sprayed. P. Wanawake in domestic mode. In neighbouring gardens, people surrounded by jugs of lemonade and children had complained comfortably about the temperature or the size of the Sunday papers.

Although it was now dark, the heat had scarcely diminished. The garden chairs had been stowed away in the clematis-covered shed. Further down the street, someone had been cutting their lawn: the scent of new-mown hay still hung like summer essence in the warm air.

In the big drawing-room, 126 pounds of Penny Wanawake lay gasping on the sofa. 128 pounds, to be exact. More or less inside a white one-piece bathing suit. Four days ago, her mother had sent several pounds of strawberries up from Hurley Court, and any fool knew that if you didn't eat strawberries immediately they'd rot. Any fool also knew that the only way to enjoy them was with sugar and cream. Neither of which came top of anyone's diet sheet.

Oh man, was it hot. There was sweat along Penny's hairline, and more under her arms. Honeysuckle perfume curtained the open french windows in a cloud of almost graspable solidity. She sipped from a glass of chilled champagne. On the stereo, Kris Kristofferson was begging her to help him make it through the night. Summertime and the living was easy.

The darkness outside the open windows was filled with stars. They simmered in the sky, their size and brightness intensified by the heat. The plump libidinous burps of frogs came from the pond. In one of the neighbouring houses, someone softly played a Viennese waltz.

She tugged the edges of her swimsuit down as far as they

would go. It wasn't very far. The phone rang.

She picked up the receiver.

'Yo,' she said.

'How are the frogs?' It was Barnaby.

'I want to tell you those darn things are a big disappointment,' Penny said.

'Why?'

'I spent the entire afternoon kissing them and all I got was sore lips.'

'No handsome princes?'

'Only handsome prince I want's on the phone right now, sugar-baby.'

'Do you miss me?'

'And how.'

'Do I miss you?'

'So it hurts.'

'Thought so.'

'Hurry home,' Penny said softly. 'I'll kiss it better.'

'I don't suppose it'll turn into a handsome prince.'

'As good as.'

Hanging up, she poured more champagne. Barnaby's best. Salon de Mesnil. You need an orgy once in a while. And Barnaby wouldn't mind. He never minded anything she did. Hadn't, since the first time they met. That'd been in Paris. She'd had a stick of bread under her arm, fresh from the *boulangerie* down the road from her *apartement*. He was examining the contents of her jewel-case. When he said he was from the gas company, she laughed. 'This place is all-electric,' she'd told him. He laughed too, before making a dive for the window. She saw him again at Cartiers. Watched him palm a couple of diamond rings under the careful eye of a salesman. She caught up with him a boulevard later. 'I like your style,' she said. 'I like your looks,' he said. Sexist, maybe. Even patronising. They'd been together ever since.

Barnaby was the red-headed son of a South Africa diamond merchant who had decided on leaving Eton that his mother-country's attitudes did not accord with his own views on freedom of expression for all, be they black, white or coloured. With a little help from his father's safe, he had returned to England where his liberal interpretation of the property laws, particularly as it applied to other men's jewels, had landed him with a nine-month stretch in Parkhurst. He'd been let out, unreformed, after serving six. He stole only the kind of stuff that was heavily insured and easily recreated. Occasionally some small bibelot of worth would also disappear from the homes of those he burgled. Often the disappearance was not noticed for some time. The bibelot itself would end up in the steel-lined room below Barnaby's antique shop in Mayfair, to be gloated over by someone who appreciated it all the more for the risk involved in its acquisition.

His meeting with Penny had far-reaching consequences. She persuaded him that a life of crime took on a new dimension when most of its proceeds were channelled towards those who needed it. When he became a partner in Miss Antonia Ivory's not very successful employment bureau, renaming it the R. H. Domestic Agency, business for both of them boomed.

Penny loved Barnaby. No question. That didn't mean she trusted him. In case of need, there was no certainty that her own jewels would be any more sacrosanct than those of strangers. She kept them carefully hidden. He had no morals whatsoever. She didn't mind that. She didn't have too many of her own. But if he took her stuff, she'd feel obliged to shop him. That would undoubtedly mean him being sent down again, perhaps for longer. She would miss him dreadfully.

She had just finished thinking of him when the telephone rang again. Heavy night down at the exchange. When she lifted the receiver, someone at the far end of the line moaned.

Heavy breathers, yes. Like everyone else who lived in London, she knew all about them. But heavy moaners? 'Who is this?' she said, speaking kind of sharpish.

'It's appendicitis,' said a tiny voice.

'A what?'

'Or might be, if I'd got one. But as far as I remember, it was removed when I was seven.'

'Fascinating.'

'Otherwise I would have said that it was grumbling.' Another little moan. 'Fairly loudly.' The voice wavered. There was a sharp gasp, a rustle, a faint crunching sound. At a shrewd guess, someone not a million miles away from the basement flat was popping Rennies like they were M & Ms.

'Miss Ivory,' Penny said. 'Is that you?'

'Possibly, dear.' Two floors below, Antonia Ivory, one of Penny's two Sitting Tenants, coughed apologetically. 'I'm afraid I'm not absolutely sure. I really do feel most unwell. Could it be peritonitis?' The voice faded again.

'Did you eat out tonight?'

'As a matter of f—'

'Then it's much more likely to be indigestion brought on by gross self-indulgence,' said Penny.

She turned over on her back. Without Miss Ivory's firm refusal to move from her flat, despite the previous owner's blandishments in the form of turds through the letterbox, bricks through the window and threats through the mail, Penny would never have been able to afford to buy the house in Chelsea. In addition to which, without Miss Ivory, her own personal campaign to bring a tiny measure of relief to Third World unfortunates would never have gotten off the ground. The sudden death of Sir Caspar Ivory, the flamboyant horse-trainer, due to a sudden seizure as the horse (Coming from Behind, by Gay Hussar out of Nancy Bell) on which he had just put his shirt fell at the second fence, left his daughter with a string of debts and a scandal connected with a kidnapped horse to live down. Plus a way to make in the world. The R. H. Domestic Agency, operating out of her basement flat, had now established itself among such agencies as the fillet steak to everyone else's hamburger. Miss Ivory placed girls in a variety of posts. Not just as nanny or cook or simple mother's help. She also supplied executive boardrooms with cordon bleu cooks, and hotels with staff from florist to chambermaid. Recently she had branched out into such seasonal or temporary placings as ski chalets and hospitality tents. She never touched what she called Colonials and always warned prospective clients against any hanky-panky. Bit of a waste, really. Most of her clients wouldn't have known a hanky if she'd embroidered it with strawberries and dropped at their feet. Let alone a panky.

But there were other facets to this successful business venture. Penny knew that Miss Ivory was unaware of them. She wanted to keep it that way. Didn't want her to start wondering why a break-in so often occurred at houses where a RHDA girl had just taken up employment. Why only jewellery was taken, though frequently some small portable *objet de vertu* also vanished. Didn't want her to start making connections between Barnaby's interest in the files and the large sums of money he later handed over to her for maximisation. Meaning bets on dead certs.

For Miss Ivory had another priceless quality. Her knowledge of horseflesh was phenomenal. While her father had lived it up

16

in the European fleshpots of the time, she spent long hours with his stable lads, absorbing their expertise. She made use of it by placing 50p bets at the local betting shop. Plagued by an uncertain digestive system, it was her boast that she had never once lost money – except for a shaming occasion at Folkestone, caused by a doubtful salmon-paste roll, which she preferred to forget. She could recite the form-book the way other people could recite the Lord's Prayer. Barnaby Midas, antique dealer and jewel thief, found her invaluable. By handing her the results of his negotiations with various fences, he was able to maximise his profits. The money ended up in Africa, feeding the needy. It was symbiosis at its best. Easily as efficient as the food chain in any Chelsea lily pond you cared to mention.

Obviously Penny felt responsible for her Sitting Tenant. Anyone would. Poor old lady like that. No family. Alone in the world. On the other hand, it was difficult to feel sympathetic towards someone who'd dined on caviar, which Miss Ivory invariably did when taken out. Especially when one had oneself made do with scrambled egg on toast. Even if one was probably the second-best maker of scrambled eggs in the entire universe. One conceded that Barnaby Midas was probably the best.

'Indigestion? I can't believe that,' Miss Ivory said. 'The restaurant has an international reputation.'

'Which one is that?'

Miss Ivory told her.

'The chef's that guy with the hair that looks like he last washed it the day John Lennon died. No wonder you're ill. Ever inspected the kitchens?'

'Of course not.' There was another cough, followed by another moan.

'What exactly did you eat?' Penny asked.

There was a pause. After it, Miss Ivory spoke placatingly. 'Perhaps I should explain that, out of the blue, a friend of my father's telephoned me this afternoon and asked if he could take me out for dinner.' She tried to titter. 'Well, actually, Penelope, to be perfectly candid with you, he was more a friend of mine, if you know what I mean.'

'I'm rather hoping I don't,' Penny said. She turned over. It was lonely under the duvet. Barnaby was in Yorkshire.

'And since the gentleman in question is exceedingly well off, I didn't feel I need stint myself,' explained Miss Ivory. 'The food really was rather superb.'

17

'In other words, you absolutely pigged out.'

'Yes.'

'What on?'

'Caviar,' sighed Miss Ivory. 'Bouillabaisse. Lobster. A terrine of salmon and pistachio nuts that was worth dying for. Which I'm very much afraid I am about to do, unless you can get me to a hospital immediately.'

'Are we talking stomach pumps here, Antonia?'

'Penelope, unless you get down here at once, we are talking graves, worms and epitaphs.' The telephone receiver clattered suddenly, as though dropped from a nerveless hand. The noise of someone throwing up sounded horrid in the night.

'I'm so dreadfully sorry. An appalling breach of manners.' Miss Ivory lay back against the hospital pillows, brittle as a brandy-snap. White carnations sprawled in a glass beside her, looking hung-over. She held a glass in one hand, a pencil in the other. There was a copy of *The Sporting Life* on the bedcover.

'Don't give it a thought,' Penny said. 'I'm delighted to spend the small hours cleaning up after greedy spinster ladies of a certain age.'

'There's nothing certain about *my* age,' snapped Miss Ivory. 'It's the most uncertain thing about me, and I fully intend it to remain so. My dear mother always taught me that it was one secret a woman should keep to herself. Tell people how old you are and they immediately label you.'

'Like a parcel, do you mean?'

'More like a bottle of wine, dear. Complete with vintage.' Miss Ivory pressed a hand to her stomach. 'Oh dear. I doubt if I shall ever be able to face caviar again.'

'Don't even think such a thing. It could cause a commercial crisis in Beluga.' Penny did a bit of Nightingaling. Plumped up a pillow. Fluffed out a carnation. Ate a grape. 'OK. I'm out of here. Is there anything else I can do for you?'

'Yes. You've saved my life, I know. Now I need you to save my business.'

Penny groaned. 'Isn't it enough that the whole house smells of Lysol because of your incontinent appetites?'

'The hospital says it was food poisoning,' said Miss Ivory. 'Nothing whatsoever to do with over-eating. And I've got to stay here for at least another three days. For observation, they said.'

'Good. I'll be able to catch up on my sleep.'

'There are two matters which concern me,' Miss Ivory said firmly.

She wasn't taking any nonsense from Penelope, thank you very much. A dear girl, despite the unfortunate matter of her colour – not that she herself was in any way prejudiced, of course, and the fact that there were no – uh – *coloured* girls on the Agency's books was simply because none had ever applied, apart from that really rather frightful creature who tried to pass herself off as some kind of royalty – but she and Barnaby Midas didn't realise quite what a downy bird she herself was. Nor would they, if she had anything to do with it. *Always keep 'em guessing, old girl*, her father had advised her, in one of his rare moments of paternal *bonhomie*, and she hoped she had always done so.

'One matter that concerns me is that Mr Midas asked me to put some money on for him,' she said.

'How much?'

'Fifteen thousand.'

'Wow.'

'Exactly. And you, my dear, will have to place the bet.'

'No way.'

'I've written it all down for you. I'll tell you exactly what procedure to follow.'

'The only thing I'm going to follow is the EXIT sign,' Penny said. She stood up.

'I don't suppose Mr Midas would care too much for that,' said Miss Ivory. She placed two fingers on her lips. Her shoulders lifted minutely in a genteel eructation. 'Incidentally, I see that they're predicting further famine in the Sudan next year. Those poor suffering people.'

Penny glanced at her. Miss Ivory didn't glance back. Instead, she smoothed down her copy of *The Sporting Life*.

'What was the second matter?' Penny said. Darn it. The old girl was tougher than concrete under that vicar's-daughter disguise.

'I'm desperately worried about the Agency,' Miss Ivory said.

'Why?'

'This is the busiest time of the year. I simply cannot afford not to be there.'

'You should have thought of that before you stuffed half the contents of the Black Sea down your throat.'

'What am I to do?' Miss Ivory said. Her eyes were wide and anguished. She pressed the back of her hand against her teeth in the gesture of a woman distraught. Or was it a woman suppressing a burp?

Penny knew what was coming. 'No,' she said. 'Whatever it is you're going to ask me to do, I won't.'

Miss Ivory ignored her. Five minutes ago the glass in her hand had contained three inches of Bacardi and orange. Two of them had gone.

'I need a stopgap. Someone I can trust,' she said. 'Someone who understands the workings of the Agency. Who has some interest in maintaining its high standing.'

'There's only one kind of high standing interests me.'

'Try not to be coarse, Penelope.' Miss Ivory brushed some small debris from her bed-jacket. 'I need to follow up on several of the new recruits. And UniChem was on the telephone only yesterday, positively begging me to find two girls to deal with their executive lunches over the holiday period. I take it you know how to use a computer.'

'Uh ... actually I—'

'Log in or drop out, Penelope.'

'What?' Sometimes you wondered where the hell the old girl picked this stuff up.

'This *is* the final decade of the twentieth century, you know.'

'Yeah.'

'But my main worry is this dreadful business of Fiona McIntosh.' Miss Ivory heaved a sigh of heavy wretchedness.

'What's she been doing.'

'Disappearing, the silly child.'

'What's that supposed to mean? Disappearing isn't a continuous action, is it? Unless you're a rainbow.'

'A rainbow?' Miss Ivory raised a hand bewilderedly to her head.

'Coming and going.'

Miss Ivory nodded. 'That's exactly what she did. Came, when the baby was born. Then up and went. Two days ago. The family rang just as I was closing and, what with my dinner engagement and the next day being Sunday, I was hardly in a position to do anything about it. But tomorrow ...' She frowned. 'The trouble is, as far as I remember, we have no more nannies available on our books.'

'Good thing too, if they're all like this Flora Macdonald.'

'McIntosh. Fiona.' Miss Ivory shook a disapproving head. 'Went off without a word to anyone. Left them completely in the lurch.' Big sigh. 'I should have realised.'

'Realised what?'

'That she wasn't reliable. With a mother like that, she was bound to be irresponsible. I ought never to have taken her on to our books, although I have to admit she had impeccable references.'

'The mother disappeared too, did she?'

'The mother ran off with a South American cricket-player,' said Miss Ivory. 'It comes to much the same thing in the end.'

'South Americans play guitars, not cricket.'

'This one played cricket. Only as an amateur, of course. He brought a side down to my father's place one year.' Miss Ivory sighed pleasurably. 'I can't tell you what a dash he cut in his flannels.' She tossed back the remains of her rum-and-orange. 'He's dead now. Shot in a hunting accident, as I recall. But that's beside the point. Here I am, a sick woman loaded down with responsibilities, and not a single person I can turn to in my hour of need. I tell you, I'm at my wits' end.'

'You don't look like it,' said Penny. 'You look much more like a salesman who thinks he's seen a sucker and is about to move in with the pitch.'

'My dear Penelope, I have no intention of putting any moral pressure on you whatsoever.' Miss Ivory fumbled in her bag for her antacid tablets. 'If, of course, you felt like helping me out, knowing, as you do, how much I hate to let down UniChem who are, after all, one of the R. H. Domestic Agency's biggest customers, then naturally I should be exceedingly grateful. If, on the other hand, you don't, then I beg you not to feel in any way guilty about the damage my failure to provide the personnel they want will do to my Agency's reputation.'

'I won't,' Penny said.

'That's perfectly all right.'

'I suppose you don't remember that I'm involved with the organisation of this BlackAid concert thing at Wembley in four weeks' time. Not to mention the big Amnesty International exhibition.'

'Of course I haven't forgotten. But I would ask you, Penelope, to consider seriously whether universal charity is more, or less, important than charity towards an individual.'

Good point. Faith, hope and charity. And the greatest of these is charity. Which begins at home, right?

Tears had formed in Miss Ivory's eyes. She allowed one to slip with slow pathos down her cheek. 'The best years of my life ...' she murmured brokenly.

'That's going back a bit.'

' ... dedicated to building up the Agency. And now a moment's indiscretion is going to wipe out all my hard work. Unless I can find someone who—'

'No,' Penny said.

'Penelope, plea—'

'No. I have far too many other things to do.'

'Three days, Penelope. Just three days.'

'No. I'm busy.'

Miss Ivory shrugged. 'Very well, Penelope. I understand how you feel. I must say I had hoped that the services I've cheerfully rendered you and Mr Midas in the past, plus the very full use you have both made of my admittedly meagre horseracing expertise, might have persuaded you to help me out for this short period of my incapacitation. However, I quite understand.' Silently she poured two fingers of Bacardi into her glass, added a smallish slug of orange and sipped it carefully.

'Oh, God,' Penny said.

'Please, Penelope. Don't say another word. If you're too busy to help out an old friend, you're too busy. That's all there is to say about it. Naturally, next time Mr Midas approaches me, I myself may find I am too busy. We'll just have to see, won't we?'

'Blackmail, Antonia?'

'Indubitably, Penelope.'

'Got me by the curlies, Antonia.'

'You bet I have.' Miss Ivory knocked back what was left in her glass. 'And please give urgent attention to the matter of Mrs Osman. It's the top letter on my desk.

'Mrs Who?'

'Osman. The mother of Joshua, Fiona McIntosh's little charge. Barely three months old and he's been left high and dry without any kind of professional care. I'm most concerned about it.'

'There's always his mother.'

'Worse than useless, I shouldn't wonder. Mothers usually are. Some sort of actress, wasn't she? Well, I mean.'

'Whaaat?' Penny grabbed Miss Ivory's drinking hand.

'Actress? Do you mean Mrs Zachary Osman?'

'Of course.'

'The former Chrissie Cooke?'

'I believe that may have been the name under which she —'

'Uh-oh.'

'What's the matter?'

'Nothing.' Penny closed her eyes and scrunched the corner of her mouth up in exasperation.

No strings attached. She'd absolutely insisted. Ludo had *sworn*. Yet if what she was hearing now wasn't the authentic sound of attached strings being tugged, before being tied in a complicated and unravellable knot, she was a Carmelite nun.

3

She'd never for a second wondered why she didn't take a nine-to-five job. If she had, two minutes sitting behind a desk in the offices of the R. H. Domestic Agency would have made the answer abundantly clear. She looked round her. Filing cabinets stood against the wall. A picture of the Queen in tweeds with corgis hung crookedly above a Pembroke table. On either side of a filled-in fireplace were two upright chairs the V. and A. would have gone bankrupt for. On other walls were photographs of jockeys and horses. The jockeys had signed theirs. Shelves held the reference books necessary to Miss Ivory's trade. There was a coffee-maker, and a discreet array of bottles – sherry, whisky, gin – on a silver tray, alongside clean Waterford glasses. On the windowsill, half a dozen pots of Venus fly trap yawned serratedly. A small computer stood on a table made of hole-punched black steel, above a curl of continuous print-out paper. Already the persistent dust of London had settled on the surfaces. It could have been any office, anywhere.

And as close to the prison house as Penny ever hoped to be. Her own career as a photo-journalist didn't seem to count as a proper job. Mainly, she had decided, because there was money in her background and she worked freelance. The two facts were entirely unconnected. People assumed she had access to her parents' bank account when in fact she earned her own keep, sometimes with something left over at the end of the month, sometimes not. But in the eyes of the world, unless you had a room with a desk in it, and probably some kind of visible filing system, not to mention a swivel chair, it wasn't Real Work. The eyes of the world were full of beams. Insecurity might be a hazard of her profession, but it had to beat the deadening effect of turning up day after day, week after week, year after year, to the same workplace. Gaahd. The routine of it all. The predictability. Above all, the seductive safety of not having to think for yourself. Living-by-numbers, Penny would have put it, had some thought-provoking columnist approached and asked for her views on regular hours.

Only last night, she and the Literary Gent up on the top floor of the house had debated the same issue. Peter Corax, her other Sitting Tenant, was one of Britain's leading novelists. He was talking about the years he had spent as a schoolmaster prior to his first book being published.

'There was a marvellous security about knowing where you were supposed to be and with whom at any given moment of the school day,' he told her. 'It took real courage to pack it all in for something most people don't even consider real work.'

'What were you, one step ahead of the lynching committee?' Penny asked.

'What *can* you mean?'

'Knowing your views on lovely lads and sunburned thews and all,' Penny said.

'Nonsense, my dear.' Corax filled his own empty glass with supermarket whisky and ignored hers. He fixed her with a globular glance from his oyster-coloured eyes. 'Sometimes I almost regret the safety of the weekly pay packet.'

'Come off it, Peter,' she said. 'The only thing you regret is the Classical Sixth.'

'You're right, Penelope, as you so often are. The Classical Sixth.' He mused a little space. 'Funny how a love of the Ancient Greeks in a boy always seemed to go hand-in-hand with the most stunning looks.'

'I've got nothing against Ancient Greeks,' said Penny. 'It's the modern kind I can't stand. Especially when they're throwing bottles out of the top-floor windows at three o'clock in the morning.'

'Why do I feel you are being barbed, Penelope? Could you be referring to the young man I was entertaining the other night?'

'That was no young man. That was a bit of rough.'

'Buggers can't be choosers, my dear.'

'Perhaps not. In which case they should avoid being boozers.'

'I've already apologised profusely for that little incident. It won't happen again.'

'I wish I could believe that.'

They smiled at each other. Not having a proper job seemed like the ideal every right-minded person should be striving for.

So far, however, there had been a marked absence of columnists in and around Chelsea demanding her views on this or any other subject. Which left her more time than she wanted to get on with handling the day-to-day office routine. And also with gasping quite a bit at Miss Ivory's business acumen. The Agency was élitism at its most virulent. Only girls with the highest of references were taken on to the books. Their references were always checked out by Miss Ivory herself and included background as well as qualifications. But the grilling they went through was as nothing compared to that of the prospective employers. Miss Ivory's standards were exacting. The families to which her girls went were always wealthy. It wasn't enough that a nanny was offered a room of her own with Laura Ashley wallpaper and Jane Churchill bed-linen. The head of the family to which she was sent must be in receipt of a certain minimum income below which Miss Ivory was not prepared to entertain him as a client. In addition, she wished to know what make of car was allocated to the new nanny's use. Was there a swimming-pool? Where did the family winter? And summer?

She rarely seemed to touch clients from abroad. Not unless they dripped oil from every pore or had diamonds on the soles of their shoes. As she had frequently remarked to Penny, you could rely on your own sort, whereas you couldn't really be responsible for foreigners. She made it sound like running sores.

Priority obviously had to be given to finding a replacement for the missing Osman nanny. Before Penny could even start wondering how to start, the phone rang. She picked up. 'Yo . . I mean, the R. H. Domestic Agency?'

There was a breathless little cry. 'That's not Miss Ivory, is it?'

'Quite the opposite.'

'Where can I reach her?'

'I'm afraid she's temporarily out of the office,' said Penny. She figured Antonia would prefer to keep her gastronomic excesses to herself.

'Oh God, isn't that just typical?'

'What is?'

'I mean, you can't rely on anyone these days. First of all they send you someone absolutely useless – I shouldn't think that girl knew any more about babies than I do, which God knows is absolute zip – and then she cuts out, leaving me to cope entirely on my own.' In the distance, behind the over-aspirated voice, there was a continuous wailing noise. 'Oh God,' the woman said. 'Can you hear that?'

'Yes. It sounds like a baby.'

'Sounds like a baby. Looks like a baby. *Smells* like a goddam baby.'

If ever Penny had heard teeth gritting, she heard them now.

'Frankly, I've got a good mind to sue,' the voice went on. 'I've had a whole weekend of looking after it and, frankly, I'm going stark raving mad.'

'Sue who?'

'You.'

Sounded like one heck of a dissatisfied customer. 'Who's speaking, please?' Penny said. In the background the infant wail rose by a couple of thousand decibels.

'This is Chrissie Cooke.' There was a short pause during which Penny was tacitly invited to scream with rapture, or at least make some sound of appreciative recognition. She let it hang. 'Chrissie Osman, I guess I should have said.'

'Ah yes.'

'That nanny you sent me's taken off – I already told you that – and I don't know the first thing about feeding schedules and diaper-changing. Don't want to, either.'

Whatever happened to looking after my own child, of *course*? 'Quite,' said Penny, stalling.

'Are you going to find me someone else or am I going to have to slit my throat?'

Penny restrained herself from saying that of the two alternatives, the second sounded infinitely more pleasing. 'I shouldn't do that, Mrs Osman,' she said, prissier than a corset saleslady. 'I'm sure we can find someone to suit.'

'When?'

'Uh—'

'Can you absolutely guarantee someone by tonight?'

'I - uh—'

'Otherwise I shall start ringing round the other agencies.'

Antonia would have a fit if one of her clients went missing during Penny's caretaker government. 'No, no.' she said hastily. Someone will be down there by – uh – by sundown.' Thank God they were on British Summertime.

'I just hope so.' The phone was slammed down.

Penny looked round the office. Jesus. What a bitch of a thing. How was she supposed to set about finding another trained nanny? She got up and went over to the files. Somehow she had to get hold of a replacement for – what was her name? Fiona

27

Something, whose mother had run off with a Peruvian cricket-player. She searched the files, pulling the folders out here and there. They all seemed to relate to the employers rather than the employed.

She flipped up the lid of the grey plastic box on the desk. It was full of cards with names on. More Emmas and Charlottes than you could shake a stick at. Each name was followed by personal details filled in with Miss Ivory's tiny hand, followed by a kind of code. It took Penny a while to figure out what MH and CB stood for, but N was simple, especially once she had followed the cross-referencing and discovered that girls with N after their name went to families looking for someone to help with new babies. Or old ones. The sort that have grown into toddlers and are presumably in need of the kind of nannyish exhortations she remembered all too well from her own childhood. 'What a nice picture *that* would make for the *Tatler*,' was one of Nanny Simpson's favourites, reeking of a class structure that should have broken down years ago yet still survived against the odds. And Ludo Fairfax's nanny, a fearful old battleaxe who locked him into cupboards on the slightest provocation, was always inspecting his fingernails and demanding to know whether he was in mourning for the cat.

Poor Ludo. Amabel was his stepmother, as well as, in some complicated way, his cousin. Ludo's mother had died shortly after his birth; his father had not remarried until Ludo was nine. Penny shuddered. Ten minutes with Brigadier Sir Hervey Fairfax was as much as she could stand at any one time. He used to make her feel as though death-watch beetle had attacked her extremities and was advancing remorselessly on her vital organs. That Ludo had survived nine years alone with his father was something of a miracle. Rigid, humourless, stern, he could have stepped right out of a Victorian three-part novel. Amabel, fifteen years younger, had softened him to some extent and in so doing had taken the edge off the chill that had been Ludo's home life. No wonder he adored her.

She looked for Ns. She found plenty. However, as Miss Ivory had warned her, every one of them was already in full employ. What the hell was she supposed to do about it? For a moment she contemplated calling up Lucas, her cleaning lad, and ordering him to man the phones while she went down to Mrs Zachary Osman's place herself. There were two strikes against that idea. First, one close encounter with a soiled diaper and she'd probably lose her lunch. Second, Lucas was playing Ariel in *The Tempest* at Darlington Civic Theatre and was therefore not available.

Darn it. She started going through the cards again, looking for the girls with MH against their name, even though the odds were that the former Chrissie Cooke would curl her pouty little lips at a mere Mother's Help. She found a Lucinda Mackworth-Box who seemed to be currently unemployed. When contacted, she wasn't. The next card was Fiona McIntosh's.

Already intimately concerned with this missing stranger, Penny read her details with interest. Fiona was twenty-two, single, with both parents living, though at different addresses. There was also a sister one year younger. Both had been educated at the same minor private school for girls. Fiona had spent a year in Australia and another working in Spain as an au pair before taking a course in nannying. Her training had been completed just over a year ago. Further particulars could be found in the Osman file.

A head-and-shoulders colour photograph was attached to the card with a paper-clip. Fiona McIntosh was not what Penny had expected. The name implied some large raw-boned creature with big teeth and a broad brow. The girl in the picture had soft blonde hair curling round the edges of a sweet-faced expression. It was not a beautiful face but eyes of a spectacularly deep blue made it immediately memorable. Not just because of their colour. There was a pathos in them which Penny had seen before, in photographs of refugees or slum dwellers. The girl's mouth was a surprise. It didn't go with the rest of her. It was long and generous. A mouth determined. A mouth ready to speak up for itself.

Not, Penny would have thought, the mouth of a girl likely to run out on her job.

She moved on to the Hon Venetia Masterton, and on again to Caroline Mauncey-Smith. Venetia was coded CB. Caroline was F. It seemed fairly obvious that the last thing Chrissie Cooke Osman wanted right now was an Hon who catered after-theatre suppers, or a Double Barrel who'd graduated from some of school of flower arranging.

The telephone rang.

What now? Another duke needing a housekeeper? A further earl searching for kitchen staff? Miss Ivory's clientele was not only noble but cackhanded, seemingly in constant need of domestic help. When she answered, a girl's voice said hesitantly: 'I'd like to apply to be put on to your books.'

Penny pulled a pad towards her. 'What sort of work are you looking for?'

'I'm a trained children's nurse.'

'You are?'

'I've been told that your Agency is the best in its field.'

'You betcha.' Penny tried to keep the relief out of her voice. Talk about nannies from heaven. She must have piled up more credit with the Universal Architect than she thought. 'Where are you speaking from?'

'Chiswick,' the girl said cautiously. 'I'm staying on a friend's houseboat.'

'Great. When can you start?'

'I'm free now, but—'

Penny was about to tell her to take a train straight down to wherever it was the Osmans lived and get stuck in on the nappy changing. Second thoughts prevailed. Assuming the girl's qualifications were OK, she still ought at least to check her out, see she didn't have a wooden leg or some facial disfiguration so hideous that it might frighten the horses. Let alone the baby.

'Why don't you come and see us?' she asked.

'Now?'

'Strike while the iron's hot,' Penny said heartily, hating herself. 'No time like the present.' Offhand, it was hard to decide which phrase was more repellant.

'All right.'

'Find yourself a taxi and come straight round here. We can discuss things then.'

'When would you want me to start?'

'Depending on arrangements, we do have one or two immediate vacancies, as a matter of fact.'

'Wonderful.'

'Mmm-mm,' Penny said. The trouble was, even answers to prayers needed references. But if she was to fulfil her promise to Chrissie Cooke Osman, she would not have time to run a check on the girl. Nor give her the full Ivory-style background treatment. But a nanny in the hand was worth twenty-two anywhere else. A *hundred* and twenty-two. Surely Antonia would understand. 'What's your name, by the way?'

'Vanessa Carrington.'

'See you in a minute, Vanessa.'

It was all go in the domestic agency business that day. No sooner had she finished speaking to Vanessa than the telephone sounded again. She picked up the receiver, reminded herself of Nanny Simpson's strictures about well-brought-up little ladies, gave the words an upward lilt. 'The R. H. Domestic Agency?'

The voice belonged to a male. North-of-the-borderish and young. 'What time do you close tonight?'

Penny hadn't really thought about it. 'Uh—'

'If I came down at six o'clock, would someone be there?'

She thought rapidly. If the Carrington girl checked out ... 'Normally speaking, yes. This evening, no,' she said firmly. 'What was it in connection with?' She hoped she sounded right. Complicated tenses were something telephone receptionists learned at their mother's knees.

'One of your girls.'

Rats. Another dissatisfied customer? 'I could see you tomorrow morning,' she said.

'How early? I have to get to work but ...'

'Eight o'clock?'

'Fine. I'll see you then.' He rang off.

Vanessa Carrington proved to be exactly what was wanted. No new-born mother who was into nannies in the first place could have failed to entrust her with their offspring. Penny herself might well have done, supposing she had offspring to entrust. Which she did not, nor ever would. Not that she didn't like children. Quite the opposite. Though, again, she stopped far short of the kind of generalised enthusiasm women often came out with: *I love children*, as though they were all identical, all lovable. But to Penny's mind, there were already far too many of them around, not being taken adequate care of. Senseless, therefore, to add further to the world's overcrowded population.

Vanessa had an open honest face that not even her mother could have called beautiful, and the kind of hips usually known as childbearing. The way she took her coat off sent a frisson down Penny's spine. Just so had Nanny Simpson removed her good wool coat after church on Sundays before putting it on a hanger on the back of the nursery door. And when Vanessa sat down, the frisson frissed again. The not-all-that-distant-past crowded in on her. Just so had all the other nannies of her youth spread their legs when they sat, making a lap designed for the efficient dandling of infants. Just so had they offered a tantalising

31

glimpse of knicker to their disrespectful charges.

'Well now,' Penny said. She tried to look elsewhere than straight up Vanessa's sensible skirt. She wasn't quite sure what she ought to say.

The girl handed her a thick envelope. 'I expect you'll want my references,' she said. 'They're all in there.'

'Quite.'

'And, of course, you'll want to know who I've worked for and what my background is.' Fluently she ran through details that seemed almost too good to be true.

Eventually, Penny said: 'This may seem a little sudden, but we do have a bit of an emergency. Would you be willing to start immediately?'

'How immediately?'

'Like – uh – now?'

The girl regarded Penny from intelligent brown eyes. The suddenness did not seem to faze her. 'All right,' she said. 'I've got some things in a bag with me, as it happens.'

Penny made a quick decision. It was getting near to closing time. Those still in need of cooks and companions, housekeepers and help with the children, or cleaning ladies of an upscale kind, would have to wait until tomorrow. 'I'll drive you down there,' she said.

It would give her a chance to look – all right, to *snoop* – around, see what kind of poop she could pick up on Fiona McIntosh. She waved at the telephone. 'If there's anyone you'd like to call, explain where you're going . . .'

'That's all right. I can do it after I've settled in.'

'Fine.' It seemed very self-possessed. But then this girl was. A mite more so than Penny cared for, if the truth be told. She snuck a look at the girl's particulars. Twenty-five. She seemed older. Several decades older.

The drive down to the Osman place was silent for the first fifty miles or so. Vanessa Carrington sat staring straight ahead of her. Glancing sideways, Penny couldn't help noticing the relaxed way she did it. It seemed at odds with the impression she gave of someone ready to spring into action almost without thinking. Perhaps that's what listening out for babies all the time did to a person. It was a twenty-four-hour, seven-day-a-week job, on full alert, her mother had once told her. It wasn't really surprising that those who could afford it hired someone to help stand watch.

She herself was trying to figure out where to start finding clues to Fiona McIntosh's disappearance. Not that it was any of her business, of course. But it seemed rather odd that she should have walked out like that, without explanation. Perhaps Little Miss Chrissie could add more information. Which reminded her.

'I forgot to ask,' she said. 'I don't know if you're supposed to wear a uniform.'

'I have something with me, in case, but the family may wish to provide their own,' the girl said.

'Don't you feel this whole nanny scene is a bit of an anachronism?' Penny said.

'Not at all.' Vanessa's voice was composed. 'As a new class of rich develops, so the need for help to support the increasingly complicated fabric of their lives returns. In the old days of the First World War, the so-called Golden Era, the great houses of England couldn't have survived without the infrastructure of their servants, from boot-black to butler. You could say the working classes made the whole thing possible.'

'Is this part of your doctoral thesis or something?'

'We're seeing a return to the same sort of social hierarchisation with today's newly rich, of course. Except that this time, it's the servants who have the upper hand. An ironic reversal of relative positions, don't you think?'

'Positively metaphorical.'

My Gaaahd. Whatever happened to old-fashioned nanny-speak? Had the new breed of child nurses or whatever they called themselves now thrown simple phrases like 'Who's She, the cat's mother?' and 'I want doesn't get' out of the window in favour of sociological analysis? Was this what they called progress? However irritating, there had always been something reliable about Nanny Simpson's predictable responses. No kid, asking where babies come from, wanted to be handed a full-scale discussion of the sexual act and its consequences. The old stork and gooseberry-bush version was much more satisfactory.

An image popped into Penny's mind. Then popped right out again. But not before she had glimpsed a table, people behind it, a disembodied voice, this very same girl. Where had it been?

'So you don't find it demeaning to be a servant?' she asked.

'Not in the least. It would only be demeaning if I felt

demeaned. Which I don't. Besides, everyone in the market-place is a servant of some kind, don't you think, in the sense that he or she is working for someone else?'

'True. What about the ethics of handing over your kid to someone else to bring up?'

'That's a much more complicated question, and a matter of individual preference. If the need is there, and I have the skill, I don't see why I shouldn't fill it.'

'Like beauty queens.'

'Exactly. What else can girls like that do? And how long can they do it? Beauty is ephemeral, and once the first flush of youth has gone, very hard work.'

'A bit like nannying, I should think.'

'Yes.'

'Everybody's mother but nobody's wife, sort of thing.'

'Perhaps,' Vanessa said equably. 'We'll have to see, won't we?'

At least the words sounded more like something an authentic nanny would come out with.

There was an entry-phone at the entrance gates to the Osman residence. That meant either affluence or arrogance. Penny spoke into it. Shortly afterwards, the gates swung open and she motored up a drive of what felt, from the grip of the tyres, like clinker. Looked like it, too, stretching away to a house that had obviously been built while Queen Anne was still alive. Attractive without being vast. And considerably more modest than a man with millions at his disposal might be supposed to own. Its pleasingly classical façade of red brick with white trimmings, set behind a formal display of rose beds, exuded stability and peace. It was an illusion swiftly dispelled. They could hear a baby shrieking even before someone who was not quite a butler had opened the front door to them. The hall was wide, its sanded floor of broad pine planks covered with oriental rugs. Behind the smell of woodsmoke given off by the logs burning languidly in the fireplace, there was a discreet sense of first-class central heating ready to spring into action whenever needed. The scent from bowls of pot-pourri decorated the air.

As they stood there, a door opened and Chrissie Cooke raced through. Red hair artfully mussed, designer jeans tight over her cute little butt, she stopped short at the sight of them. She stared at Penny, raising one faltering hand to her lips.

'Oh my God,' she said. 'You didn't tell me she'd be—'

Before she could complete a remark that would have had the Race Relations Board spitting tacks, Vanessa stepped forward. 'Are you Mrs Osman? I'm Vanessa Carrington.'

'Thank heavens. Great.' Chrissie turned to Penny without missing a step or clarifying why she was giving thanks. 'And, of course, you're Lady Helena's daughter, aren't you?'

'You dined with us in the spring,' Penny said.

'The day Joshua was born. Such a beautiful house,' sighed Chrissie. Boy, she was smooth. She turned again to Vanessa. 'Let's go into the morning room and talk – though I can see at once that you're going to be perfect with the baby.' She glanced upwards at the source of the noise, wrinkling her cutesy brow. 'I had no idea when I went into this that babies could be so *noisy*,' she said.

The room she led them into had been expensively colour-coordinated in shades of raspberry and cream. Trouble with a place designed from scratch is, the past tends to get shoved to one side. With everything homogeneous, there's no room for natural growth and development. Penny didn't like breathing artificial air.

For a while they discussed terms and duties. It was supposed to be a get-acquainted session but it was a foregone conclusion that Chrissie would take Vanessa on. Once the girl had been shown to the nursery and Chrissie had returned, Penny put on her Captain-of-Industry look.

'We're most concerned about Miss McIntosh,' she said.

'Believe me, lady, so am I.' With the new nanny safely installed, Chrissie felt free to drop the Bo-Peep veneer and was allowing the Wicked Witch beneath to show. 'It certainly wouldn't do your agency much good if I spread that little story around. Running out on me like that.'

'We're not entirely convinced that she has,' Penny said. Although she had no reason to believe otherwise, she felt that someone should go in to bat for Fiona. Innocent until proved guilty, etc.

'Well, she sure as hell ain't hanging round here, let me tell you. The noise that kid of mine makes would raise the dead.'

'Which let's hope she's not.'

'Not what?'

'Not dead.'

'Don't be ridiculous,' Chrissie said. She stood up, smoothed her hands over the buttocks of her jeans, checked out a fingernail, sat down again.

'Did she take all her stuff with her?' Penny asked.

'As a matter of fact, she didn't.'

'What did she leave behind?'

'Just about everything.'

'Doesn't that indicate that something is slightly off-key?'

'Hell, no. I've got a sister that sort of age. It didn't surprise me in the least.'

'May I see her things?'

For the first time, Chrissie looked uncomfortable. There were faint lines around her eyes, and a deeper one between her eyebrows, as though she frowned a lot. 'I don't know about that.' She wriggled about in the corner of the chesterfield where she was sitting. 'Fact is, ever since the baby arrived I've been liable to lose my cool. I'm afraid I just chucked everything of hers I could find into a pile and told the butler to get rid of it.'

'I see.' Penny shifted to her undertaker's expression, the serious one that needed a spot of chin-stroking to make it look just right. 'Wasn't that a bit premature?'

Chrissie waved tiny hands in the air. 'Like I said, I got mad.'

'Would your – uh – butler still have the stuff?' Penny asked gravely. She stroked her chin.

'He might.' The wriggling stopped. The brow wrinkled. 'You sound like you think something seriously major's gone wrong. What exactly do you think could have happened to her?'

'I don't know. Kidnapping, maybe.'

'Are you *crazy*? Who'd want to kidnap a nanny, for God's sake?'

'Perhaps she was only pretending to be a nanny.' Penny said it lightly, not really serious.

Chrissie thought she was. 'That would explain a whole hell of a lot,' she said slowly. 'Not that she didn't take good care of the baby, or anything. I just never felt she was one hundred per cent sure what she was doing. She was kind of ... kind of amateur, rather than professional. Feeling her way more than anything.'

'I find that hard to believe,' Penny said. Miss Ivory would surely have checked Fiona out as thoroughly as she did everything else. It would have been difficult for her to have got on to the books of the R. H. Domestic Agency if she wasn't what she said she was.

'I didn't mind that so much. I'm kind of amateur myself where babies are concerned. I figured she was probably nervous in a new job, she could do without me bugging her the whole time.' Chrissie took a cigarette out of a box on a table. Raspberry pink paper, gold initials: CCO. *Très vulgaire.* She lit it, took a puff, then ground it out again. 'I keep forgetting. I'm not supposed to smoke while I'm still feeding Junior.' She looked down at her front. Two wet stains were spreading across her sweat-shirt. 'God, I hate all this,' she said. 'I can't wait to get Joshua off me and on to the bottle.'

Penny wanted to say that in the Sudan, women were dying slowly of starvation, nursing babies too weak to suck at breasts that had long ago dried up. But where would be the point? It wasn't Chrissie's fault. Wasn't anybody's fault.

'Sure,' she said.

'Anyway, like I say, it was the girl's snooping that really got on my nerves.'

'Snooping?'

'Not quite that, I guess. Just an impression she gave, every time you went into a room, that she'd just that second finished going through your old love-letters or rifling Zachary's desk or something. Really got up my nose, if you want the honest-to-God truth.'

'But you never actually saw her doing it?'

'No. But I'm darned sure she did.'

'Mrs Osman. As you can imagine, such a breach of responsibility reflects very badly on the R. H. Domestic Agency.'

'I'll say.'

'Can you think of any reason why Miss McIntosh should have left like this?'

'You mean was I bawling her out every two seconds? Or was my husband groping her? The answer's no to both questions. Especially the second one.' She grinned. 'I take good care that he doesn't have enough energy left over for that sort of thing.'

Ho hum. Penny rolled her mouth about in a disapproving kind of way.

'Or,' said Chrissie, 'a letter arriving from foreign parts? Or a mysterious stranger turning up on the doorstep. As a matter of fact, some rather dishy guy *did* show up that morning. Said he wanted to take her out to lunch. She gave him the runaround and he left.'

'Any idea who he was?'

'None at all. Nor did I ask. The help have a right to their private lives.'

The help. Penny loved it. She pulled out the photograph of Fiona McIntosh she'd removed from Miss Ivory's files. 'I take it we're talking about the same girl.'

Chrissie looked. Grinned. Said: 'Yeah. That's ol' Fee, all right. Looks like she's just about to have it off with some guy, doesn't she?'

'I should remind you that Fiona has gone missing, Mrs Osman.' Boy, could Penny be glacial when she wanted. If you have leers, prepare to shed them *now*. 'I don't suppose you've searched the grounds, have you?'

'Damn right I haven't.'

'Perhaps you should.' Penny said coldly.

'Hey, what is this? The nanny goes missing, I don't immediately call out the bloodhounds and dust off my magnifying glass, you know. She chooses to hightail it out of here with some guy, she's welcome. Just don't expect me to start crying about it. Find me another nanny's all I ask.'

'It doesn't seem a very responsible attitude.'

'Look. Some man rang up and said she wasn't coming back. Put down the receiver before I had a chance to practise my vocabulary.'

'What did he say?'

'Just that Miss McIntosh wouldn't be coming back.'

'I see. Mightn't it be a good idea if someone did take a look around.'

'What for?'

'Just in case.'

'But what about the phone call?' Chrissie didn't ask in case of what.

'Yeah, well,' said Penny.

'Just hang on a second, will you. I thought you were just joshing when you said about her being kidnapped.'

'I was.'

'But it could be true.'

'It could.'

Chrissie chewed her lip. 'Jeez. I guess that means calling the cops. Zach's gonna really love that. I suppose they'll be swarming all over the place, taking fingerprints and nosing into things.'

'It might never happen, Miz Osman. Meanwhile, I'll take her personal possessions back to London with me. If she should show up, she can pick them up from there.'

'That's assuming Shane still has them.'

'Shane?'

'The butler.'

'*Shane?*'

'Yeah. I know. He's only a *sort* of butler.'

Vanessa Carrington's lecture on current sociological trends notwithstanding, it looked like the servant problem was still as acute as it ever was if people like the Osmans had to make do with a butler called Shane.

'What was Fiona like?' Penny asked.

'As a person?'

What else? As a lawn mower? As dental floss? 'Yes.'

'I mean, I already told you what she was like as a nanny. As a person ...' Chrissie paused a moment in girlish thought ' ... well, very sexy. I mean, that's the chief thing I remember about her. Men fell for her like ninepins. She wasn't especially beautiful, and she didn't dress sexy or anything. It was just her – attitude. yeah. She was sexy. Even I could see it and God knows I don't go for women.'

'How exactly do you mea—'

'It was as though she switched it on. Not that she did it very often but when she did, it was really something to see. We had an old friend of mine from Hollywood over recently and suddenly the shy little nanny turned into this smouldering inferno of – well, sex. Nothing obvious. She didn't throw herself at him, or give him the big hallo. Scarcely even looked at him. But by the end of the evening he was absolutely – wow!'

'And do you think it went any further?'

'Not under my roof it didn't. Probably not at all, since he flew back to the States the next day. Same with the people Zachary had invited here last Friday. I mean, the guy's wife is right there with him, but that doesn't stop Miss Hot Twat strutting her stuff.'

'What did the wife think about it?'

'I didn't notice. I was too busy wondering whether to send Shane for the fire-extinguisher in case her husband suddenly burst into flame.' She laughed. 'Could've caused an international incident.'

'How?'

'Well, he was attached to some embassy. As a matter of fact, I'm not sure it wasn't the same guy who was at your mother's house that time. Anyway, like I said, the Fiona thing wasn't that obvious, unless you were looking at it. Or having it beamed at you. I wouldn't have noticed myself if our Hollywood friend hadn't told us about it later.'

'I see,' Penny said, although she didn't really. It all sounded kind of weird, to tell the truth.

She followed Chrissie upstairs to say goodbye to Vanessa. As with the rest of the place, everything in the nursery was, like, two minutes old. Despite the age of the house, there was no sense of other babies having been here before. It was as if Zachary and Chrissie had no past to give their child, only a gold-plated present. Penny leaned over the designer crib and stroked Osman Junior's velvety cheek. As well as velvety, it was red. Looked like the Tooth Fairy better start saving up.

Into the back part of the house, they found Shane wrassling with the intricate text of a Superman comic. Turned out he'd stashed the McIntosh effects in his sort-of-butler's pantry. Penny took them and stowed them in the back of her car.

She left.

* 4 *

She was up early the next morning. With Barnaby still in York-shire, there was no point lingering in bed. She went down to Miss Ivory's offices. They seemed less negative in the pale light which filtered through from the street to the basement. She fed the plants on the windowsill, dropping minute crumbs of mince into their gaping green throats and watching the saw-toothed jaws slowly close round them. She poured rainwater into their saucers. Miss Ivory had explained that the inferior stuff from the tap was not to pass their lips.

Something about Fiona McIntosh was bothering her. It didn't make sense. Why take off like that? Why not give proper notice so there was a chance to find someone to take her place? And in any case, what would make a girl walk out on employers who, however she might feel about them personally, were offering top whack in terms of conditions and wages? There had to be more to it than a boyfriend. If, indeed, that was what the man who'd telephoned the Osmans really was. Her wrists tingled, as though lightly electrified. This was all too heavy. Too full of stress. The more logically you looked at it, the more obvious it was that something was very wrong. Should she call the police about it, or give it a couple more days? Antonia would have known what to do.

She took out the Osman file and sat with it at the desk. It contained masses of cuttings about Zachary Osman and his various businesses which Miss Ivory must have culled from the newspapers. There were photocopied letters from what appeared to be friends – or maybe enemies – of both Zachary and Chrissie. There were interviews with Chrissie, taken from women's magazines, wanting to know her views on the role of the wife and mother in today's increasingly lawless society. There was 'A Day in the Life Of', 'A Room of My Own'. That sort of thing. Unbelievably, there were even copies of bank statements. Penny didn't bother feeling surprised. Antonia Ivory

41

was a resourceful woman. Just what form her resources took was hard to guess. Given her age and looks, the sale of her body in exchange for privileged information was probably not a front runner. Or was that being ageist? Older women did it too, she reminded herself.

At the back of the green folder, she found the names of Fiona's references.

Both had replied to Miss Ivory's follow-up letters. One of them, Sir Fingal Hamilton, wrote on thick cream-laid paper embossed with some small item of noble headgear. According to him, what England needed was more Fiona McIntoshes. Regiments of them. Armies. Put the running of the country into Fiona's hands, and Britain would once again be Great. Or so he implied. He might have been more enthusiastic if Fiona had been the Archangel Gabriel, but not much.

Attached to his letter with a yellow paperclip was another one, equally glowing. It made Fiona sound like a cross between Mother Teresa and Mary Poppins. Penny looked further through the newspaper cuttings in the Osman file. Most of them charted, via the gossip columns, Zachary's romance with Chrissie Cooke. Flamehaired, they called her. Sultry. Lovable. It wasn't a word Penny would have used.

Several of them analysed Zachary's business dealings in close detail. The financial editors of the quality papers couldn't leave him alone. The time he floated a new share issue. The takeover bids. The acquisition of a small publishing house. The chain of cut-price drugstores he purchased almost by accident. The travel agents spreading across the northen half of England, like a spider slowly weaving its web. Rumours concerning his reliability, his honesty, his judgement, his acumen. What nobody disputed was that he was rich. And getting richer. A Sunday paper profiled him. *Time* and *Newsweek* did features on his financial empire.

Despite what Ludovic had told her, nowhere was there ever any overt mention of impropriety, though *Time* wondered about the mysteriousness of his meteoric rise into the ranks of the seriously rich, and one financial editor hinted at a past not entirely free from shade. As she was putting the file back, she saw a small clipping, no more than three lines, saying that senior officers of the Fraud Squad were travelling to Bradford to question the manager of a travel agency suspected of illegal transfers of money to the Indian subcontinent. It was dated Saturday, the day Miss Ivory had been taken ill. There was nothing to link it with Fiona's former employer beyond the fact that the travel agency was referred to as belonging to the Osman empire.

She went back up to her own part of the house. She pulled on a white warm-up suit and a pair of Reeboks. She set off at a fast trot down the street towards the Embankment. Despite the sunshine, it was cool, a reminder that autumn lurked. Her breath dragoned out ahead of her as she ran across the bridge towards Battersea Park. The river was thick and opaque, toffee-coloured against its heavy retaining walls. On mornings like this, the city had a translucent quality, its roofs and spires airy in the fragile light. In the park, she pounded past bushes, hoping the drop in temperature had kept the flashers and meaningful grinners in their respectable suburbs. The bells on the Temple of Peace tinkled as she headed towards the lake. There were ducks: mallards, mostly. Black red-beaked swans floated colourfully. Grey geese squabbled.

Ludo. She forced herself to concentrate on him. She wished now she had taken more notice of what he had told her about Zachary Osman. Money-laundering, he'd said. The phrase always conjured up the wicker hampers in which the Hurley Court dirty linen was dispatched to be washed. Illegal transfers of huge sums, he'd said. A hundred million pounds min per annum. It was a good round figure, if too vast to grasp. What did one do with so much cash? What was there in the world to spend it on?

Money cast a spell she could not imagine being enthralled by. Yet those with lots of it seemed always to want more. Why? There were only so many houses you could live in, clothes you could wear, cars you could drive, food you could eat. Good you could do? Spending-wise, most of the super-rich seemed not to consider that an option. As for those at the opposite end of the scale, they viewed money as a universal panacea, a cure-all, a solution to all problems. Murder had been committed for sums less than the cost of the average hardback crime novel.

What little brightness the day had begun with was evaporating fast as she ran back along pavements already spotted with rain. She stopped to pick up a newspaper and ran on with it folded under her arm. Home again, she lifted a few weights, showered, went down to the kitchen. Now. What should she have for breakfast? She never had the same thing twice. Yesterday she had eaten a custard-apple, skin-thin slices of Parma ham on hot rolls, and dill sauce. The tea had been Darjeeling laced with a little Lapsang. Today, she would settle for convention: half a pink grapefruit, a bowl of muesli, Earl Grey. Just as proximity destroyed love, she believed, so routine killed spontaneity. Breakfast was the best way she knew to beat the rap. Also, to assert your personality. If you had one. Sometimes she thought she didn't. Unless it was multiple. How else to explain why she sometimes fancied cheese puffs and fruit *compote*, sometimes OJ and a Danish?

Her relationship with Barnaby was like that. Sometimes free-running as table salt, sometimes snagged up on spikes of personal quirkiness. Never the same thing twice. It took a lot of hard work to keep the spontaneity in a relationship that had continued now for six years. Plus a little casting of the eyes in other directions. Partly for the fun of it. Partly because it made you appreciate what you had. Sometimes the two of them didn't meet for weeks on end. She liked that.

She plugged in the kettle and went out to the pond. Haricot, the neighbour's tomcat, was sitting on the edge, studying the yellow kingcups. He blinked at her, lids heavy, pupils tiny with lust and daylight. His apparent interest in botany was a blind. He knew it. So did she. There were nine goldfish in the pond, orange streaks in the murky water. If Haricot had his way, there would shortly be eight. Barnaby had told her that if he managed to get hold of one and she rescued it in time, she was to feed it brandy and cover it with a towel. The fish, that is. There were many parts she hoped to play in life. Providing first aid to goldfish did not figure among them. She shooed the cat away and scattered flakes of fishfood on the water, as Barnaby had instructed her to do. A chill breeze caught her across the eyes. Somewhere beyond the houses in the next street a siren wailed. Her bones felt cold. She shivered.

Back in the house she filled a kettle and plugged it into the wall. She slipped a C. & W. cassette into the player on the counter and sang along at the top of her voice. If you wanted the *mens sana* as well as the *corpore sano*, nothing beat the three S words: singing, smiling and sex. She spooned long eccentric tea-leaves into a pot and added boiling water. Sugar-free muesli, bowel-movingly wholesome. One pink grapefruit, hot from Florida. Breakfast. Except – she looked at her watch – she'd have to eat on the run. It was already 7.42 a.m. and she had an appointment at 8.00 a.m.

At 7.59 a.m. it was time to get below. She had just settled behind Miss Ivory's desk when someone ran down the outside steps leading to the Agency's entrance. Although there was a neat sign ordering callers to walk in, the knocker was rapped impatiently. The bell buzzed.

Penny glanced up at the wall clock. 8.00 a.m. If the guy could time his arrival so exactly, he could certainly read two simple words. She sat tight. The buzzing and rapping continued for a moment, then she heard the door whish across the bristles of the doormat as someone pushed it open.

'In here,' she called.

The young man who appeared in the doorway had thick caramel-coloured hair and glasses with frames to match. There was a high colour on his flat smooth cheeks. He looked as if he probably shaved once a month and then only to make himself feel grown-up.

'Miss Ivory?' he said. He hesitated into the room, fingering the buttons on the jacket of his well-cut navy-blue suit. She could see Jermyn Street stripes under it, and a regimental tie of some kind.

'Hi,' she said. 'I'm Penny Wanawake.'

'Ah!' Good breeding would not allow him to show surprise, but she was clearly not what he expected. 'I was – uh ...'

'Miss Ivory's in hospital. I'm office-sitting for her.'

'Oh. Right.'

'Do sit down, Mr Uh.'

'Yes. Sorry. I'm Ewen Hamilton.'

'Son of Sir Fingal?'

He looked surprised. 'Yes. I work in the City.'

'I'm afraid we don't handle that kind of position,' Penny said firmly.

He stared at her, then laughed. 'Good Lord. I haven't come about a job or anything. It's Fiona.'

'Fiona?'

'McIntosh. I'm a friend of hers. Well, actually, I'm madly in love with her, to tell you the honest truth.'

'Do sit down, Mr Hamilton.'

He took a chair and brought it close to the desk so he was sitting right opposite Penny. 'I've been ringing that place where she was working but all I get is some hysterical woman screeching about nappy liners and accusing Fiona of jumping ship or

45

something. I thought I'd come here and see if you made more sense.'

'I'm kind of in the dark myself.'

'It's been two days since I heard from her, you see.' He looked at his watch. 'More.'

'That's not really long, Mr Hamilton. Not in the Missing Persons game.'

'Far too long in the Madly in Love game,' he said. He tried to smile.

He had large red-knuckled hands. He clasped them together in front of him. That didn't stop them shaking. Penny could see from his face that he had already reached through fear the same conclusions that she was reluctantly beginning to reach through deduction. Nannies don't disappear, leaving all their stuff behind, except for the very worst of reasons. Like abduction. Like death, sudden and unanticipated. Like, maybe, murder.

'Obviously you've called her parents,' she said.

'Obviously. Her mother's actually over here in London at the moment. Has been for about ten days. She hasn't heard from Fee recently but didn't expect to. Paco – that's Fiona's step-brother – saw her on Saturday morning. They're not too worried.'

'What about her father?'

'Dr McIntosh? I called him last night.' He hunched his shoulders. 'He hasn't heard either. I don't know about Dymphna because she's on holiday.'

'Dymphna?'

'That's her sister.'

'And Fiona's friends?'

'Naturally I went round to the flat she used to share but the girls there said she hadn't been in touch with them since she got the job with these Osman people.'

'It's only two days, Mr Hamilton. While I agree it's a little strange, you can't really call it anything else at the moment. There could be all sorts of explanations.'

'Such as?'

'Perhaps she's done something like this before.' Penny was aware that as examples went, it came under the heading 'Poor'.

'She certainly has not.'

'Are you sure? How long have you known her?' she asked.

'All my life.'

'Oh.'

'The girls were only about two and three when their mother ran off and their father moved back to Scotland,' Hamilton said. 'He's the doctor in the village near where my people farm. We all grew up together.'

'Perhaps something unexpected came up.'

'She would never go off and leave someone in the lurch. Let alone me.' Hamilton's voice, faintly Scottish about the vowels, shook slightly.

Penny remembered what Miss Ivory had said about the girl's unreliability. Or had it been the mother's? 'You're sure of that?'

'Of course. For one thing, she adores children. I can't believe she'd abandon a baby like that. For another, her mother ran off when Fee was only a child. After seeing first-hand what happens when you let people down, she'd rather die than do it herself.' He saw how unfortunately chosen his words were as soon as he'd spoken them. Unclenching his big hands, he said, 'Oh God. If anything's happened . . .' The colour suddenly drained from his cheeks.

'Mr Hamilton, how about a drink?' Penny got up and poured him a stiff whisky. Early as it was, if there'd been some of that sippin' sweet bourbon around, she'd have poured herself a stiff Jack Daniels, but there wasn't.

He took it from her and swallowed half in one go. She watched the way his Adam's apple knocked against the starched collar of his shirt. 'Where can she be?' he said quietly. Although he was not of a class or an age – or even a sex – that would show much emotion, Penny was nonetheless aware that he was close to breaking down.

'Look,' Penny said. 'The best I can do is to make some enquiries. Have you thought of contacting the police?'

'I don't want to do that.' Hamilton brushed a hand down one of his broadcloth sleeves as though hoping to wipe away the gathering fears which Penny knew she could do nothing to allay.

'They are professionals, you know.'

'Yes. Of course. But, it's like . . .' he fixed his gaze on the print of Her tweed-skirted Majesty ' . . . once I contact them, it makes it real. Her disappearance, I mean. And then there's . . .' he turned appalled eyes to Penny ' . . . I mean, what they might find, once they start looking.'

The thought had also occurred to Penny. She felt maternal. It might have been all the talk of babies. Or because he seemed vulnerable. She didn't want him to be hurt. 'Please don't worry,' she said. 'I'm sure she'll be all right.'

He didn't believe her. She didn't expect him to. She wondered whether to tell him about the phone call that Chrissie Osman had received and decided not to. For the moment.

When he'd gone, she sat thinking. The police were the obvious people to get in touch with, yet she could understand Ewen's reluctance to make concrete something that for the moment still remained nebulous. After all, the girl had only been gone a couple of days. Perhaps, when Miss Ivory returned – tomorrow or the day after – she might look into it a little further. If Fiona hadn't shown up by then, of course.

She spent most of the morning working through the CB annotated names in the card-index files. She needed to find a couple of Cordon Bleus to handle the UniChem lunches during the summer season. She could only find one. When she called her, the girl offered to bring a recently qualified friend. Thankfully, Penny agreed, and started on the necessary paperwork.

The rest of the time, when she wasn't fielding calls from folk who featured at the top end of *Debrett's*, she grazed through the extensive office files. Some of the stuff they contained was dynamite. What the hell sort of clout could a little old lady like Antonia wield, to get hold of so much info? Especially when it was on the kind of people you wouldn't think had info to be got hold of. It wasn't just the low-down on ordinary things like credit ratings and share portfolios. It was also fascinating little items like disreputable pasts. Not to mention presents. How people treated their spouses. Who they adulterously slept with. Their sexual preferences. Even prison sentences and youthful indiscretions. Those files could have started major scandals in any of a dozen City boardrooms. In the case of one foreign ambassador, maybe even a minor war. There was enough hot gossip to fill the tabloids for the next five years.

Over a cup of Earl Grey, she opened the envelope that Vanessa Carrington had given her the day before. It contained two letters of reference. The first, from someone in the Scilly Isles, was written in the same adulatory terms as Fiona McIntosh's had been. So was the second. Penny read:

To Whom It May Concern
Miss Vanessa Carrington came to us on the birth of our daughter, Laura, and proved a most capable and loving

nanny not only to her but also to our son, Dickon, then aged three.

Her ability to run the nursery and organise the new baby with both efficiency and enthusiasm, and yet, at the same time, to give my son the warm-hearted but firm treatment that he needed, impressed my wife and myself most favourably.

We are extremely sorry to see her go, which she is doing only because my wife has decided to take over the full-time care of the children herself. I most heartily recommend her and consider any future employer to be highly fortunate in obtaining her cheerful and reliable services.

It was signed: Harry Surtees-Brown.

Say *whaaat*? My wife. My son. What a load of baloney. Laura, for chrissake. *Dickon*. What kind of a name was that. Penny slapped the folder shut and returned it to its file.

The top of her head felt hot. She was mad. As a wet hen. She might not be President of MENSA but her nose was in good working order and sensitive to the smell of rotting fish. She should have realised before. You don't get the real good breaks more than twice in a lifetime and she'd already used up her quota. No wonder Vanessa Carrington turned up in the nick of time. She wasn't a nanny but a plant. A Venus fly-trap-type plant, soft green wings agape, ready to catch the Osmans in her sticky embrace and softly crush them to death.

How did Penny know?

Because of the address at the top of the letter was how. Wrestebury Hall, Wrestebury, Norfolk. Plus the name. Harry Surtees-Brown. She knew all about Mr Surtees-Brown. Like Penny, he was a childhood companion of Ludo Fairfax's. Like Penny, he was big and dark. Unlike Penny, he was a velveteen teddy-bear.

What bothered her most was how Ludo had expected to get away with it. She glanced up at the shelf of reference books. *Debrett's*, *Burke's Peerage*, *Walford's County Families*, *Crockford's*. Wrestebury itself was famous enough. So was Miss Ivory's bloodhound instinct. Seeing that letter and its signatory, Antonia would have been running a finger down the pages of one or other before you could say 'tumbril'. Ludo must have realised that. He would never have risked using the false name unless – the qualifier hit her like a blow from a croquet mallet –

unless he had known that Antonia herself would not be checking it out.

How was that possible? Why had he lied about baby Laura and three-year-old bloody Dickon? Did he know Fiona McIntosh had gone missing? Was he, perhaps, even behind her disappearance? She didn't want to think about possible answers to that one.

There was plenty to do. She did it. It wasn't until nightcaptime that she was able to open the newspaper she had bought that morning. She'd never drunk a nightcap in her life. She had a Jack Daniels instead. As usual, the world was full of politicians being boring. Moslems were demonstrating in Bradford. The exhibition which had opened the day before at the Royal Academy was reviewed by someone who hadn't enjoyed it much. A South American diplomat was meeting with the Queen. He looked rather like the guy she'd met at her mother's dinner party in the spring. In a juxtaposition which must have been editorially deliberate was a piece about the misuse of diplomatic immunity as practised by the foreign embassies, particularly with regard to parking tickets.

On an inside page, a paragraph described the finding of a woman's body in undergrowth at the foot of a railway embankment near Norwich. The autopsy had not yet been completed.

Bloody men, Penny thought. She was about to turn over when the name of the victim caught her eye.

She had been identified as a girl called Fiona McIntosh.

Shiiit.

She called Ludo Fairfax at his London flat. There was no answer. Nor was there for the rest of the evening until she gave up and went to bed. Though not to sleep, much.

* 5 *

Even though it was still early, a word must be had with Ludovic
Fairfax. A confrontation, even. And soon. She picked up the
telephone. Whatever they taught at Private Peepers school, only
twenty per cent of investigation is about trudging down mean
streets, knocking on doors and being dogged. The other eighty
per cent is knowing whom to call and then calling them. She
looked up Ludo's London address in her book then hit the
buttons. She wanted an explanation. Or perhaps a reassurance.
After a long while, someone sleepy answered in the kind of voice
they hand out to yuppies, along with the filofax and the Barbour.

'Is Mr Fairfax there?' she asked.

'No.'

'Where is he?'

'No idea.'

'None at all?'

'No. Hang about. Didn't he say he was off to Spain again?'

There was a pause. After it, Penny said, 'Well, did he?'

'God knows.'

'And you've no idea where he is?'

'None.'

'Were you at Eton?'

'Yes.' The voice heated up a joule or two. 'Were you?'

'Actually, no. I just recognise that old Etonian charm.' Penny
slammed the phone back on to the receiver. *Quel* nerd. She
looked at the small diamond watch on her wrist. 6.17 a.m.
Hmm. Perhaps that explained the lack of real warmth on the
guy's part.

Other thoughts occurred to her. If poor Fee McIntosh had
already been identified, the police must almost certainly have
been in touch with the Osmans. Next stop might well be the
R. H. Domestic Agency. Before they arrived, she had to find out
what game Ludo Fairfax was playing. She stared again at the
telephone. Far as she was concerned, she'd have bought shares

in Alexander Graham Bell any time he issued them. Without the phone, she'd be dead. Besides, how else did you keep in touch? On the other hand, calling people gave them the chance to be evasive if they wanted to. She needed hands-on contact with Ludo if she was to get the truth out of him.

Before that, before anything else, she better take a look at Fiona McIntosh's luggage. Two big suitcases, one smaller one. An overnight bag. Assorted carriers into which the exasperated Chrissie must have chucked anything she couldn't fit in anywhere else. The two big suitcases contained clothes and shoes. Dresses, jackets, a wool suit in dark green, another in coral. Skirts and sweaters, blouses, underwear, a raincoat, a Puffa. Penny felt in all the pockets and along the seams. She didn't know what she was looking for but it seemed a worthwhile thing to do. She came up with air.

She turned to the smaller case. Lingerie. Plenty of workaday knickers and bras in various shades of white. A grey-tinged panty-girdle – and whose wasn't, Penny told herself, feeling for the first time the humanness of the dead girl – and various pairs of tights. More surprisingly, there were also a couple of satin teddies, four flimsy suspender-belts in various colours including green and red, several bras of an exotic nature and several panties ditto. Exotic was probably the right word for nippleless and crotchless. Penny held them up and looked more closely. Cripes. Did women really wear that sort of thing? Did men really require them to? Chrissie Cooke Osman had said Fiona was sexy. This seemed to bear it out. But when would she wear them? Was Ewen Hamilton only able to get turned on to her when she wore such erotica? It certainly provided a new slant on both halves of the engaged couple.

The overnight bag contained personal items: letters, diaries, photographs. A small blue bear with a tartan bow round its neck. A jewel case. Penny opened it. There were scores of pairs of earrings, most of them cheap. Two pairs were not. One was an antique pair set with opals. The other was made of diamonds with a small ruby in the middle of them. Expensive, but not thrillingly so. There were several rings, too, most of them Victorian. Garnets, moonstones, seed pearls. She leafed through the letters. Without taking the time to read them, she deduced nothing whatsoever from them beyond the fact that Fiona didn't get a lot of mail, and most of what she got was either the official kind or from her parents. The photographs, too, seemed no more than the standard family snapshots. The diary was entirely blank. The only slight oddity was the fact that there were three different chequebooks, each from different banks. Fiona was one of those people who keep a running total. The total she ran made Penny's tonsils feel weak. The girl had thousands of pounds stashed away in high-interest deposit accounts. Where from? It couldn't have been saved from her nannying wages, surely? Perhaps she'd inherited it.

Penny shovelled everything back and went downstairs. She picked a mango from the bowl in the kitchen, slapped smoked salmon between slices of brown buttered bread. Breakfast. OK. So the telephone was a terrific invention. But she'd changed her mind on something. The guy who *really* deserved the Oscar was the one who first thought of hanging fresh salmon from a beam over a peat fire.

Placing every shirt she had plus her new Jasper Conran jacket on Ludo being down at Wrestebury, she left town.

Wrestebury was magnificent, if you liked that sort of thing. Penny had nothing against it, long as she didn't have to live there. Too grand, too large, too cold. She preferred rooms where space did not gather in corners and lower at you. Where invisible lengths of red plaiting did not implicitly rope off access to Axminster, Sheraton or Cotman. Even to *books*, for chrissakes. If you couldn't take a book off the shelves without feeling that some unseen attendant was liable to give you the bum's rush, what was the point? That this huge place should be home to only two people seemed anachronistic. Not to say showy. It was enough to turn even Margaret Thatcher to communism.

The approach to the house was dismal. It sat in acres of waving grass which should have been mown and in happier times was. Newly planted saplings sprouted here and there, each one guarded by a gothic iron arrangement that could have doubled as an instrument of mediaeval torture. Or a corset. Boy, the things women did for men. Away in the distance, the striped rumps of deer added a touch of the veldt. A brace of scraggy white peacocks was on show as Penny drove up the drive, acting supercilious under some of the many cedars. Behind the house, there used to be gardens of several kinds. Some of them sloped down to the river where she and Ludo used to swim. Rose, kitchen, herb, topiary. Also a maze. Around them all spread plenty of the kind of landscaping which had kept local artisans in full employ throughout most of the first half of the eighteenth century. Earth had been shifted, lakes excavated, trees planted, follies erected. The result was a series of prospects that most definitely pleased.

Penny drove round behind the house. The various out-buildings were built of the same pale stone. With the advent of the combustion engine, some of the stables had been converted by an Edwardian Fairfax into garages. It was years since she had last visited Wrestebury. Then, with the Brigadier in ferocious charge, the place had been immaculately kept up. Weeds had been kept at bay. Woodwork was painted at least once a year. Windows shone. A string of twenty-five or thirty horses occupied the main block.

All was changed. Now, only a couple of horses leaned over the stable doors. Grass and weeds sprouted between the cobbles of the stable yard. The oak half-barrels outside each loosebox, formerly kept full of seasonal flowers, held only moss-bound dirt. The need for paint was evident everywhere. Such unwanted neglect was sadder than any deliberate lack of care could be. It spoke of purse strings tightened, of wolves slavering at doors. Like a woman who had once been beautiful but could now no longer afford the cosmetics to keep up appearances.

Penny was right out in front there, when it came to admitting that she herself was privileged. She never felt guilty about it. The wealth of her parents was no more or less her fault than blue eyes might have been, or six toes. Nonetheless, she spent the greater part of her time in making some effort to compensate for it. Being poor wasn't much fun. Neither was having been rich once, as Ludo had, and now not being. Far worse was minding so much, being so wrapped up with a state which had been but was no longer and the need to get back to it. This she found both desperate and painful.

Getting out of the car, she saw a man open the kitchen door and walk towards her. He had rather more dark hair than seemed appropriate for someone of his age, which she guessed at about fifty-five. His face was obscured by a pair of glasses so thickly lensed that his eyes appeared huge behind them, soft and brown like those of the better sort of cow.

'Have you come to look at the table?' he said.

'Which table?'

'The mahogany dining table that was advertised for sale.'

'I'll be glad to look at it,' Penny said politely, 'but I already have one, thanks.'

'I see. Only Mrs Fairfax is out and she asked me to . . .'

Penny held out her hand. 'I'm Penny Wanawake.'

'Martin Harding.' He had a deep voice and a professionally positive manner. He sold something, she was certain. It could have been double glazing. It could have been himself. Whichever, he was good.

'Should I react?' Penny said.

He smiled. The action produced long cracks in either cheek, like starved dimples. 'Not unless you're something to do with the teaching of English as a foreign language.'

'I'm not.'

'I didn't think you were.' His magnified eyes lingered for several seconds longer than was necessary in the region of her rib cage then slid rapidly towards her legs. Despite the spectacles, there was nothing much wrong with *his* vision. Nor his libido, either. 'May I ask where you're from?'

'I'm in charge of a domestic agency,' Penny said. Well, it was true. No need to add that it was a short-term responsibility, due to end in the next forty-eight hours.

'Are you indeed?' Harding's face brightened. 'Just what I need. I'm short a cook. Luckily the first course is a small one. Could you find me someone suitable for the end of next week?'

She remembered now: Ludo saying that they'd rented part of Wrestebury to a language school. This must be the guy in charge. An extra gold star or two wouldn't hurt when Antonia returned. 'I might have,' she said. 'I'll give you a ring when I get back to the office. But I came to see Mr Fairfax. Is he home?'

From open windows to the left of the house came the sound of someone using an electric drill. Two distinct hammers were also in play.

'Yes. Is he expecting you? He didn't say anything about—'

'No. No, he's not.'

'I'd take you up but it's such a big place. You really need a motor-scooter to get about. He's in what I gather used to be the day nursery.'

'I know it well.'

'Good. I should just go on up. I'd take you myself but . . .' He did vague things with his hands. 'There's such masses to . . . '

'Right.'

Penny walked through to the front of the house and the main stairs. She peeked inside what used to be called the morning-room. Its superb panelled ceiling had been put in by a home-improving Fairfax of the Tudor period. She gazed up at its painted carvings, glad to see that this at least had not suffered from the recent downturn in family finances.

Ludo and his stepmother had clearly been forced to create a home within the house. Like the Christians in Cordoba, plonking their cathedral slap bang in the middle of all those Moorish arches. Walking along corridors, climbing stairs, passing closed doors, Penny felt the palpable presence of decay. Crumbling plaster. Invading damp. Spreading rot. And empty spaces. Hadn't there been a picture there, once? A Claude, or something similar, a vast landscape populated with pert shepherdesses and smug sheep? And an Elizabethan linen press there, heavily carved with fat little kids cavorting amid foliage? Sad. The Fairfaxes' loss had undoubtedly been Sotheby's gain.

The nursery door was half open. She could see an unnecessary fire burning in the big hearth. Apple logs. Penny recognised the smell at once. Seated beside it was Ludo, in an armchair of battered brown leather. His feet were up on the brass-tipped fender over which Nanny used to hang Viyella undergarments to air. A flat board was spread across the arms of his chair and scattered with papers. A brown leather attaché case leaned against its legs.

For a moment she watched him signing cheques. He was using the heavy brown-mottled fountain pen that had once been his father's. Like the aristocratic Brig himself, it was solid, dependable. Thick, too . . .

She went in, 'Hello, Ludo,' she said.

He leaped to his feet, knocking the board to the ground. Dramatically, the colour drained from his face. 'Jesus . . .' he said. 'What the hell . . .'

'Aren't you supposed to be in Spain?'

'What are you doing here, Penny?' He sounded very different from the Ludo she knew. Rude. Hard, somehow. Was that shock? Or guilt? His eyes were very bloodshot.

'Just passing, Ludo.'

'Really?'

No, not really. 'Thought I'd pop in, see how little Dickon was.'

'Little who?'

56

'Dickon.'

'Never heard of him.'

'How about his baby sister Laura?'

The red colour he had lost returned. Fourfold. 'Ah,' he said.

'Quite.'

'How'd you hear about that?'

'I'll tell you if you tell me something.'

'What?' He was wary.

'Who you had dinner with last Saturday.'

'I can't imagine why I should tell you, but as it happens I was with old friends of the family.'

'Friends?'

'I do have some, you know.' Ludo was annoyed. Or pretending to be. 'I'll give you their number if you don't believe me, so you can check it.'

Was he bluffing? 'You swore that if I got my mamma to invite you to dinner, there'd be no comebacks,' she said.

'You imply that there are.'

'I'd say false references and a dead nanny were comebacks of a sort. Wouldn't you?'

His line in perplexed enquiry was a classic of its kind. 'Am I supposed to know what you're talking about, dear heart?'

'Have a stab.'

He made his mouth go wry. 'Where to aim for?'

'Try the jugular. If you don't, I will.'

'Thought you were a photographer, Miss Wanawake, not a pit bull terrier.'

'That too. Especially when I'm agency sitting.'

'Ah,' he said again. 'I see.'

He knew. She was certain of it. He was perfectly aware that Fiona McIntosh was dead. Knew already about the semi-naked corpse lying among the willow herb and dead-nettle while the Intercity trains gushed past along the embankment above. Knew, too, about the dark-blue – Nanny-blue – stocking which had been used to throttle her, and the fact that the back of her head had been crushed with something blunt and heavy before death.

'When did you find out about Fiona McIntosh, Lude? Before the newspaper report appeared, or after?'

He covered his mouth with his hand, a quick movement designed to hide its sudden uncontrollability. She watched him think of something to say. She could practically hear the cogwheels spin as his brain meshed into action, working out the permutations before he came up with an acceptable answer. Shall I lie? Can I get away with a version of the truth? What does she want?

'In case you're not absolutely clear, I'm talking,' she said, 'about the girl who was erstwhile nanny to the Zachary Osmans.'

'What about her?'

'Knock it off, Ludo. You know she's dead.'

He gave a strange harsh cry. He bent over and began massaging his calf. 'Cramp,' he explained through gritted teeth. He pointed at the wicker chair opposite him where his own nanny used to sit, twenty years ago. He sighed. 'Yes. I saw it in the paper.'

'Thing is, why?'

'There you have me.' He stroked his smooth yellow hair.

'And who killed her?'

'Poor girl,' he said. 'It's dreadful, truly dreadful. But these things do occur from time to time, however much we wish they wouldn't. There are so many perverts nowadays. It could have happened anywhere.'

'Get outa here,' Penny said, disgustedly. 'Are you trying to make me believe that her murder has damn all to do with you being so hot to meet Zachary Osman a couple of months back?'

He frowned. 'Of *course* I am.'

'Did you plant her there?'

'Don't be ridiculous.' He started to pick up his papers. 'I've never met the girl. Never heard of her, either, until I saw about it in the newspaper.'

'What about Vanessa Wotsit? You certainly sent her along to the Agency with forged refs.'

'It's hardly a hanging matter, Pen.' The sound he made was meant to be a rueful kind of laugh. 'Jesus. If I'd realised you'd be taking over from old Ma Ivory, I'd have used a different address on that reference.'

'And name, Ludo? Or should I call you Harry?'

Again the laugh. Not awfully rueful. More like embarrassed. 'Yes. Well . . .'

'Is all this still to do with the money you think Osman is laundering?'

'Naturally. The new baby seemed the perfect excuse to get someone I could trust – like Vanessa – into the centre of things. When you mentioned the R. H. Agency at your parents' dinner party, the whole thing fell right into place. Unfortunately this McIntosh girl got in there before I could get anyone organised.'

'How did you know?'

'Know what?'

'That Fiona was dead? Vanessa Carrington contacted the Agency the day before yesterday. I took her down to the Osmans that evening. There was nothing about Fiona in the paper until yesterday morning.'

'I didn't know,' Ludo said, his voice as smooth as satin camiknickers. 'I asked Vanessa to get herself on the books. The idea was that she would prove to be busy or something, unless it was the particular job she wanted.'

'You're seriously asking me to believe that?'

'Yes.'

There were so many objections to it as a plan of action that Penny didn't bother pointing them out. Ludo knew what they were as well as she did. 'Do you get danger money?' she asked, leaning heavily on the sardonic button.

'How do you mean?'

'I always thought banking was among the safer professions. An occasional rubber cheque. The odd hold-up. Apart from that, I thought it was all a totter towards a golden handshake and a retirement pension, followed by the grave.'

'Banking's changed, Penny, like everything else. When there are millions at stake, the criminals can get pretty ruthless with anyone who gets in their way.'

'Is that what happened to Fiona?'

'I doubt it. I told you, these sex-killers choose victims at random.' His eyes were not happy.

'And I told you you're full of prunes.' Penny tapped him on the knee. 'Ludo. Who killed Fiona?'

'I already said I don't know.'

'Not you?'

'Don't be ridiculous.'

'Swear.'

'I swear.' He passed a finger across his throat. His voice broke as he added: 'I absolutely swear.'

Penny looked into the heart of the fire. Ludo was lying. Not neces-sarily about murdering Fiona, but about something. Ludo was playing his cards so close to his chest that even he couldn't see them. 'Do you think Zachary Osman was responsible?' she asked.

Suddenly Ludo looked old. 'Penny, I honestly don't have any idea.'

'But if he did – doesn't that mean Vanessa Carrington could also be in danger?'

'I don't want to believe that,' he said slowly.

The nursery door opened. A woman came in, carrying a tray with coffee fixings. A dog snuck in behind her, sliding round the edge of the door and heading straight for Penny. On the tray was a plate of iced biscuits stencilled in sugar, the sort Ludo had always asked for when he came home for the hols.

'Mr Harding said you had a visitor, so I thought you'd like something,' she said.

Ludo got to his feet and took the tray from her. 'Thank you, Mrs Heath. How kind.'

She looked round the room. 'Don't often get up here,' she said. 'Dear me. You could certainly do with a lick of paint up here, couldn't you?'

Penny saw Ludo wince. 'I like it like this,' he said.

Penny did too. Long lines of Fairfax children streamed away from the present back into the past. Nannies, nursemaids, governesses, maybe even mothers had sat in this same battered chair, wiping noses and tears, reading stories, kissing places to make them well. Every stain on the dun-coloured walls was a memory. Every mark on the battered paint was a reminder of former occupants. Nothing in it had changed for years except the personnel. Its very shabbiness welcomed.

'But those curtains,' Mrs Heath said. 'Look at them. Practically falling off the rails.'

'It'd be a bit pointless to replace them. At least until there are some more babies up here.'

Mrs Heath looked at Penny. 'He ought to find a nice girl to marry,' she said.

'No nice girl would have him,' Penny said back.

'Then a nasty one. It's about time there were some babies here again.'

'I'm doing my best to oblige,' Ludo said. 'I really am.' He spoke lightly. The lightness did not offset the impression he gave of someone silently screaming.

The dog snuffled at Penny. She wished it wouldn't. Although she had nothing against dogs, she didn't like them much. Especially insistent ones. On the other hand, it was kind of hard to shove a dog aside when its owner was watching. She let it snuffle, wondering how many swallows it would take to drink her coffee. Coffee was another thing she didn't like much.

'Only instant, I'm afraid,' Mrs Heath said. 'We keep the beans for best.'

It was one of those remarks that grew ruder, the more you thought about it.

'Are you staying to lunch, Pen?' Ludo said.

'That's very kind.' Penny would have gone straight back to London if she hadn't thought there might be more to find out. 'Yes, please.'

Martin Harding joined them for lunch. 'I shouldn't really,' he said guiltily. 'But my Course Director has taken the students on an excursion to Stratford so I'm freer than usual.' They ate a ginger shepherd's pie and overdone broad beans. Compensated for to a certain extent by the fresh strawberries and thick cream which followed. After them, Harding showed Penny the alterations in the right wing. 'They had to put in extra bathrooms and loos,' he explained. 'Health and safety regulations. But apart from that, it was mainly an exercise in slapping on paint.' He opened the door of a large room on the ground floor. 'This used to be a games room. It's converted rather well to an office, don't you think?'

'Great,' Penny said. She walked over to where three large corkboards had been fixed to the walls above a couple of cheap office desks. 'How long've you been in occupation?'

'Only a month. My secretary and I needed to be on the spot for the final three weeks or so before the first course started,' Harding said.

The room was crowded. Three or four computer terminals. A copier. Piles of English-language readers. VCRs with attendant cassettes. Boxes of stationery. In a corner leaned a dozen tennis racquets and a heap of tennis balls sealed in cylinders. Harding pointed at them. 'We've had the tennis courts put back into some sort of working order. I wish they kept this place up: I'd be happy to take it on every year.'

'Did you tell them?'

'I mentioned it to Mrs Fairfax, but she seemed to think her son would object so I've said no more. Pity, really. It's got everything I want, including that authentic English stately home atmosphere. Just what my students want. Or their parents do. The younger ones don't give a damn, really, as long as they can watch *Police Academy 92* on the video.' He picked up one of the cellophane-wrapped racquets and mimed a serve.

'I thought the people were coming to learn English, not play tennis,' said Penny.

'We like our students to play hard as well as work hard,' said Harding. 'Lots of activities going on in the afternoon, after the classroom work in the morning.'

Penny read some of the pinned-up notices. Timetables. Bedroom allocations. Names of teachers. Lists. Lots of them. She read one through. It contained only eight names.

'Ludo told me several groups would be passing through during the summer,' she said.

'Yes. What you're looking at there is the current adult course. They're more expensive because there are fewer participants and a higher ratio of staff to pupils.'

'What's an adult defined as?'

'Anyone over twenty. Once that course finishes, we have younger children – between eight and eighteen – for six weeks. Then another short course of adults to finish up with.'

'I hope it all works out.'

'My God, so do I. I have a reputation to maintain, apart from anything else.'

'For the Fairfaxes, I meant.'

'Yes.' He looked at her sideways. 'They do seem a bit skint. I suppose trying to keep these huge places up is a terrible drain on the finances. Incidentally . . .' He changed the subject without hesitation. 'I meant it, about the girl to cook for us.'

'I meant it too.'

'Sorry?'

'That I'd look through the files when I got back to London.'

'I don't mean anything in the cordon-bleu line, of course. Just what my mother used to call a good plain cook.'

'I'll telephone you.'

'And come and visit us again, if you'd like to. We're always glad to see visitors.'

'I might do that.'

Ludo walked Penny out to her car. The noise of sawing and hammering echoed back from the stable yard. 'Is Amabel enjoying all this?' Penny said.

'She seems to be.'

'Isn't that a good thing? The more enthusiastic she is, the

more successful this whole venture will be.'

'Maybe. But she's tried to go into business before and it didn't work.'

'I remember the hats.'

For friendship's sake, Lady Helena had bought one. It made her look like Mary Queen of Scots. After the axe had fallen. Remarking fairly forcefully that loyalty to friends stretched only so far, she'd given it to Miss Ivory. Miss Ivory looked great in it. Like Lady Jane Grey.

'And the antiques,' Ludo said gloomily.

'I must have missed those. How did they go?'

'Rather rapidly. She hasn't got much business sense, I'm afraid. By the time she decided to pack it in, she'd been done by just about everyone. Especially the woodworm.'

'You know, Wrestebury would make a superb hotel,' Penny said. 'People would pay anything you liked for the chance to stay in a place like this. The ceiling in the drawing-room's worth twenty quid on anyone's bill, let alone the—'

'Shut up,' Ludo said. His tone was savage.

'Let me guess,' said Penny. 'You don't want to talk about it, right?'

'Right.'

'Because it's Amabel's home, right?'

'Right.'

'She might actually enjoy it, you know. The activity. The responsibility. Especially if you brought in some kind of professional help.'

'Over my dead body.' Ludovic was looking terrible. His face was blotchy. One of his eyelids fluttered minutely. You could have planted leeks in the lines round his mouth.

'Ludo,' Penny said softly, 'you look like someone on the verge of a breakdown.'

'Thank you very much.'

'I should have thought your love and loyalty to Amabel over the years has long since wiped out any debt you might have felt you owed.'

'It's none of your business.'

'True. But Fiona McIntosh is. At least while I'm standing in for Miss Ivory.'

He pulled a long breath in through his nose. 'I should leave the poor girl to the police.'

'I probably will. But if anything happens to Vanessa ...'

6

'So tell me about her,' Penny said.

She sat in the drawing-room in cotton calf-length trousers and an over-size T-shirt printed with the opening sentence of the *Iliad*. Both were white, like all her clothes. Like all *Gandhi*'s clothes. And for the same reason. White meant peaceful. White meant good vibrations. Her legs were long. Her drink was stiff.

Opposite her, tucked into a corner of the chesterfield, sat Ewen Hamilton. His legs were longer. His drink was stiffer. It needed to be. He was clearly shattered by the news of Fiona McIntosh's death.

He had been waiting outside the Chelsea house when Penny arrived back from Wrestebury. Last time they met, he still had the freshness of a new-laid egg. Now he could have been a hundred and twenty years old. Only a monster could have ignored his plea to talk to her.

Which is what he was now doing. 'You've got to help me,' he said. 'The police don't care. I rang them up but all they would say was that they were pursuing their enquiries. They think Fiona was murdered by the same man who killed those other two girls last October.'

'Near Haslemere?'

'Yes.' Ewen spread the kind of tabloid that Penny wouldn't have wrapped her sweat socks in across the coffee-table. 'Look.'

'FOURTH NANNY SLAIN', howled the headline. Underneath, in measured tones and typeface suitable for the partially sighted, the text insisted that this beast must be caught before he struck again. There was a picture of Fiona looking smudged. Others showed Chrissie Osman looking glamorous and Zachary looking rich. Further down, the writer demanded to know how much longer the carers in our society must walk in fear. A footnote at the bottom of the page invited people to turn to page five where there was an editorial on 'Women at Risk'.

The Nanny Murders. Uh-oh. Give a journalist a peg and he'll

hang his typewriter on it. The first victim, who had died in circumstances similar to Fiona's the previous July, had been a young woman walking home after baby-sitting her nephew. The two Haslemere victims were au pair girls from Düsseldorf. Yet they were all being lumped under the same occupational umbrella as Fiona. Now, with the Osmans involved, the Nanny Murders had taken on a new dimension. Money plus glamour plus sudden death meant unlimited opportunities for slease, the stuff every newspaper proprietor dreamed of. Slease sold papers. On the inside pages of this paper, there were pictures of the Osman house and another of the Osman wife, this time dressed in fishnet tights and a top hat, doing a tap dance for a charity revue.

At the bottom of the page a further photograph showed a smiling woman holding the reins of what was probably a horse. Double-thick type, boxed in black, revived the scandal of the former Mrs McIntosh who had abandoned husband and babies for love of Rodolfo Esteban, international playboy. The article managed to make several implications about the lady's morals and manners without being in the slightest way libellous.

'The point is,' Ewen said, 'it's like the Yorkshire Ripper.' Tears began to roll down his pink face. He didn't bother wiping them away.

'How?'

'The police will sit in front of their computer terminals, collating millions of pieces of evidence, and getting thoroughly bogged down. It'll be at least a couple more murders before they finally get the break-through they need. And once they get him, they'll charge him and that will be that.'

'Possibly.' Penny leaned over and refilled his glass.

'Definitely. And Fiona will be – will be swept under the carpet, just another victim.'

'Isn't that what she is?'

'I don't think so. At least, not of this so-called Nanny Killer. Even if he exists I'm convinced he had nothing to do with Fiona dying.'

'Why?'

'I can't really explain. But it's more than just a feeling. For a start, he stripped all the clothes off those other poor girls and took them away from the scene of the crime. Fiona wasn't ... she'd been left half dressed, according to this story. And the others were stabbed and' – he swallowed – 'mutilated. Fiona was

65

strangled. They'd been sexually assaulted, too. Fiona wasn't.'

'How do you know? They haven't said anything.'

'Exactly. That means there's nothing obvious, whereas with the others they were able to say immediately that they'd been raped.'

'What exactly are you asking me to do here?'

'Maybe there's nothing *to* do. But at least look into it for me.' Ewen put his hand inside his jacket and pulled out a wallet. 'I'll pay you. I'll be glad to. With Fee dead, there's no point in saving money.' He stared beyond Penny's head to the open french windows. Behind his toffee-coloured spectacles his eyes were desolate. She could guess at something of what he felt. She could hear a bird singing in the garden and the sound of frogs. One day there would be another Fee McIntosh in Ewen's life, but for the moment his days stretched bleakly ahead, intolerable expanses of loss and loneliness to be somehow survived.

'What are you hoping I'd find?' she asked.

'I don't know. Something. Anything. All I know is, there's something not right about it.'

'Whatever I found, if anything, I wouldn't want money. Not for myself.'

Ewen stretched a chequebook over his knee. 'Name your charity,' he said. A fountain pen hovered.

'Let me think about it,' said Penny. 'First off, tell me more about Fiona.'

He did. At length. Earnestly, expanding on what he'd told her the last time he'd come around.

Turned out he'd never met the mother. Once she'd disappeared with her cricket-playing lover she had not, until now, returned to England, though news of her filtered through. It was known that the lover already possessed two sons by his dead first wife. The McIntosh girls used to fly out every summer to spend the holidays with their mother and stepbrothers.

'One big happy family,' commented Penny.

'I don't know about that. I gather that this Esteban character – the new husband – had a bit of a temper.'

'What's that mean in English? That he was violent?'

'Fairly. So I understood from Fiona. Threw things. Threatened people with shotguns. That sort of thing.'

'How old was she when he died?'

'Sixteen or seventeen, I think. She told me about it once. There was a row about something and he stormed out of the house, apparently, and didn't show up at dinner that night. That was quite normal, I gather. It wasn't until the next morning that they sent a search party out for him and found him shot dead somewhere up in the hills.'

'Who did it?'

'They never found out. As far as I remember, it was put down as a hunting accident. Which it might very well have been.'

'You sound doubtful.'

'It's just I gather he wasn't terrifically popular, locally. Fiona didn't like to talk about it much. Anyway, there were always people out hunting – local landowners and so forth – and I suppose her stepfather was in such a rage when he marched off that he might well have been careless. Walked into someone's line of fire.'

'I suppose she was pretty upset.'

'Yes.' He stared into thin air, furrow-faced. 'I can't quite remember but she may even have been the person who found him.'

'One of those experiences every adolescent needs.'

'And later she never went into au-pairing and children's nursing?'

'She'd always wanted to work with children. She told me once that children didn't – uh – fuck you up.'

'Man hands on misery to man,' Penny said.

'Quite.'

'It deepens like a coastal shelf.'

'What?' Hamilton stared at her in bewilderment.

'Get out early as you can and don't have any kids yourself.'

'Yes.' Ewen worked his eyebrows a bit as though clearing space around himself. The average Brit's response to anything said seriously. Or anything potentially embarrassing, like a stranger quoting poetry. 'It was a bit of a waste, really, I always thought. She was awfully bright.'

'Just a minute,' Penny said. 'There are those who'd argue that looking after children is one of the most fulfilling jobs around. If fewer people thought like you, the world would be a better place than it is now.'

Ewen took off his glasses and stared at her. His eyes were large and water-logged. Without the protection of the lenses they seemed destitute. 'You know what I mean.'

Unfortunately she did. The implications were that caring for children required instinctual values rather than intellectual ones.

Which meant that child-care was often left to those considered to be at the lower end of the intellectual scale.

Had Ludo Fairfax been lying when he said he didn't know Fiona? He'd sure as hell been lying about *something*. If he had been, and if Chrissie Osman's suspicions about Fiona snooping were correct, might it not mean that Fiona had been got at by Ludo to see what dirt she could turn up about Zachary Osman? And now here she was, dead.

'Does her mother know what's happened?' Penny asked.

Ewen shifted forward. His hands, clasped around his glass, hung between his knees. 'I don't know,' he said. 'Perhaps, if she reads the papers. Otherwise ...' He shrugged. 'Dr McIntosh doesn't know where she is, so he couldn't have said anything.'

'Does anyone know where she is?'

'I do. Fiona told me which hotel she's at in London. Apparently she and Paco – the eldest Esteban son – have brought the younger son over. It's his first visit to England. He's supposed to be taking some kind of training course over here.' He gave Penny a speculative look. 'Someone ought to tell her ...'

'Won't the police have been to see her?'

'I'm afraid they probably won't.'

'But they'd never release the name of a victim without informing the next of kin. Which means someone has identified her for them.'

'Yes.' He coughed apologetically. 'That was Dr McIntosh. I called him yesterday. But the reason they might not have told her mother ... I asked Dr McIntosh about it and he said that Fiona lost her mother years ago.'

'And if he said the same thing to the police, they'd assume there was no mother to inform.'

'Exactly.'

'So are you going to see her?'

'Uh – she doesn't know me.'

'What about Fiona's sister?'

'Dym? I told you. She's just finished one of those cookery courses. She's on holiday with some friends at the moment, taking a break before she starts working.'

'Do you know where?'

'No. But on a boat, I think.' His gaze slewed away as though he felt guilty for not knowing. 'Oh Lord. Unless they buy the papers, they won't know what's happened, either.' He set the glass down carefully on the floor and then turned and buried his face in his arm. 'What am I going to do?' he said, his voice muffled by the sleeve of his jacket. 'I loved her so much. How'm I going to tell Dym? How's her father going to manage without her? Or any of us?'

Penny went and sat beside him. She put a hand on his shoulder and pressed down hard. The cold comfort of strangers, she thought. Impossible to convey how deeply you felt for someone in mankind's worst predicament. No blow was more cruel than the death of a beloved. No pain was sharper. Death, after all, was implacable.

'I'll do what I can,' she said. 'But it might not be much.'

The hotel was opposite the back gates of Buckingham Palace. Penny took the five shallow steps up to its entrance in a single stride. Inside there was a lot of dark mahogany and a fair amount of disapproval as she crossed the lobby. Hard to see why. She was wearing her white knee-length shorts and a crisp white cotton shirt with a button-down collar. A belt of scarlet webbing encircled her waist. What more did they want? Ermine? She walked past a flower shop, past a small display case containing cultured pearls and silver filigree brooches, and across a square yard or two of deeply polished parquet flooring. The low panelled ceiling and lack of windows lent a Dickensian gloom to the place. Tourists paid handsomely for that kind of thing. She stood at the reception counter, watching the paunchy clerk behind it register some strong emotion. Difficult to say which. Indifference, probably. He elaborately slotted mail into pigeon-holes for a while, oblivious to the needs of the clientèle. In this case, Miss Penelope Wanawake. Who might, for all he knew, want to book the bridal suite for a month, but wasn't being given a chance to do so. She thought she might be about to get mad if she wasn't given it very soon.

Be fair. Perhaps it was too dark in there for him to see her. She picked up a representation of the Tower of London fashioned from a metal that was probably base, and rapped the counter-top with it. He reacted violently, clapping a hand to his chest.

'Yes? Can I be of service?' he gasped.

'Let's just say you can tell me Mrs Esteban's room number.'

'Why?'

'Guess.'

69

'We don't hand out information to anyone who walks in off the street, you know.'

It was one of those occasions when Penny wished she owned some dreadlocks. She leaned on the counter. 'Hey, man. What you think? I be gonna mug 'em? Steal their travellers' cheques or something? Break their eardrums with my blaster? *That* be what you think?'

'It's simply that we have to protect our guests.'

'Well, I believe in that, man. And I gonna protect myself, too. How about you call me the manager right now.'

'The what?'

'Manager, man. Know what I mean?'

'That isn't necessary.' He gave her the hairy eyeball for a moment then turned to the wall behind him. 'Room 204,' he muttered.

'Thanks. Can I call Mrs Esteban from down here.'

He pointed away to the right at an old-fashioned kiosk of wood and glass set halfway down a dimly lit passage. She walked towards it and dragged open its folding door. The clerk had already turned away. Swiftly she walked further along the thick-piled carpets and round the corner. Somewhere there would be stairs or lifts to the second floor. When she found them, she'd use them. Knocking at doors had it every time over telephone calls. It was difficult to tell someone to bug off when they already had one of their white canvas shoes stuck in your door.

Three left turns further on, she found what she was looking for. Upstairs, the landing widened out sufficiently to accommodate the odd side-table with flower arrangements on. The flowers were real. Three windows offered a glimpse out over royal leafage.

Room 204 had double doors painted white with the number in gold. She knocked and waited. After a while, she heard a key turn on the other side. The door opened.

A man stood in front of her. He stared at her without speaking. She stared right back. Either she had vision problems or this guy was the hunkiest thing she'd seen for years. Would he be the elder Esteban? She'd imagined some dewy-faced kid, hairs just sprouting on upper lip, a zit or two somewhere near his mouth. Instead, she was checking out some serious good looks here.

'Hey,' she said. 'You can park your moccasins in my wigwam any time you like.'

'I beg your pardon.'

'Mr Paco Esteban?'

'Yes.'

'I'm looking for Mrs Esteban.'

'What for?' He drew his heavy black eyebrows together. Before he did that, they had been lying above dark brown eyes and a bushy moustache. Although he must have been close to thirty, there wasn't a single line on his smooth tanned face. Not that Penny could see. Not from here. She was willing to get a little closer, see if she could pick up on one or two. What made him stand out was the fact that his hair was completely white.

'Does the name Ewen Hamilton mean anything to you?' she said.

A sneer of the kind most people keep for inadvertent shit on their shoes briefly marred the set of the moustache. 'Yes.'

Without a falter, Penny moved into barefaced deception. Her talents were few. For instance, she had only once ever managed to open a door using her American Express card and then only because it hadn't been locked. But where lying was concerned, she was top-drawer. 'He's engaged me to make some enquiries about Miss Fiona McIntosh.'

'What are you, some kind of private detective or something?' His English accent was almost faultless.

'Right.' Faith unfaithful, she told herself, kept her falsely true.

He seemed apprehensive. 'What has my stepsister done, that you need to make enquiries about her?'

'If you'd allow me to come in, I can explain.'

'All right.'

She walked in.

The Esteban family clearly didn't spend much time queuing for welfare. The room was part of a suite, and suites in London didn't come cheap. *Broom*-cupboards in London didn't come cheap. For the privilege of a sitting-room plus at least two bedrooms and presumably, attendant offices, they'd be paying a whole lot of plenty. Especially with the Queen brushing her teeth in the palace right across the street. The furnishings were mock tapestry and gilt-encrusted wood. Tables groaned under the weight of roses and fruit baskets. A magnificent honey-coloured mink had been tossed carelessly on to a window-seat. It matched the linen slub which covered the walls. Two oil paintings hung from them. One was a winter scene that could have been painted by almost any Dutch Master you could

71

remember the name of. The other was a still life featuring a Delft plate with chips in the rim on which stood various pieces of fruit including a three-quarters-peeled lemon and some peaches which made you want to rush over and sink your teeth into them. Not a single expense had been spared.

'Hi. I'm Penny Wanawake,' she said. She was standing close to a magnificent mirror, a fake Louis of some number or other, which had embossed invitations stuck into its edges, three 'At Homes' from people with high-class names. A private view. A wedding invitation.

He took the hand she held out and dropped it again. Amy Vanderbilt would probably not have listed the manner in which he did it under Ways To Make A Woman Feel Good.

'Katrina – Mrs Esteban is not yet up.' The voice reminded her that there was work to be done.

'That's your stepmother, right?'

It's difficult to make brown eyes look icy but he managed. 'That is correct. What exactly do you want to know?'

So far, no mention of Fiona had been made. With a curl of apprehension, Penny saw that they hadn't heard about the murder, which meant she was standing there with her butt in the wringer. Few positions were less envious. Nobody liked being the messenger who showed up with the bad news.

Paco quirked a handsome eyebrow. She'd seen the way he did it on the covers of a hundred Harlequin romances. 'So,' he said, 'why is Mr Hamilton sending private detectives to interview us at this time of day?' He spread his hands so that she could take in a gold watch on his wrist. 'Or, indeed, at any time, of any day?'

She would have found the whole thing a lot easier if he had not been wearing a plum-coloured bathrobe of a material that several tons of silk-worms had spun themselves to death for. The edges kept drifting apart so that she could see most of his torso, plus tantalising glimpses of the rest.

Where to begin. 'It's – uh – it's about Fiona.'

He nodded encouragingly, moving towards a phone. 'I'm about to order breakfast,' he said. 'Would you like something?'

Now he mentioned it, she was ravenous. She snuck a look at her own watch. 8.05 a.m. She wished she wasn't a morning person. It was a real handicap. Sometimes she thought she would have preferred a glass eye or no thumbs. Something more obvious in the way of disablement. When you were the sort who was ready to go at five o'clock and you knew the rest of the world wouldn't have switched itself into gear for another three or four hours, it could be pretty frustrating. Talk about marching to a different tune. 'Yes, please.'

'What?'

The full English breakfast, she wanted to say. With a side order of kippers and a double portion of devilled kidneys. 'Whatever you're having.' She prayed that he wasn't one of those melba toast 'n' black coffee freaks.

For the first time he smiled. 'Miss Wanawake, you look like someone who has not had a square meal for at least twenty-four hours.'

'Shows, huh?'

'Why don't I order you the full English breakfast?'

The man was a miracle. 'Why don't you?' she said.

He picked up the phone and began ordering.

'I don't drink coffee,' she added quickly.

When he had replaced the receiver, he came and sat opposite her. He adjusted his dress. Penny looked modestly to one side, but not before she had caught a glimpse of boxer shorts patterned with leaping frogs. Darn it. That reminded her. She'd left home without checking out the ones in Barnaby's pond.

'Now,' he said, 'what about Fiona? You were about to tell me why Mr Hamilton has taken it upon himself to rouse us from sleep.'

'You sound like you don't care a whole lot for Ewen.'

'I have no feelings either way. I have never met the man, though I have heard Fiona talk of him. He is besotted with her, is he not?'

'Isn't it mutual?'

'What?'

'I understood they were planning to get hitched.'

She'd heard of ready smiles. This guy had ready frowns. He displayed one. 'Do you mean ...' he paused ' ... *married?*'

'Right.'

'Tell me, Miss Wanawake. Are you a successful private detective?'

'Wouldn't exactly go—'

'Because I want to tell you you have got things completely wrong. Fiona has no intention of marrying Mr Hamilton.'

'How do you know?'

'Because she is going to marry me.'

73

Penny crossed her long shiny legs. There was no need to but it gave her a chance to show off a bit. People with good gams shouldn't hide their tights under a bushel. Also gave her time to think. If she'd still had her braids, now would have been the perfect time to shake them about a tad. Two men claiming to be engaged to Fiona? *Très* bizarre. Finally she said: 'Did she know that?'

It was the right question. It disconcerted him. 'Certainly she does. there is no doubt about the matter,' he said stiffly. 'Mr Hamilton is nothing to Fiona.'

'She actually said that?'

'Frequently. She finds the man's attentions irritating and intrusive.'

Oh Jeez. There it was again. The present tense. Signifying he definitely did not know about Fiona's murder. If you thought about it, it wasn't hard to see why. The police had only just identified the body. Her mother wasn't home since she was visiting London, and the father – according to Ewen – didn't know his former wife's whereabouts. There was no reason why anyone official would have got on to Ewen Hamilton yet. And the sister was temporarily of no fixed abode, out of touch.

As she'd feared, someone was going to have to tell Paco Esteban what was what. And then deal with the consequences.

For someone, read Penelope Wanawake.

'Look,' she said. Her hunger had vanished. There were various ways she could handle it. 'I don't know how to tell you this, but—'

There was a knock on the door, followed immediately by the rattle of wheels as a waiter pushed into the room with a cartful of covered dishes. 'Room service, Mr Esteban,' he said. Just in case Paco thought it was the Queen's Own Highlanders come to pipe him into the shower.

'Just leave it,' Paco said. He'd picked up on the gravity of the situation.

Penny wanted out of there. She didn't have to be here, doing this, damaging peoples' hearts, causing grief. This wasn't her problem. This was nothing to do with her. Except that Ludo had made it so by turning up three months ago and asking for a dinner invitation.

Once the waiter had left, she got it over with. Esteban heard her out in silence. Once he covered his eyes with his hand, pressing thumb and forefinger into their corners and bowing his head. When she had finished, he didn't ask any questions. He laced his fingers together and looked at them for a few moments. Hard to tell whether he was praying or fighting for control. A bit of both, probably.

When he spoke, his voice was thick. 'This will be hard for my – uh – for my stepmother to hear.' He shook his head.

'Were they close?'

'Not particularly. There had been ... problems. Katrina had hoped that this visit would give them a chance to become friends again.'

You didn't have to read between the lines to grasp the situation. Penny stood up. The smell of fried mushrooms seeping out from under the covers on the trolley was making her feel faint. 'It'd be better if I went,' she said. 'I'm really sorry to have been the one to tell you.'

'I don't imagine it was easy,' he said. He stood too. 'Is there somewhere I can get in touch with you when I've had a chance to – to take in what you've told me?'

'My card.' Penny handed it to him. He propped it on the mantel, alongside several more invitations to grand affairs. One of them she could see from here was ambassadorially crested.

He came to the door with her. 'I'll call you in the next couple of days.'

He opened the door into the passage outside. As he did so, one of the inner doors opened. A sleepy voice said, 'Darling, what are you doing?'

The woman who appeared was stunning. If she was Fiona McIntosh's mother, she had to be in her early forties. Yet, from where Penny was standing, she looked more like a luscious twenty-year-old. The force of gravity had not yet begun to tug down either breasts or belly. Blond hair curled about her head. She had one of those wide, sensuously-lipped mouths that set the blood racing as the mind invents things for it to do.

She was wearing a robe that matched Paco's. When she came into the room it hung loosely about her body. Seeing Penny, she pulled it together, but not before Penny had observed that the blonde was for real. Her voice had been ripe with sex, either recently fulfilled or about to be. Now it sharpened.

'Who're you,' she said. 'Paco, who is this girl?'

Penny wanted to say she was a full-grown woman, thank you very much. Now, however, was probably not the time for feminist dialectic.

'What does she want?' The woman had some kind of a faint accent. Scandinavian, it sounded like.

Penny edged through the door. She definitely did not wish to be around when Katrina Esteban heard about her daughter's death.

Paco took Penny's elbow and put his face close to hers. 'I'll talk to you later,' he murmured. She could smell his toothpaste and, from the opening in his robe, a headier, franker musk. Recently fulfilled, Penny surmised, rather than about to be. Or possibly both. Either way, as she turned into the Mall towards Trafalgar Square, it provided her with food for thought.

Later, in her Chelsea kitchen, providing food for sustenance, she thought about it some more. She took a tray out into the summer-lit garden and sat on the edge of the pond. Disturbed from his contemplation of the lily-pads, Haricot stirred, stretched, shoved off. Penny watched the plopping frogs as they waved tiny hands in the air and jumped about, or sat panting on one of the rocks Barnaby had provided for them to pant on.

She thought about Paco Esteban. God, he was attractive. And made more so by the fact that, unlike so many of the men who possessed good looks over and beyond the call of duty, he made no conscious use of them. It would be a cliché to say he seemed unaware of them. Only a man with the brains of a ping-pong ball could have looked into the mirror for some thirty years and not seen that he was film-star class.

What was far more interesting, what made the pulses really sing, however, was the fact that he appeared to be involved with both mother and daughter at one and the same time. Nothing wrong with that. Men had done it for ever. But on the whole, when they were doing it they tended to avoid entanglement. To be arranging to marry one while bonking the other seemed to be coming it a bit strong.

She wondered if Fiona had known.

She wondered if Katrina Esteban had. Even more, she wondered what, if they *had* known, either of them felt about it.

7

What now?

And what could she do about it, anyway? The notion that
the police were an incompetent bunch of idiots, only too grateful
to be helped by the gifted amateur detective out of the impasse
into which their blundering incompetence had led them was
long dead. It was no longer a question of whipping out a
magnifying glass and making a deduction based on the state of
a man's dandruff or the contents of his turn-ups. No amateur
could hope to compete with the vast crime-solving resources
which the police now had at their disposal. No amateur with
any sense would try to.

She decided it was ridiculous for her to go poking into something about which she knew so little. If there had not been
the connecting links of the Osmans and Ludovic Fairfax –
tantalisingly simple, probably, though for the moment obscure –
she wouldn't have spent two seconds listening to Ewen Hamilton. Let alone agreeing to look into the matter of Fee McIntosh's
murder. For one thing, what exactly was there to look into? For
another, you just knew the cops were biting their nails, praying
that some big black bint would barge in on their investigation
and give them a hand. She'd probably wind up on a charge of
impeding the course of justice or something.

Scattering fishfood, Penny considered Fiona McIntosh. When
she'd done that, she considered Ewen Hamilton. Was Paco
Esteban correct when he said the only feeling Fiona had for
Ewen was irritation? Or was it the natural reflex of a man who
senses a rival? And if it was true, what sort of a woman had
Fiona been, if she could give Ewen reason to believe that she
loved him when she didn't? Or was she one of those people who
can't bear to hurt anyone and end up hurting everyone in sight?
And what kind of a guy was Paco that he could betray the
woman he intended to marry with her own mother?

Betray. It was an old-fashioned notion. But however state-of-the-art you were, it still didn't fly right. A man who slept with both mother and daughter was the stuff myths are made of. And jokes about travelling salesmen. Same thing, really.

By the lily pond, the frogs quivered. Some sat on the cool green leaves, little hands spread in front of them ready for immediate lift-off. Half a dozen peered unblinkingly at her from under some grey-green foliage with kind of spiky leaves. It was cool in this corner of the garden. Several of the edging stones had moss on them, a miniature acreage of plant life. A ladybird nosed out from under a leaf and began the long trek towards the next one. Best place to be. Penny wouldn't mind spending the day under a leaf.

She came to a decision. She would call Ewen Hamilton up and tell him the deal was off.

There was nothing she could help with. Besides, she had a heap of things to do. Miss Ivory needed picking up from the hospital. Admin for the BlackAid concert was hotting up by the minute. There was a new Sara Caudwell waiting to be read. And the weathermen were predicting still more sunshine. Yeah, telling Hamilton she was pulling out was the only course of action to take.

So get in there and take it.

Something fluttered around her mind like a moth trapped in a jar. She could see it clearly, trying to get out and not making it. Something to do with the Estebans. She wondered about hitting Ewen Hamilton with what Paco had said about Fiona. Someone had got their wires twisted and it would be kind of interesting to know who. But where was the point if she was opting out?

The cordless telephone she had by her rang. The open air reduced its vibratory noise almost to nothing. Nonetheless, several startled amphibians hit the water in a running dive as she reached for it,

'Miss Wanawake?'

'Yup.'

'This is Paco Esteban.'

'Give me a moment to get my breathing under control.'

'I'm sorry?'

'What can I do for you, Mr Esteban?'

'I have called the police but they are being most unhelpful.'

'What did you ask them, the cricket scores?'

'Why should I do that? I do not play cricket.'

She remembered. 'Your father did.'

'I cannot imagine how you know that, but yes, he did. Among many other things.' An indefinable something crept into his voice. That didn't stop Penny trying to define it. Without much success. There was certainly some anger in there. Plus a soupçon of hurt. Fleetingly, she wondered whether Esteban Senior's murderer had ever been apprehended. 'Why I rang them, in fact, was to ask them to find my stepsister, Dymphna. They did not seem inclined to take on the task.'

Paco sounded as though he were using his sneer again. She hoped sneering wasn't something he did a lot of. It would be too bad if Nature, having pulled out all the stops in the looks department, fouled up with too big a dose of pomposity. A little was OK. It gave a woman a chance to retain a sense of proportion. It cut a guy down to size. After all, there wasn't a man on this earth could be pompous and not be ridiculous as well. 'Which is why I am calling you,' he continued.

'And here I hoped it was for my body.'

'What was that?'

'Sorry. I've got a frog in my throat.' Gaahd. What a thought.

'A frog?'

'It's a figure of speech.'

'Miss Wanawake. You are a private investigator.'

'Of sorts,' Penny said. She spoke cautiously. He wanted something she was probably not going to want to give. 'In a purely amateur and accidental way.'

'I want to hire you,' he said.

'To investigate?'

'Naturally to investigate. What else?'

'Just a thought,' Penny said. 'What do you want me to look into?'

'I want *you* to find my stepsister. She has gone boating with some friends, I understand, and therefore is difficult to get hold of. I shouldn't imagine a person like yourself would find it hard to track her down. It's only a question of following her route.'

'Where did she start from?'

'Somewhere on the Norfolk Broads.'

'Yes.' Penny waited. 'But where?'

'That's all I know. She wrote to Katrina – my stepmother – and said they were holidaying on the Norfolk Broads.'

'That's a pretty big area.'

'Is it?'

79

'No wonder the police weren't too keen to join the search. Haven't you got any further clues as to where she set off from?'

'I have her letter in front of me: *"The four of us have hired a boat and are going to mooch around the Broads for a couple of weeks as soon as we've got our diplomas. Might even see something of Fee since her new job's not that far away. We're really looking forward to it, though I've put on so much weight in the past year I'll probably need a new swimsuit."*'

'Mooch,' Penny said.

'Yes,' he said impatiently. 'Will you take the job?'

She wanted to say no. Now was the time to tell him she'd opted out, she'd resigned from the Sam Spade Association, she was taking a world cruise. Anything. But curiosity won out. It was too late now. She was hooked and likely to stay that way until whoever knocked off Fiona McIntosh was found.

She sighed. 'OK.'

'Good. My stepmother is obviously deeply upset by the news. The sooner Dymphna can get here, the better.'

'For whom?'

He thought about that one. Then said: 'At times of trouble, people need their family about them.'

'I'm sure Dymphna would agree.'

'Please start looking for her immediately.' He sounded stern. Tell the truth, he sounded downright bossy. It was the kind of sound that made her want to stamp her foot and say 'shan't'.

'I do have other commitments,' she said. With restraint. 'But tomorrow, I'll drive over to Norfolk and see what I can come up with.'

Putting down the receiver, Penny felt pretty certain of one thing. She didn't go much on rules for running her life. Nor on principles. Too many of those and you could end up as an elder of the Free Presbyterians or something. Only the weak needed principles to provide props for their uncertainties. It was best to go with the flow. Play it by ear. Be ready to change when circumstances required it. But one rule she tried to stick to was that of being non-judgemental. Quite apart from anything else, she loved the way it sounded, rolling off the tongue. Non-judgemental. Great.

And being non-judgemental, she was reluctant to form an opinion about a woman who deserted her young children for the sake of a classier screw than the one she was getting. She didn't know enough about the circumstances. However, Fiona's mother apparently needed Dymphna around as some kind of support system rather than because the girl herself might need supporting. The Colonel's Lady and Judy O'Grady might be sisters under the skin, but it was damn clear to Penny Wanawake that she and Katrina Esteban were not out of the same crate of oranges. Or was she being unfair? Perhaps it was Paco Esteban's selfishness she was picking up on, rather than his stepmother's.

She went into the house. On her desk were various telephone numbers that Ewen Hamilton had given her. She found the one she wanted, came back outside, pressed the number buttons.

A brusque voice answered. 'Dr McIntosh?'

She was brusque. 'My name's Wanawake.'

'So?'

'I'm a private investigator, Dr McIntosh. I'm trying to locate your daughter Dymphna.'

'On whose authority?'

She wondered how he felt about his former wife. Using the Esteban name might not produce the best results. Divorced friends of hers spoke about the sense of failure and rejection they felt when their husbands walked out. It must be much the same for a man when his wife left. She dodged answering that one. 'I'm very sorry about . . . about what's happened,' she said.

'Yes. Well. It's a family matter. You need not concern yourself about it,' he said. If this was a sample of his bedside manner, his patients probably slept in hammocks.

'The thing is, the police haven't been able to get hold of your younger daughter to let her know. That's where I come in. I was wondering whether you—'

'You're working for the police, are you?'

Gulp. Good as she was at prevarication, she tended to crumple under direct questioning. Not that it happened very often. Most people were too afraid of challenge to say that they didn't believe her. Not to mention being too polite to suggest she was lying. 'Absolutely,' she said. And simply for confirmation added: 'Fiona's mother ought to—'   'My daughters lost their mother when they were very young,' the cold voice interrupted. 'Are you from the newspapers?'

'No.'

'Hrumph,' he said. Or something pretty close. It was so exactly the sort of noise made by crusty old Highland doctors with hearts of gold that she could practically smell the haggis.

'So,' she said, before he could start making further noises of

the sort that sounded like crusty old Highland doctors slamming
down the phone. 'I was hoping you might have some clue as to
where I should start looking for Miss McIntosh. All I know is
that she's on the Broads.'

'Potter Heigham.'

'What?'

'Potter Heigham, woman,' he said impatiently. 'She started
from Potter Heigham.'

'Right. Thank you. I hope—'

He hung up.

She tried to analyse the way he did it. Was it a slam? Not
quite. In fact, as receiver replacements went, it could be classed
as not entirely unfriendly. On the other hand—

Stop! This was displacement activity of a ludicrous kind. She
found the road atlas and looked up Potter Heigham. It looked
kind of small. The sort of place where they'd be sure to remember a group of four brand-new cooks going off for a fortnight
on the river. She hoped.

At the pond's edge, the telephone cheeped again. The garden
was full of loud batrachian reproach. It wasn't what they were
used to. Birds, yes. Birds, they could cope with. Telephones,
definitely no. They told her so. A goldfish moved about,
bumping at the surface of the water like an aquatic carrot. She
picked up.

'Hello.'

'How're the frogs?'

'Croaking.'

'Oh Lord. You're not going to tell me you forgot to feed
them.' Barnaby didn't sound too thrilled.

'Got it in one. I'm not.'

He was being slow.

'I don't mean turning up their toes,' she added. 'I mean they're
doing what frogs do best. Second-best. Listen.' Penny held the
receiver closer to the piebald chorus. It immediately shut up.

'Can't hear a thing,' Barnaby said.

'How about asking if I'm OK?'

'Are you OK?'

'No.'

'What's up, honeybun?'

She told him.

When she'd finished, he said: 'Know what I like about you?'

'Yes.'

'Apart from that?'

'Tell me.'

'For most people, death comes as the end. For you, it's just the beginning.'

'Barnaby, I really wish it wasn't. I don't exactly like dead people, specially when they die before their time, like this Fiona. I don't like the grief death causes. I particularly don't like the way violent deaths always seem to involve prising the lids off people's private cans of worms.'

'You could retire.'

'I never hung out a shingle in the first place. And no one takes me seriously when I say I don't want to do whatever it is they're asking.'

'Just a girl who can't say no.'

'Dead right. Which is why I'm off to Norfolk tomorrow, to hire a boat.'

'You and boats don't exactly hit it off.'

'I can't think of any other way to locate the sister. All I know is she's on the river somewhere. Started from Potter Heigham. Talk about a needle in a haystack.'

'Funny phrase,' Barnaby said. 'If I had a spot of sewing to do, a haystack's probably the last place I'd choose to do it in. Matter of fact, I can't think of anything I would choose to do in a haystack.'

'Can't you?'

'It'd be so prickly.'

'Exactly, big boy.'

He laughed. 'Antonia's back today, right?'

'Right. I'm picking her up from the hospital this morning.'

'Have fun on your boat.'

'Oh, sure.'

At eleven o'clock she was helping Miss Ivory into the car. Not that Miss Ivory needed helping. In fact Miss Ivory had already indicated that the only thing she needed was a stiff rum-and-orange and a chance to bitch about the way Penny had run the Agency in her absence. She took the news of the Fiona McIntosh murder as a personal slur.

'I knew I shouldn't have taken the girl on in the first place,' she said. 'I could tell at once that she was deeply disturbed.'

'Hey. What about a little compassion here?' Penny said.

'Of course, I'm very sorry for her family and everything. It's

83

a most terrible tragedy.' Miss Ivory fiddled with her hat. 'Oh dear. If only I'd been around.'

If you told yourself that Miss Ivory was childless, that the Agency stood *in loco infantis*, you could just about choke back the words lurking on the tip of your tongue.

'It's guilt,' Penny said, sliding behind the wheel. She turned the key and listened to the hiccup as the engine caught. It'd been doing that ever since she converted to lead-free.

'What is?'

'The way you're acting like I'm personally responsible for bumping off one of your nannies.'

'Guilt? I have nothing to be guilty about.'

'Oh yeah?'

'Oh yeah,' said Miss Ivory. She rummaged in her bag for a couple of Rennies and placed them carefully in her mouth. Any minute now she'd burp.

'It's not how *I'd* feel, if I'd thrown up all over my apartment and then left someone else to clean up.'

'Please, Penelope. I'm an invalid. Barely discharged from my sick bed two minutes ago and already you're berating me for something that was beyond my control.' Miss Ivory raised a Bernhardtian hand to her brow.

'Anyway, I got a replacement for Fiona.'

'What is she called?'

'Vanessa Carrington.'

'Carrington? Not those people from Surrey, I do hope.'

'I can't remember.' Penny swung into the Scylla of the Hyde Park Corner traffic lanes. No need for a Charybdis. If you got out of that alive, you'd get out of anything.

'You checked out her references, of course.'

'What do you think I am, Antonia, some kind of slouch? Went down personally and had a word with the guy.'

'You mean there was only one reference?'

'Only one within reasonable reach of London. 'Course, I could've got the sleeper down to the Scilly Isles but in view of the urgency ...'

'I suppose you're right.' Miss Ivory spoke grudgingly.

'Anyone ever tell you that with a moustache and a cowlick, you'd be a dead ringer for Hitler?'

'Not so far.'

'Better watch it, that's all.' The traffic spat the car out into the turbulence of Grosvenor Place and down the length of the

Buckingham Palace garden wall. Penny patted Miss Ivory's knee. Four, five years ago, she would have exchanged a word or two with her Sitting Tenant, neither of which would have been particularly civil. She was more tolerant now, aware not only that most of the old don't much like being that way, but also that she too would be old one day and grateful for the understanding of the young. Not that Antonia was particularly ancient. Sixty-four? Sixty-five? She said: 'What's sixty-plus these days?'

'Sixty-plus is sixty-plus,' said Antonia, burping gently. 'You never think for a minute you'll ever be that old. And then around forty-six or so, you begin to realise that if things go on the way they have been you'll be fifty any year now. And after that, it's a clear run towards sixty. Not much fun really. Especially when you perpetually feel like a sixteen-year-old.'

'Does one stay the age one enjoyed most?' Penny said. 'If so, guess I'll always be nine. That was the year I was given my first bike and got to watch *Doctor Who* on TV, and Nanny Simpson helped me make scones which my parents said were the most delicious things they'd ever eaten in their entire lives.'

'They were probably lying.'

'Thank you, Antonia. You just destroyed my dream of taking over when Raymond Blanc mothballs his egg-whisk.'

'I don't know why adults lie to children,' said Miss Ivory. 'Children always know when they're not being told the truth, and lying's hardly the kind of behaviour one wants them to imitate, is it?'

'Check.'

'Anyway, this Carrington creature was all right, was she?'

'Ace.' Penny turned a corner so sharply that Miss Ivory lurched to one side. She wanted to avoid discussion of Vanessa Carrington. She was fairly sure she wouldn't make it. The minute Antonia looked at those references she was going to sense that something wasn't quite jake about them.

Just as well she couldn't read Antonia's mind. Something's not quite jake about this Carrington girl, Miss Ivory was thinking.

She held on to her hat. It was green. Also netted. There was a good label inside. Picking it up in a jumble sale, she had thought for one wild moment that the Queen Mother must have discarded it. It went very nicely indeed with the new dress she'd bought for Ascot. She would have to go through the In-tray very carefully when she got back because as sure as she was sitting there, Penelope was hiding something. It was simply a matter of finding out what and then putting it right.

'I got the two cooks for UniChem,' Penny said. 'Their personnel officer rang yesterday to say how pleased they were with them.'

'Good.' Unless Miss Ivory's antennae were on the blink, there was something slightly dodgy here, too. She decided that perhaps she was getting too old for caviar. Or for caviar in the quantities she'd hitherto been able to consume. 'Well done.'

'And there's a man called Martin Harding who wants a good plain cook. I've left the details on your desk.'

'Thank you, Penelope. You seem to have coped very adequately.'

'Please, Antonia. This fulsome praise is making me blush.' Penny swung round a corner, almost hitting a leather-jacketed motorcyclist straddling his stationary machine in the middle of the road. 'Tomorrow I'm leaving for Norfolk.'

'Why?'

'I've got to find Fiona McIntosh's sister.'

'Why you?'

'Her stepbrother asked me to. Paco Esteban.'

'Esteban?' Miss Ivory sat up so sharply that the green netting tangled with the edge of the sun-shield on her side of the car. 'Oh, no, dear. I'd steer well clear of the Estebans if I were you.'

'I thought you got the hots for Esteban Senior when you were a girl,' Penny said.

'That's one way of putting it. Not the way I personally would choose, but it reflects the situation as it was, I suppose. The point is, he was a bad lot, what with one thing and another. It was just as well he didn't live in this country, all things considered.'

'Why was it?'

'So he had somewhere to run to when the police began to investigate.'

'I'm not quite following this.'

'Try and concentrate, Penelope. The point is, Rodolfo Esteban was a crook. Very high-class, of course. Very suave and charming. But a crook all the same. I don't know how many people he defrauded before he finally left the country.'

'Widows and orphans left penniless, sort of thing?'

'Hundreds of them, I should think. He certainly left a trail of bad debts behind him. Funny thing is, I was thinking about him the other day.'

'From what you've said about his looks, I'm not surprised. I may say the son is pretty damn sexy, too.'

'I'm not talking about sex, for goodness' sake. But that place where Fiona McIntosh went ...'

'The Osmans.'

'Yes. I knew the name rang a bell. Unless my memory serves me wrong ...'

'Which it never does.'

' ... the Osman husband – Zachary, is it? – was in partnership with Esteban in one of his deals.'

'Seriously?' Penny turned off the King's Road. There was a space right in front of the house. Somebody loved her. She parked and turned off the engine.

'Yes. I'm not sure he didn't go to jail for a while.'

'Zachary?'

'I think so. Or did he get a suspended sentence? Or am I thinking of someone else? I shall have to look it up. Certainly I'm sure that Esteban left his partners to take the rap. Most of them hadn't any idea what was going on.'

'How come the Press haven't picked up on it?'

'I don't know.'

'I see.' It was true. She definitely saw something. Even if it was only that the plot, whatever it was, seemed suddenly to have thickened.

Almost certainly.

8

The citrus green of spring had long ago given way to the darker green of high summer. Recent rain had freshened the hedgerows, holding back for a while the inevitability of autumn. As Penny drove further from London, the land flattened. The horizon grew wide and full of sky. Puddles lay in the road, reflecting the sharp blues and whites of the scudding clouds.

Penny's mood flattened, too. Just as Miss Ivory had once felt the grip of fifty closing on her, so she herself felt the cold bite of thirty. Thirty was a watershed. Beyond it, whatever you felt, you could no longer pretend to be youthful. Although she still had a couple of years to go, thirty was there on the edge of her consciousness. Quite a lot of the time, it loomed.

When it did, she thought of Barnaby. Of marriage. Of the things women want. Or seem to. Are expected to. What bothered her occasionally was that she didn't. Not marriage. Not babies. The reasons for rejecting them at twenty-five would not change when she hit thirty. Marriage was a tie. Babies were unnecessary. Tell the truth, babies were an unbearable responsibility. Just the thought made her neck muscles tense. She untensed them. Producing another being, taking on the job of creator, of psyche-moulder and prejudice-former, of shaping attitude and expectation: it was too much. Too powerful a magic. And when you considered that, having hand-crafted this tiny torpedo, you launched it into the world to damage or be damaged . . .

A magpie landed in the road ahead, its long tail momentarily fanning out as it touched down. One for sorrow. She shook her head. She simply did not have the arrogance to consider herself a suitable candidate for parenthood.

She ate lunch in a riverside pub. Chairs and tables made from what could have been the ruins of Abe Lincoln's log cabin had been set out on the grass. Although it was damp from the recent rain, she sat on one of the seats. It smelled of wet forests. From time to time small spiders edged out from beneath bits of bark on it and shook a leg. The river ran flatly between wooden edgings, neat as a nursery-rhyme. Small craft moved slowly up and down it. People sculled. Other people passed by in rowing boats shaped like peapods. They shouted a lot. Some of them drank from bottles and splashed their companions with water. Directly across from her, an old man fished from a collapsible stool outside a shack of weather-greyed planks. Fun, fun, fun.

Further on, Penny stopped at a Pick-Your-Own place and picked her own raspberries. They sat punneted on the passenger seat as she drove deeper into a landscape full of trees and distant individual spires, giving off what – along with the scent of willows – she thought of, would always think of, as the true smell of summer. Because Nanny Simpson had once said so, it remained a given. It was not a question of believing or not believing what Nanny said. It was a matter of acceptance. Oh, so *that's* what summer smells like.

By the time she reached Potter Heigham, she'd eaten all the fruit. She found a space in the crowded parking lot by the water and stepped out into a puddle. Darn it. She was wearing what had until then been white leather boating shoes. Now they were yellow with industrial sand. She squelched down to the river. A boat was slewed across it, the wind hammering at its sails and driving it rapidly towards the stone bridge which straddled the water. A balding man with the nose and expression of an angry eagle stood on its deck, tugging at bits of rope and shouting obscenities at a teenager in cut-offs. The teenager wore a personal stereo and had considerable quantities of blond hair. The longer parts were attached to the front of his head, the back of which was shaven closer than a lawn. Various locals leaned over parapets and against railings. Watching part-time yachties was clearly an entertainment they never tired of.

A glass-and-wood information office squatted at one edge of the parking area. 'REGISTER HERE', it said. She went in. Racks of tourist leaflets hung in plastic-coated wire frames, along with brochures of various boat-hire companies. Hoseasons. Waveneys. Blue Bird. She picked one out and looked through it. Talk about Mission Impossible. There were hundreds of boats, hundreds of different classes. And that was just one company. Asking at the desk would be pointless. It was one of those fallacies that only worked in detective fiction. Ticket sellers and the like might possibly remember the red-haired man with the severe nervous tic, or the woman disfigured by a strawberry birthmark, but they would never be able to recall where such characters had bought a ticket *to*. Especially in a busy place like this.

She glanced across at the two women behind the counter. Totally hopeless. They were working through a queue of some ten families anxious to get aboard their hired craft and away. Since it was probably like this most days of the season, there was no way they were going to recall the four newly qualified cooks signing on. Even if they'd been distinctively marked – oh yeah? With pink beards, maybe, or silver lamé body stockings? – the most they'd remember was that they'd been there. Which she knew already, thanks to lovable old Dr McIntosh.

Seemed like she had two choices. Either she hung around, waiting until Dymphna reappeared. Or else she could get hold of some kind of vessel herself. She groaned. She was too tall for water-borne craft. If there was one thing she hated, girl like her, it was low roofs. If there was another, it was motor boats. And here she was, stuck with both.

Enquiries produced the name of three yards close by where she could hire a boat. It was a reasonable assumption that one of them was the place Dymphna McIntosh had set out from. The first was a couple of hundred yards downstream. She tried it. Turned out not only did they have nothing for hire, they'd never heard of the name McIntosh. With or without the Dymphna. Why should they? She'd been assuming that Dymphna had organised the boat trip but it could just as well have been one of her chums.

'Four girls?' she said, looking down at the wizened child in oil-stained dungarees who appeared to be in charge.

He shook his head. Shrugged his shoulders. Wiped a smudge on his cheek.

Walking back to her car, she saw that the aquiline yachtsman had managed to get on course again and was heading upstream, his teenage son at the helm. The bald head was covered with a nautical cap that emphasised his amateur status. But what the hell, there's nothing wrong with being an amateur. She was one herself.

At the second boatyard, which was bigger than the first and manned by three personnel in royal-blue flyingsuits, two male and one probably female, it was made clear to her that if Dymphna McIntosh had started her holiday from there, they didn't know about it. One of the males showed her their booking chart. It didn't help a bit. Nor did they have anything for hire at that precise moment. If she wanted to come back in a couple of weeks ...

The third place was a couple of miles out of town. She drove along leafy lanes, following the course of a winding stretch of water. It was lonely out here, and intensely rural. Occasionally a house could be seen behind hedges, its beauty self-conscious, as though waiting for a photographer from *Country Living* to arrive and make its name. Otherwise, human habitation had dropped to zero. At bends in the road she softly pressed the horn. It was so narrow here that there was not room for two vehicles to pass. Saucers of elder blossom sat among the overwhelming green. Even above the noise of her engine she could hear birdsong.

'In this high pastoral,' she said to herself. 'This Blunden-time ...' Saying it did absolutely nothing for her. It ought to have moved the soul. Some might have been uplifted by so much evidence of God's busyness. Not P. Wanawake. Take her this far out of the city and she felt endangered. She needed walls at her back, preferably graffiti-covered. She liked the smell of diesel and the hiss of air-brakes. She liked shop-fronts and neon signs and bus-stops. Perhaps she just preferred Man's busyness to God's.

At a gap in the hedges, she saw a sign subsiding into a bank of nettles and Queen Anne's Lace. Faded blue letters, almost indistinguishable from the white background, informed her that this was Bardwell's Boats. She turned in, crunching over a yard or two of gravel before the path degenerated into potholed soil over which someone had laid a thin coating of sand. The recent rain had turned it into a yellowy mud which splashed up as high as the car windows. She stopped in front of what looked like a condemned Nissen hut. There were boats everywhere, some in the water, some out, as incongruous on dry land as swans. Rusty lifting gear stood about. There was a petrol pump, a dripping standpipe, a pile of tyres. One end of the hut had a window set into it with a sign above so corroded by weather that it was illegible. She pushed open a door beside it. Concrete floor. The smell of fuel and plastic. Gleaming hulls of boats rearing out of the gloom. Somewhere in the murk, green water caught a spray of light and tossed it gently up and down. She called.

Nothing. She came back outside and listened. Near by, she could just hear the sound of rock music being overlaid by the manic antipodean babble of a DJ. Edging between oil drums and tarpaulin-covered piles of planks, she tracked it down to its source. This was a tall blue-eyed man in a navy Guernsey so old that it was turning white. His hair was doing much the same thing, for much the same reason. He was fiddling away at the jib of a small sailing boat tied up to a poured-concrete slipway, whistling between a set of teeth so improbably coarse and yellow that when he turned them in her direction, she thought at first they had been cut from orange peel and inserted into his mouth as a joke.

'Hi,' she said.

He looked up and nodded. Seldom had she seen a more contented expression. If you wanted uplift, this was the place to come. She smiled. 'Mr Bardwell?'

He nodded again, pressing the Off button on his transistor radio.

'There's two things,' she said.

'Name them.' His voice matched his fine aristocratic face.

'First, I need to hire some kind of craft.'

'Sail or . . .' He stopped before uttering the blasphemy.

'Sorry. It'll have to be motor. I have to find someone on the water.'

'What's the other?' His teeth moved about independently of the rest of his mouth.

'To find out whether by any chance you hired a boat to four girls recently.'

'One of them fat?' He let go of whatever he was holding and curved his hands round the outlines of an invisible woman. A big woman, ample of breast and generous of hip.

'I don't know.' She remembered Dymphna's letter. 'Possibly.'

'One of them called Ford-Harrison?'

She shrugged.

'How're you going to find them when you don't know their names or what they look like?' The teeth bobbed around as he spoke. They didn't actually clash together. Just looked that way.

'I'll manage,' she said.

His blue eyes moved up and down her body in a way that was so frankly lascivious it was impossible to mind. 'I'm sure you will,' he said.

'Did they leave from here, then?'

'There were four girls, about a week ago. This huge fat one, as I said. Three others. One of them rather plain, the others pretty damn beddable, not to put too fine a point on it.'

'They didn't mention being cordon bleus or anything did they?'

'If they did, I didn't hear them. Too busy giving them the once-over.' His blue eyes heated up suddenly, as though someone had lighted a candle behind them. 'Their papers and so on. Not to mention their, you know, natural assets.' He stepped suddenly off the boat on to the slipway. 'I say, you wouldn't like to make an old man very happy, would you?'

'Get outa here,' Penny said.

His face sagged. 'Didn't think you would. Don't think anybody realises what it's like. Just because you're old doesn't mean you lose your, you know. Trouble is, the women my own age can't be bothered, and the ones your age don't want to go to bed with someone my age. I can't blame them really.' He looked depressed.

'Keep trying,' Penny said.

'Believe me,' he said, 'I do. Matter of fact, I proposition every woman that comes in sight. If you only get a point one per cent response, it's still a damn sight more than most old codgers are getting.'

'And do you?'

'Not to put too fine a point on it, yes.'

'If you did something about those teeth, you might even bring it up to nearer five per cent. You're a good-looking guy.'

'Oh Lord,' he said. 'I've got my working teeth in. Excuse me.' He turned away from her for a second, raising a hand to his mouth. When he turned back, he'd been transformed into a dead ringer for John Gielgud.

Working teeth? What the hell was the difference between them and any others? She refrained from asking. Truth to tell, she wasn't sure she wanted to know the answer. Instead, she looked at her watch and said: 'This Ford-Harrison party ...'

'Yes.' He came past her in a gush of cigar smoke and something rather fine and old. Brandy, it might have been. Of a superior kind. 'Let's have a look.'

She followed him into the Nissen hut. He found a dangling string and pulled it. A light came on. There was a desk with papers on it and a surprisingly serious-looking double filing cabinet. He pulled out a buff folder. 'Ford-Harrison, Ford-Harrison ...' he murmured. 'Here we are.'

She'd struck oil. Four names were written into the space

headed 'HIRER'. One of them was D. McIntosh. 'What's the boat called?' she asked.

'*Ecstasy.*'

'You're kidding me.'

'I most certainly am not.' Bardwell straightened. 'They started off upstream. But they could have branched off in any direction, or even turned round and gone down river. God knows where they'd be now.'

'If you were four girls who'd just got a cordon bleu diploma, where would you aim for?'

He frowned. The two vertical lines above his nose sharply increased the likeness to Gielgud. 'Judging by the look of them, they liked eating as well as cooking. But I can't imagine such young creatures would be in a position to afford fancy restaurants, would they?'

'Depends. Maybe after all that hard work they feel like eating something someone else has cooked, and hang the expense. Maybe they get a big allowance from their parents. Who knows.'

'The reason I ask ...' He fixed his blue eyes on her breasts. 'The reason is, there are a couple of well-known restaurants further along the river. The Owl and the Pussycat's one of them. Poncy sort of place, run by a couple of queers. Damn good food, though, whatever they choose to do with their dicks.'

'So coarse.'

'Have to be, m'dear. It's the only way to go on. Keeps the blood running freely through the veins. Otherwise it'd be wheelchairs. Or one of those gharsely Zimmer things.'

'What's the other restaurant called?'

'The Harrison Arms. Used to be a riverside pub, until these people took over. Been tarted up with orangeries and piped Mozart and the like. Can't say I care much for the chap who runs it.'

'Why not?'

'Spends most of his time pottering about in a boat with a bottle, leaving the whole place to his partner – or housekeeper, or whatever she is – to run, then shows up at drinking time and gets abusive.'

'A piss artist, huh?'

'And a bully. Twenty-four carat. I don't like men who abuse their womenfolk.'

'I don't understand womenfolk who let them.'

'I'm sure you don't, m'dear.' The blue eyes moved fondly

around her figure. 'Not everyone has your obvious confidence. Anyway, the place's got all sorts of recommendations from these Good Food Guide johnnies, thanks to poor Mary's efforts.'

'Mary?'

'Ford-Harrison's other half. Not his wife, but might as well be, from what I hear.'

'Hm-mm.'

It wasn't stretching credibility too far, was it, to suppose that there might be some connection between a girl called Ford-Harrison who'd just got a diploma in upmarket cooking and a restaurant called the Harrison Arms with a reputation for gourmet food?

'How about letting me squeeze your breasts,' Bardwell said.

'How about renting me a boat,' Penny said. 'Then we'll talk.'

As she nosed out into midstream, she saw the eagle-nosed man from Potter Heigham. He was lying back in the cockpit of his boat, a bottle of beer at his lips. The teenaged son was holding the wheel and staring fiercely into the distance. Or was it the future? She waved at him. He waved back without smiling. Oh, the angst of youth. Some of his front hair fell over his face. With a practised movement of his head, he flipped it back again.

She was making for the Harrison Arms. As a place to look for Dymphna, it was no more than a wild guess based on even wilder conjecture. On the other hand, it was somewhere to start. When Bardwell said 'abuse', did he mean physical abuse? She knew enough about the psychology involved in wife-battering to be aware that it took two low self-images for it to work, that the batterer was often as psychologically damaged as his victim. But perhaps Bardwell spoke merely of a brusque manner or unlovely habits.

She chugged past a row of small square chalets, each with its own slip where a boat lay moored. The river was demure here. As she moved further into the Broads, it grew less controlled. The chalets gave way to beds of reeds which obscured the land on either side. Sky and water took over, blending into one grey. Disorientating. She hated it. A wind got up, slapping against her face. Her hair was full of air, streaming away behind her. The river knocked against the prow and shivered the stems of the reeds. God, she loathed being cold. Even more than she hated being wet. On a boat, the possibility of being both was always distinct.

Across the tops of the reeds she could see more reeds. And in the distance, a spire. A windmill stood to hand. She wondered how long it would take to chug the eight miles to the Harrison Arms. At this rate, it would be dark before she got there. You couldn't go faster, not if you had any sort of an ecological conscience. Kingfishers, for instance, nested low on the water-line. And banks got eroded. She'd read about the damage that too many motorboats were causing in the area. She looked up into the grey sky. Jeez, it was chilly. Whatever happened to summer?

At least there were some people about. She could see sails moving beyond the reed beds. Even hear voices. A snatch of guitar music was carried past her by the breeze. 'California Dreamin', it sounded like. She knew just how the Mommas and the Poppas must have felt. She looked over her shoulder and saw the blond teenager competently go about. His father was not in evidence. Birds rose from the water and flapped around, looking as if they ought to be interesting. 'I come from haunts of coot and hern,' Penny said aloud. It didn't sound awfully convincing.

Somewhere distant, a bell sounded. Above the hiss of water and the thin throb of the engine, she counted five strokes. She'd at least be there in time for a drink and something decent to eat. It would be terrific if they let rooms. Other-wise she'd be condemned to sleeping in the damp little cabin of her temporary home. And – oh *gaahd* – using the chemical loo.

It seemed like for ever before a foursquare building of grey blocks of stones appeared. It was set back about a hundred yards from the river, with smooth lawns and plenty of cottage garden-type flowers. The sign above the door left no room for error. This was it. The Harrison Arms.

She tied up to one of the black-and-white painted mooring posts set into the bank. Three other boats were already there, their owners presumably inside the sanctuary of the bar. With the noise of the engine cut off, the silence seemed absolute under the miles of darkening Norfolk sky. Sounds edged back towards her. The sigh of the reeds. A melancholy monotone bird. Water slapping tiredly against the moorings.

She walked between the scent of tobacco plants and phlox to the door and pushed it open. Drew a big sigh. Aaah. This was what it was all about. Warmth, comfort, soft lights, people.

While she wouldn't give a rat's ass for most of her fellow men, she liked to know they were around.

She parked herself on a stool. Ordered a double Jack Daniels from the man behind the bar. Cased the joint. Most of it was busy casing her. Of the twenty people in the room, she was the only woman. And what a woman *she* was. White trousers, white T-shirt with 'I'M FOR PEACE' on it in green letters, no bra. After a hard day's tacking up and down the water, she was just what the doctor ordered. She never minded the admiration of men. In its own way, it was life-affirming. And that kind of mindless gawking, of assumption that body was all, only served to emphasise the superiority of the female. She gave them one of her best smiles and decided to grow her hair again. A situation like this really called for her white-beaded braids. If they'd still been there, she'd have clashed them around.

The door opened. Bald Eagle, the guy from the boat she passed earlier, came in, stooping to avoid banging his head. Red marks on his forehead indicated where he had previously been too late. Several times. Behind came the son, white-shirted and clean-jeaned. Recognising her, he jerked his head in greeting, looking away with the agonised shyness of the adolescent confronted by a grown-up. Was she a grown-up? Sure didn't feel like it.

She turned to the man behind the bar. Either P. F. Harrison or M. Laurence, who were, according to the hand-painted notice above the door, Sole Props, licensed to sell ales, beers, wines, etc. The former, almost certainly. Penny had seldom seen a human being more perfectly adapted to the role of concentration-camp commandant. His head was mostly bald with stubble on either side that reminded her of a cornfield when the combine harvesters have finished with it. He wore rimless glasses which magnified the coldness of the grey eyes behind them. There was no obvious point at which his head became his neck. His mouth looked as if it could earn a comfortable living tearing the wings off jumbo jets.

'Mr Harrison?' she said.

'Yes.'

'Mr *Ford*-Harrison?'

'Well, yes, actually, although I don't use the —'

'I was hoping to find your daughter.'

'Alison? Why?'

'She's on the river, I understand.' What kind of parents called a child Alison Harrison? It was almost as bad as Daisy Cheyne. Or Meyer Meyer, for that matter.

'Yes.' He was looking wary. Perhaps he was waiting for her to whip out a maternity order or something.

'With Dymphna McIntosh.'

'Dymphna is one of the party, yes.' His hands were covered with a layer of meat so solid that his knuckles had disappeared. He used them to polish a glass with a linen tea-towel. He slotted the glass into a hanging arrangement above his head. 'Why do you ask?'

'It's a rather urgent family matter,' Penny said.

'How urgent?'

'A death.'

His mouth folded in on itself. His eyebrows moved towards each other. 'Death?'

'Her sister has been – uh – killed.' Penny couldn't bring herself to throw the word 'murder' into the warm room.

'Fiona?' He did the thing with his mouth again and looked over his shoulder. 'Mary,' he said quietly. A tallish woman immediately appeared, dark-haired and aproned, walking as though on empty snail shells. 'This young lady tells me that Fiona McIntosh – you know, Dym's sister – has met with some kind of fatal accident.'

'My God, Paul.' The woman touched her mouth with two fingers. She darted a nervous look at the man. 'How dreadful. What happened?'

These people were obviously friends of the McIntosh girls. Equally obviously, they didn't watch much television, or read newspapers. Penny didn't particularly want to be the one to enlighten them but there wasn't much choice.

'Dymphna doesn't even know yet,' she said. A doubt struck her. Perhaps she did. Perhaps she simply didn't want to rejoin a family set-up which, by anybody's standards, was unusual to say the least. 'Her stepbrother's asked me to try and find her.'

'Poor Dymphna.' The woman smoothed her apron and looked at Paul. 'I suppose that's what the man wanted. Did you tell Miss ... uh?' She looked at Penny and immediately looked away. Her glance hovered and darted like a humming-bird.

'I don't think – ' Mr Ford-Harrison began.

'Wanawake. Penny Wanawake.' Penny felt like antennae had just sprouted from her nose and were waving in front of her. 'I'm – uh – a friend of the family, trying to help out.'

'Oh,' M. Laurence – for it must be she – drew in a relieved breath and again threw her rapid glance at her almost-husband. 'I thought you might be with the police, or something.' She had a thin voice, its deeper tones dragged upwards by what Penny took to be fear.

'Heavens, no,' Penny said. She acted casual. 'Which man are you talking about?'

'The one that rang this morning. He didn't say what it was about but it must have been ...' Her voice trailed away. 'Oh dear. This is horrible. Not that we knew Fiona particularly well, though the girls were all at the same boarding school. It was Dymphna who was Alison's friend, the two of them being about the same age. What was it, a car accident?'

'I didn't hear the phone ring this morning,' Ford-Harrison said. He was frowning.

'You were in the garden, dear. Perhaps I should have called you but he was ringing from a call-box. I thought by the time I found you, he'd have run out of money.'

'Why didn't you tell me about it?'

'I forgot.'

Suddenly, she looked terrified. Her expression made Penny feel sick. Was the guy going to beat up on her later, when there was no one around? Was she one of those women whose best friends were the sunglasses with which she hid her bruises? One of the silent screamers?

She said quickly: 'This man. What kind of a voice was it?'

'I really can't remember much about it,' the woman said doubtfully. 'I didn't take much notice of his voice, just that he wanted to speak to Dymphna and thought she might be here.'

Was that someone using a map and some logic? An enterprising reporter, perhaps? Or was it someone with inside knowledge? Someone who knew Dymphna was with her old schoolfriend, Alison Harrison, whose parents ran a restaurant on the Broads? It almost had to be the latter. Who could it have been? And did it matter? 'Did he have a foreign accent?' she asked.

Mary Laurence lifted wary shoulders, watching Ford-Harrison as she did so. 'I didn't notice. He said to tell Dym he'd called and she'd know who it was.'

Whoever, it was someone familiar enough to call the girl by her diminutive. 'Does she have a boyfriend?' Penny asked.

Again Mary Laurence looked at her partner before answering.

It was as though his permission was required for her to speak. 'She did have. Until ...' she paused. 'I don't know if she's got a new one or not.'

'What happened to the old one?'

'It was all rather unfortunate. Dym was very upset. They'd always been such friends before.'

'Who had?'

'Fee and Dym. Which makes this business with Fiona even worse.' She stared down at the space under the counter and picked up the cloth Ford-Harrison had been using.

'What happened?'

'Fiona stole Dym's boyfriend,' she said, 'Right from under her nose.'

'And being the way she is,' said her partner – he smiled meanly – 'you can see why she was so livid about it.'

'What way is she?'

Partner stared at partner. The male half fielded it. 'Fat,' he said, brutal as a coffin. The woman made a noise of protest and he flapped a hand at her. 'No other way to put it.'

'I suppose she does have a bit of a weight problem,' Mary said.

'She's got a damned awful weight problem. Combined with having a bit of a temper problem, too, she's not likely to find another chap very easily,' said Ford-Harrison. He looked hard and cold.

'Who was the one she lost?' asked Penny.

'Hamilton, wasn't it?' The woman required confirmation again from her partner. 'Ewen Hamilton?'

'That's right. Old friend of the family.'

Uh oh.

Likewise ah ha.

9

Overnight, the weather had rethought its position. The sun was out. The sky cloudless. Even the breeze was warm. While not changing her view that Nature was basically a royal pain in the ass, Penny Wanawake, white jeans rolled to the knee under her outsize granddaddy shirt, nonetheless felt a surge of something close to pleasure as her boat ambled along between the reeds. Part of that was because it was only 5.30 a.m. The rest of Norfolk was still sacked out. Except for a duck or two, she had the entire world to herself.

Although she hadn't found Dymphna, she knew she was aiming in the right direction. The Ford-Harrisons had told her that the four girls had dropped by a couple of days earlier, to say they were heading on up the river.

'Dymphna certainly had no idea then that anything had happened to Fiona,' Mary Laurence had said worriedly.

'Wasn't she talking about the two of them meeting up somewhere?' Ford-Harrison asked.

'That's right. She was.'

They were in the comfortable sitting-room behind the public part of the hotel. The two partners. The one Penny Wanawake. Between them, they'd been fairly hard on a bottle of Armagnac that Paul Ford-Harrison had produced from his private stock.

'The two girls were good friends of Allie's – that's our daughter,' said Mary Laurence.

'Mary's looked after my girls for years,' explained Ford-Harrison. 'Been a better mother to them than the real thing ever was.' His heavy face darkened.

Mary smiled at him gratefully. She looked different when she smiled, as though she had once been strong and lusty, before it had all been beaten out of her. 'In fact, the McIntosh girls sometimes used to spend half-terms here, rather than travel all the way back to Scotland,' she said. 'I don't think they had a very satisfactory homelife, actually.' She turned her fine grey eyes on Penny. Clearer than words, they said: *any more than I do.* 'We'd seen a bit of Fiona recently. She'd been working not too far from here. Where was it, Paul?'

'Near Wymondham,' Penny said.

'That's right. As a matter of fact, she popped over – oof!' said Mary Laurence.

'Sorry?' Penny had heard sentences rudely terminated before. Not often with such force. A husbandly nudge with a shoe under the table was one thing. A savage kick was quite another.

'Yes,' said Mary. Pan-tears hung over the edge of her eyes. You could see she wanted to reach down and rub her leg but didn't dare. She swallowed. 'Popped over a – a couple of times on her off-duty days. We were glad to see her.' A smudge of red had covered the top half of her cheeks. The rest of her face had lost colour. She avoided looking at the semi-circular glasses of her business partner.

'I see. But not recently?' asked Penny.

'No.'

'Not, like a few days ago?'

'My w— Mary said no,' Ford-Harrison said sharply.

'Oh dear,' the woman said. She wiped the side of her face with one hand. 'This is going to be such a dreadful shock for Dymphna.'

Paul Ford-Harrison said nothing. He gripped his glass as though afraid someone would try to snatch it from him if he didn't. By now, drink had reddened his face. A lot of the colour had spread upwards across his naked skull. More was staining the rolls of flesh at the back of his bull neck. Anger lurked in every fold. The archetypal wife-beater, if ever Penny had seen one. Wife-*kicker*, too. Or partner-kicker.

What made a woman stay with a man like that? Economics? Exhaustion? Children? But surely Mary Laurence had none of these barriers to independence. There'd been a case in New York recently. A highly intelligent woman with a career of her own who'd been reduced to a battered, degraded hulk. At any time she could have left the man who was beating her up, but she'd stayed. It all came down to self-image. Better fists and recognition than being alone with nothing but an inner sense of worthlessness.

Thinking about Ford-Harrison now, along the quiet waterways, Penny unconsciously speeded up. The wish to put miles between her and him was strong. She'd stayed at the Harrison

Arms overnight, comfortably boarded and bedded, but she'd had to make an effort not to imagine scenes of violence, screams unheard in the night, a woman pleading for mercy, fists, feet. She wondered what Mary Laurence had been going to say before he stopped her. Almost certainly not what she did say. Almost certainly something about Fiona popping over just a couple of days earlier, i.e. very close to the time she was murdered. It was kind of interesting that ol' Paul should want to shut her up. For a moment she saw those beefy hands pulling a dark-blue stocking tight into vulnerable flesh. Imagined the way those hard eyes would watch unmoved as a girl choked to death.

But what could possibly be his motive? She wondered whether the autopsy report had appeared yet. It would be worth buying one of the tabloids just to find out. She decided she would tie up at the next mooring that looked like it sold papers. If the girl had been raped, would that not offer a reason? Say Ford-Harrison drinks too much, offers to take Fiona back to Wrestebury, is overcome with whatever it is that overcomes men when they use sexual violence on women, and strangles her. But if so, how would he explain being absent long enough to get rid of her body? Unless he concealed it in his car until a suitable time came up. '*Just off to pick up some more packets of Porky Scratchings, dear. Be about an hour.*' It wouldn't have been too difficult.

It wouldn't have been too likely, either. It was much easier to build a case against the sister. After all, Dymphna appeared to have a genuine grudge against Fiona. There was Ludo Fairfax, too. Wherever she turned. If she wanted to get really theoretical, it wouldn't be too hard to come up with a motive for him.

Is that right?

Sure it is. Matter of fact, she'd already formulated it. Like, he needed to get someone into the Osman household fast. With Fiona already *in situ*, the only way he could do it was to ice her and replace her with Vanessa Carrington. Think about it. The timing of Vanessa's application to Miss Ivory was just a little too convenient to be coincidence. Not only that, Penny was still convinced that Ludo knew more than he was saying.

OK. As a theory it was kind of far-fetched.

She pressed down on the throttle. Face it, lady. As a theory, it stank.

A flight of ducks sped past her, necks stretched against the white sky of early morning. *Très* picturesque. They dropped their orange feet like landing gear and coasted to a splashy stop on the surface of the water. She watched a heron thigh-deep in water watching her from among the reeds. Birds did a lot of that. It must be tiring to be so constantly vigilant. Like with children. Another good reason not to have any.

Looking around at reed and sky and water, at the masts of invisible yachts, at the birds wheeling above churches and distant trees, she realised this was not the wisest way to find Dymphna McIntosh. Trouble was, there was no better alternative. People on holiday didn't have schedules. The four girls were as likely to have doubled back on themselves, or nosed up some narrow inlet for lunch or whatever, as they were to have kept straight on for the sea. Using the car to search for them was out of the question. She kept a tight watch on the sleeping craft, she passed. None of them was the one she wanted. *Ecstasy*. Honestly.

She wondered if it was worth making for the Owl and the Pussycat. The Ford-Harrison/Laurence ménage had said that the girls intended to have a meal there at some point. If she found the crew of *Ecstasy* had already been there, it would at least eliminate the place as somewhere to search for them. And if they hadn't, she could maybe hang around, see what was what. There was even the chance she might get lucky and find that tonight was the very evening they'd chosen. At the thought, she groaned. Did that mean she'd have to spend the entire day cruising up the rivers looking for them? Or should she cut corners, return to Mr Bardwell, dump the boat, check by telephone? She shook her head. When the going got tough, the Wanawakes got tougher. They didn't give up easy.

The sky was growing bluer as the run rose. Ahead she could see a scatter of houses, a sign with an arrow and the word 'FUEL', a board lettered by someone unused to sign-painting which indicated that provisions were available near by. The river dead-ended into a dark circle of water under dipping trees. She nosed in to land and tied up alongside a couple of other boats whose occupants were obviously still in their bunks. Neither was called *Ecstasy*. It was still early. The rough grass of the bank was grey with dew where the shadows lay. She walked up towards the village whose roofs she could make out between trees. Tall hedges of privet and tamarisk hid well-tended gardens. Clouds of philadelphus scent drifted towards and around her. She closed her eyes and sniffed. Man, was that delicious. Orgasmic, even. What a way to die that would be, surfeiting on the scent of mock-orange and honeysuckle.

'Excuse me. Do you mind?'

She opened her eyes. Two girls were side-stepping her, their faces smeared with that look of indignant outrage the English prefer to more direct forms of bad-mouth.

One was dark and small-boobed. The other was fair-haired and huge. Both were extremely pretty.

'Sorry,' Penny said. She turned as they passed her. The dark one was carrying a pint of semi-skimmed milk in a container of plasticised cardboard. The big one hugged a loaf of fresh brown bread from which she was pinching the corners and putting them in her mouth. Could that be Dymphna McIntosh? Obviously it wasn't since there'd been no sign of *Ecstasy* moored on the inlet. She watched them walk back towards the river then branch away to the left.

She continued along the lane. Gradually it became a street. One side was narrowly pavemented. The street evolved into a square of pretty stone houses and some plane trees. A small shop was doing a brisk early trade in newspapers and bread with the local OAPs, several of whom had massed outside and were exchanging vital information about the weather.

Penny checked out the newspaper rack. None of the headlines mentioned nannies. She bought something upmarket and something not. She stepped into the plexiglass embrace of a telephone booth and dialled 192. A few minutes later she had the telephone number of the Owl and the Pussycat. When she got through, the woman at the other end sounded rural in the way that people who sell fish-fingers or turkeys on TV sound. So much so, that Penny wondered if she was putting it on.

'Sorry to bother you so early,' she said.

'Thass arl roight.'

'I'm supposed to meet up with some friends at your place,' said Penny. 'Thing is, I can't remember whether it's tonight or tomorrow.'

'Whass air name, then?'

'I don't know what name they'd have booked the table under. My friends are called McIntosh and Ford-Harrison.'

There was a spot of the kind of breathing that implies a tongue curled into the corner of a mouth. 'Ford-Arrrson?' the woman said, after a while.

'Yes.'

'Pardy of four?'

'Yes,' Penny said. 'You don't happen to know what time they've booked for, do you?'

'Today. Twelve-thirdy.'

'Lunchtime, you mean?'

'Thassit. Duck.'

'What?' Difficult to tell whether the word had been a statement or a local endearment. Or a command, even.

'They'm ordered duck with abricots.'

'Sounds fabulous.'

Penny put down the receiver. She felt elated. She might not often find parking slots when she wanted them, but at least she'd hit pay dirt on this. All she had to do now was be at the place by noon, get hold of Dymphna and, if she wanted, take her back to London. Nice game plan. Only problem was, she'd still be the one breaking the bad news. Rats!

At noon she was sitting under an umbrella on the lawn which separated the river from the Owl and the Pussycat. There was a long drink in her hand. Long on alcohol, that is. When she'd asked for a double gin, the guy behind the bar had opened his eyes rather wide and put his head on one side. He'd then assumed an expression that made her want to tear off his toupée and chuck it into the plastic drum of ice-cubes which sat on the bar.

'Dear, dear,' he said. 'We sound like we're in a bad way.' He pushed a glass against the giant bottle of upside-down Gordon's a couple of times. Penny considered herself pretty damn tolerant, but some guy in false hair and eyeglasses with rainbow-coloured rims getting on her case about what she drank was something she could very easily do without.

'You're dead right,' she said.

'Alcohol does terrible things to women, you know.' His glasses reflected things. He had to be Owl.

'So do men,' said Penny. 'Doesn't mean I'm gonna give them up.'

He tittered. 'My dear, I know *just* how you feel.'

There were miniature bottles under the counter: tonic, tomato juice, soda water. He took the top off a couple of tonics and pushed them towards her. 'Abstinence makes the heart grow fonder, I always say.'

'I wouldn't know,' Penny said. 'I never abstain.' She winked. Lewdly. Hoo, *boy*. Could she ever be one of the guys when she wanted.

106

'You're so right.' He took his glasses off and blinked at her. This was a man wasn't ever going to be one of the guys. However much he wanted to.

Another man, younger and prettier than the first, appeared. Pussycat? His hair was an interesting shade of mouse and cunningly styled. Both his middle fingers had gold rings on them. She couldn't help noticing because he waved them about a lot. He walked like he took ballet lessons twice a week.

'What's new, Pussycat?' Penny said. Cute. She leaned on the bar, acting like she'd already had a couple.

He eyed her without actually looking in her direction. Beyond him she could see a door leading into a conservatory which evidently did duty as a dining-room. At one of the pink-clothed tables was the eagle-nosed yachtsman she'd seen earlier, high forehead gleaming with the exertion of lifting a fork to his mouth. Lamb *en croute*. Penny had seen *bubbles* heavier than the puff pastry round the meat. Opposite him gangled his son, hair slicked back, pushing something ostentatiously vegetarian around his plate, while his face registered adolescent distaste for the carniverous excesses of adults.

'Disaster, dear,' Pussycat said. His accent was antipodean. 'The raspberry soufflé's just gone flop.'

'Oh no,' whittered Owl.

'Oh yes.'

'But it's your best thing.'

'Blame the heat, ducky, not me.' Pussycat's gaze slewed round the room and came to rest on Penny's armpits. She was prepared to bet that his own were Armani-flavoured. He addressed her. 'In the trade yourself, are you?'

'Not actually. What makes you ask?'

'Don't get too many of your sort round here, in the normal way of things.'

'Black, you mean?'

'That's right.' She liked him for coming out with it. 'And you've got that ... *polished* look. Usually means a professional of some kind.'

'What are we going to do about the soufflés?' Owl whined. He glanced poisonously at Penny.

'We'll have to call it a mousse or something. They won't mind.' Pussycat grinned suddenly at Penny, displaying dimples big enough to receive satellite TV. 'Even flopped, it's delicious.'

Penny guessed he was right. Sitting outside, the lunch menu in her hand inspired confidence. None of this dawn-gathered/garden-fresh crap. Nothing about tender beds of puréed this or that. The only place for tender beds was in tender bedrooms. Preferably with tender bedmates in them. She wondered how Barnaby was. *Where* he was. Sometimes she tried to imagine what life would be like without him. She never managed it.

She opened the first of the two newspapers she had bought that morning. The tabloid one. It gave full coverage to the wedding of a raddled former popstar and a teenage girl who admitted frankly that she was marrying for what she could get out of it. Accompanying photographs showed exactly what the former popstar was getting out of it. The Nanny murder made a small para way down on page five. Autopsy results were not mentioned. There was the simple statement that the police were following leads and were anxious to trace a man seen near the railway embankment.

The quality added very little more, beyond the news that though Fiona had sexual intercourse shortly before her death, she had not been sexually assaulted. Penny was never quite sure what the phrase meant, whether it was a code name for something quite specific or simply a catch-all phrase for violence that stopped short of actual vaginal penetration. Ugly thoughts for a summer day. She put the newspapers on the slatted wooden table beside her.

Did the fact that Fiona had been sexually active prior to her death change the possibilities? Probably not. There was no reason to suppose that the killer was the man involved. The girl could have been murdered some time after the act of intercourse, for reasons having nothing to do with it.

There was a burst of female giggling from the river. Looking up, she watched as a boat nudged in beside her own. Across the prow she could see the word *Ecstasy*. A private joke of Mr Bardwell's. Standing on the bow, ready to leap ashore and make fast, was the fat girl she had encountered earlier that morning. No prizes for guessing that this was Dymphna McIntosh. She wondered where the four girls had tied up overnight. She must have passed them on the way, or else there was another inlet leading to the village. Not that it mattered much. She was reluctant to tell Dymphna what she had to say. But it seemed indecorous to leave it until after lunch.

As the four girls stepped ashore and walked across the grass, she stood up.

'Dymphna?' she called softly. The big girl in well-cut jeans and a loose pink top looked over at her and then back at the small dark girl she'd been with in the village.

'Yes?' She had a great deal of curly blonde hair and the same astonishing blue eyes as her mother. She was tall. Under the denim, her legs were good, too. Fat peoples' often were.

'Paco Esteban ...' Penny paused, waiting for the look of recognition to appear. It did. But not before another had preceded it. One of what she was prepared to swear was contempt. '... asked me to find you.'

'What does *he* want?' The voice was cold. Behind her, the three friends stood like a bodyguard.

'Look, I'm real sorry but I have bad news for you.'

'What sort of bad news?'

'The worst kind, I'm afraid.'

'Oh God.' Dymphna crossed her arms across her body, clutching at her own elbows. 'It's my father, isn't it? Something's happened to him. His car's crashed. He always goes too fast down to the main road. I've told him ...' She was talking to stop Penny telling her whatever it was she had come to say. After a couple more sentences, she dried up. Her pale skin had grown paler. 'What is it?' she said softly.

'Not your father. Your sister.'

'Fee? What's happened?' She looked wildly round at her friends. 'What's wrong with her?'

Jesus. This was the bit Penny choked on. The ugly finality of the word 'dead'. She vowed that she would never again allow herself to be put in the position of destroying other peoples' lives like this. Somehow she managed to convey the stark outline of what she had to say. To stand while Dymphna stared incredulously then sank weeping to the ground. To watch while the friends, after glaring at Penny with loathing, patted and stroked and hugged, tears forming on their own faces. Later, Penny knew, there would be the appalled disbelief, the demand for detail, the agonising readjustment to a world in which someone known and loved no longer had a place.

'I'll drive you back to London, if you like,' she said.

Dymphna took this offer in one word at a time. 'No.' She swung her hair violently from side to side. 'I don't want to go.'

Penny didn't blame her. 'Your mother is very anxious to see

you,' she said. 'I'm sure the two of you can help each other through this time of ...' She mumbled to a halt. Cliché, cliché. It probably wasn't even true.

'No. I can't.'

'You'd better go, Dym.' It was the small dark girl who'd been with Dymphna in the village that morning.

'I suppose I'll have to,' muttered Dymphna.

'Do you want me to come with you?'

Slowly Dymphna shook her head. Her cheeks quivered. 'Thanks, Allie.' She stared at their boat, motionless on the river. 'My things ...'

'We'll get them.' Allie organised the others. Anxious to get away, to have something to do, they headed for the riverside.

Dymphna suddenly took a couple of steps forward and another backwards, crushing some pinks in a flowerbed. Her head dropped. She moaned.

'Stay here.' Penny shoved her into a seat and ran towards the house.

Pussycat was behind the bar. Elsewhere in the house she could hear Owl going on about crêpes. She ordered a double brandy.

'Those soufflés came out beautifully,' Pussycat told her. 'I've slopped on some kirsch and decorated them with fresh rasps. Terrific. You'd never know that's not how they were meant to be.'

'Do you know anything about Paul Ford-Harrison?' Penny said rapidly. Through the small diamond-paned windows she could see Dymphna, still slumped in her seat.

'Oh, my dear, yes. Goebbels, we call him. Isn't he too terribly *brutal*? Terrifies the pants off me. In a manner of speaking.' Pussycat set the brandy glass down in front of her. 'Not that he'd care if he did. Literally. I mean, it's women he goes for. The more the merrier. The younger the better.'

'Really?'

'Yes, indeed.' He leaned tanned arms on the counter, enjoying a chance for a gossip. 'There've been rumours about him for years, though nothing concrete, as far as I know. Sex with a minor or something. Local girls. Not a very savoury character, our Mr Ford-Harrison, all in all. And so incredibly mean to his poor wife. Not that she is his wife, of course, though she'd love to be.'

'What is she, nuts?'

'Desperate, dear.' He patted his hairstyle with one of his

110

hands. 'She belongs to the generation of women who think they're failures if they can't get themselves a husband.'

Penny didn't have time to point out that from where she was standing, he looked like he belonged to a generation of men who think things like that about women. She watched him pull the tab from the lips of an old-fashioned cash register on which he'd just rung up the charge. As the drawer below slid open, she saw the notched handle of what was unmistakably a small hand-gun. He saw her seeing.

'No need to raise your eyebrows, dear,' he said, slamming the drawer shut again.

'I didn't.'

'Everyone has them around here. It's all very well in the summer when there're lots of people around. But in the winter, well, you're pretty isolated. And there've been a lot of break-ins over the last couple of years. Mind you, they can have the money, as far as I'm concerned. We're just worried they might want more.'

'Not ...' Penny made her voice go breathless '... your virginity.'

'Cheeky thing.'

She picked up the brandy glass. As she turned to go, he said: 'Frankly, I don't know why Mary puts up with Paul. There's quite a bit of money there, far as I know, and they *say* it's hers. I suppose she stays because of the daughter.'

'Alison?'

'Yes. Poor Mary. What a life. And all for the sake of a wedding-band.' He handed her the change.

Penny took the glass of brandy outside and gave it to Dymphna without speaking. The girl drank its contents down in a single swallow and stood up. Her eyes were pink but not wet. 'We'd better get going,' she said. She went over to the little wooden landing stage and picked up the leather grip which had been put there. From the deck of *Ecstasy*, her three companions watched. 'Good luck,' one of them said. The others echoed her, subduedly. Allie suddenly stepped back on shore and gave her a hug, patting her shoulderblades as she did so.

On the downriver journey to Potter Heigham and Penny's car, she didn't speak. She stood in the cockpit, facing back the way they had come, her plump shoulders rigid. Penny let her be.

Once in the car, she relaxed a little. 'Poor Fee,' she said.

111

Penny murmured something meaningless.

'Daddy'll be upset.'

There was a pause. 'Not you?' Penny asked.

'Of course me,' she said violently.

'Right.'

Another silence. She went on: 'But in a way, I almost expected something like this to happen.'

'Isn't that rather a strange thing to say about a sister?' Penny felt a kick of excitement. Was she going to hear something that would support Ewen Hamilton's doubts?

'I don't mean murder. But something disastrous. Something terrible.'

'Any particular reason?' Keep it light, Penny told herself. Don't push. Don't intimidate the witness.

'It was the way she acted. As if she couldn't help herself. I thought she ought to have therapy – see a psychiatrist or something – but Daddy wouldn't hear of it. He thinks they're some kind of admission of failure. He thinks people ought to be able to control themselves.'

'And your sister couldn't?'

'I don't think so. Not any more. Daddy didn't know that. He'd have flipped his lid if he thought his beloved daughter had been to bed with just about everybody who'd ever asked her plus quite a few who hadn't. Including his own partner in the practice. Even Allie's father . . .'

'What? Paul Ford-Harrison, you mean?'

'Yes.' Dymphna squiggled around a bit. 'I mean, it's really embarrassing when your sister's throwing herself all over your best friend's father.'

'Do you think they ever . . . ?'

'Several times,' muttered Dymphna. 'Fiona told me Paul was besotted with her. God. I hope Allie doesn't know. And Mary.'

Penny had known already that Fiona was relatively promiscuous. Not to this extent, though. 'Why?'

Dymphna shrugged. The tears which she had held back for a while began to pour again. 'I don't know. At least, I can guess. But who knows. Perhaps Nanny Campbell was right and she was just born that way.'

'Nanny Campbell?'

'Our nanny. And housekeeper, I suppose.'

'She looked after you?'

'After we went to Scotland, yes. I hated her. So did Fee. We

112

kept telling Daddy about her but he wouldn't listen.'

'*What* about her?'

'She was obviously a nutcase,' Dymphna said. 'She had this thing about men. About how we must never let them touch us. Never be alone with boys. And any girl who did was filth, trash, a whore. You name it, Nanny Campbell had dirty words for it. She used to make us wear three pairs of knickers if we were going to a party, can you imagine?'

'Did she say why?'

'To make it more difficult, she used to say. We thought she meant more difficult to go to the loo. Once she made Fiona sleep for a whole week with her hands tied to the bedposts because she came in and found her sleeping with her hand tucked between her legs. I mean, talk about primitive. Not that Nanny Campbell was the only one. Daddy wasn't much better, what with my mother going off like that. I don't think he liked women much, which was a pretty poor lookout for us, considering we were both girls. Actually ...' She turned her marvellous blue gaze on Penny. 'Actually, I think he's pretty sick too, if you really want to know.'

'In what way?' Penny tried to keep her voice neutral. Dymphna was into words now, pouring them out, saying things that she had probably never said to anyone before because she was with a stranger, someone she would never see again, whose very unknownness was a comfort in itself.

'His attitude to Fee, for one thing. One minute all over her – I mean, literally, stroking her and fondling her like he was her lover, not her father – and the next not speaking to her for weeks on end because Nancy Campbell sneaked about something, or because he was convinced she didn't love him.'

'Did she?'

'She'd tell you she hated him. But of course she loved him as well. One does love one's father, doesn't one, whatever he does? She was very mixed up about everything, really.' Dymphna sighed. 'Sometimes I feel that if I could find out who it was, I'd kill him.'

'Who what was?'

Again Dymphna was silent for a long time. At least several miles went by, full of villages and leafy trees with sudden shining glimpses of the river between.

Finally, she said: 'The man who raped her.'

113

* 10 *

It was a damned good line to sleep on.

Or would have been, if Dymphna hadn't spoiled it by adding: 'At least, I *think* that's what happened. She wouldn't talk about it, but that's what I kind of gathered.'

After that, she'd dried up. Perhaps she felt she had said too much. Penny asked a couple more questions, but Dymphna had only shrugged. She'd spent the rest of the journey curled up in the passenger seat with her eyes closed, pretending to be asleep. Penny couldn't blame her. She left the question of Ewen Hamilton being head-hunted by Fiona. It gave Dymphna a motive, sure. But the police would tweeze it out eventually, and talking about it now would only add to Dymphna's distress.

Dicing with the London traffic after dropping her at the Estebans' hotel, Penny could think of Fiona McIntosh with nothing but pity. What a balls-up those in charge of her had made. Mother runs out on her. Father doesn't try to conceal his incestuous feelings for her though guilt makes him treat her with over-the-top severity to compensate. And as for the nanny . . . Watching a Jensen Interceptor slip into the space in front of her and then immediately slam on its brakes, she shook her head. *Quelle* fruitcake. No wonder the girl was a mess.

Ewen Hamilton was waiting outside the house again. He sat in his green sports car, staring miserably through the windscreen while she parked further up the street.

He spoke rapidly, tongue tripping over the words. 'I'm sorry. I know I shouldn't inflict myself on you. But you seemed kind and I don't know who else to talk to.'

'What about?' As if Penny couldn't guess. She called up some patience from the compartment where she stored it, and gave him a warm smile.

'Fiona,' he said.

'So talk.' There was no need to ask why he wanted to discuss the dead girl. Words shaped and defined. Words created an image. By talking about Fiona, it was possible to believe that she still survived. To feel temporarily that death had been cheated.

She led the way into the house.

An envelope lay on the doormat. It required almost no powers of deduction to realise that it had been hand-delivered. It was obvious that it was urgent since the word was printed twice on the outside. She picked it up and ripped it open.

'*Must see you at once,*' it insisted. Once had been underlined three times. She stuffed it into her pocket.

'There was something magic about Fiona,' Ewen said.

Penny was beginning to feel she could argue the toss on that one. Magic was one way to put it. Insatiable was another. She left it. Ewen's eyes were shiny with tears that any moment now he was going to shed. She poured him a stiffish Jack Daniels, in the hope that he would volunteer the information that until the older sister began casting her spells, he had been an item with the younger one. Otherwise she'd have to prise it out of him.

'Had you always been together?' she asked. Although she knew the answer, honey couldn't have been sweeter. 'You said you'd known her most of your life.'

'Yes.'

'Childhood sweetheart sort of thing, was it?'

He coughed. 'No, actually.'

'I thought you said ...' Penny paused deliberately. Pauses encouraged.

'I did. But the fact is, before she and I, before we ... I was engaged to Dymphna, actually.'

'Why did you stop being?'

Moving his shoulders about as though trying to dislodge a burr, he said: 'You can't imagine how awful I felt about it all. But Fee – I don't know what it was. Like being under a spell. Enchanted. I couldn't help myself. She'd never even looked at me before. Nor I at her. Dym and I had been a couple for years. And then this one time I had tickets for something and Dym was ill. She told me to take Fiona instead, so I did. I helped her into the car and went round to my side and got in, and she turned to look at me.' He stared across the room at Penny, trying to explain the inexplicable. 'I can't really describe what it was like. As though I was high on something. As though I'd just showered in sunshine.' He used the flowery phrase without embarrassment. For him, as for Romeo, for Abelard, for Dante, that's what it had been like.

'So you took her to the movies and got engaged, huh?'

'There was a bit more to it than that,' he said. He was embarrassed.

'Why then? You'd known her for years. Why hadn't you felt like that about her before?'

'I can't imagine. I must have been blind.'

Or had Fiona suddenly decided to give him the treatment? Had she set out to seduce him away from Dymphna? And if so, what was her motive: jealousy of her sister? Or was she just practising? Just checking that the equipment was still in working order? Because lovable though he might be, Ewen couldn't begin to compete with the charisma of Paco Esteban. If Fiona was already engaged to Paco, there could be no reason for her to ensnare Ewen. Except sheer love of mischief.

Getting up, Penny refilled Ewen's glass, and added a splash to her own. 'I hate to tell you this,' she said, 'but her stepbrother seems to think that he and she were going to get married.'

Ewen didn't seem surprised. 'She told me he had some insane idea of that sort. In fact, we kept our engagement secret for that very reason. She was afraid he might do something violent if he found out.' 'Macho sort, was he?'

'I don't know. I never met him. I just went along with Fee.'

Miss Manipulation up to her tricks again. If they were all as pliable as Ewen, it made you kind of start wondering how many other times she'd pulled the same trick.

'Mr Esteban seemed quite positive about her being engaged to him,' she said, wooden-spooning it.

'That's absolutely ridiculous.' Ewen wore a shirt of fine cotton with wide rose-coloured stripes down it, and a white detachable collar. Without the collar, the shirt would have been street-chic. The image of Ewen collarless was as difficult to imagine as the Archbishop of Canterbury with hair brushed into a green coxcomb. 'Fiona and I were at the point of discussing where we were going to live after we'd got married. She was wearing my engagement ring. At least. Most of the time she was. When we were together.'

'Not otherwise?'

'No. Because of Esteban. And her father.'

His gaze wavered. Doubt darkened his face. Was that his own lack of confidence in his ability to hold on to this demigoddess, this marvellous girl? Was it an until-now unexpressed disbelief that she could really have preferred him to all other men on the planet? Or did he know something about the character of Fiona McIntosh that led him to recognise immediately a truth about her he had not wished to face?

'Her father?' This was a new slant. Penny was beginning to feel like half a grapefruit. The sort that people stick toothpicks into with tidbits on the end.

'Yes.'

'Guess he didn't go for you, huh?'

'Oh no. Nothing like that. Quite the opposite. The thing was, Fiona wasn't too keen on the old man. She knew he wanted the two of us to get married so she – she ...'

'Wasn't going to give him the satisfaction.'

He nodded. 'That's what she said. It sounds rather petty, I admit.'

'But understandable. Was this dislike mutual?'

'Not a bit. Dr McIntosh absolutely adored her. My family thinks it was because she looked so like her mother.'

'How did he react to his wife leaving?'

'How would *you* react?' Ewen got up, making enquiring gestures at the Jack Daniels with his glass.

She nodded. 'I meant, after the initial rage, grief, whatever.'

'He was very bitter. I used to feel sorry for the girls. He was always ranting on about it. About a woman's duty to her family. About the way a woman ought to behave. And that ghastly nanny didn't help.' He snorted quietly into his drink. 'Funny, really, that Fiona chose nannying as a career when she hated Nanny Campbell so much.'

'Does this lady live as one of the family?'

'Completely. She's even worse than the doctor about a woman's role. You can imagine the kind of impression the girls got of their mother.'

'Was that why Fiona didn't get on with her?'

'Maybe. As I told you, the girls used to spend the summer holidays on Esteban's finca or whatever it's called, but Fiona came back that last year and said she was never going again. And she never did. She said she hated her mother.'

'Was that the same year that the stepfather died?'

'I can't remember. I know it was the year that – well, I was never entirely sure of the details – she wouldn't talk about it

much, but according to Dym some man tried to rape her or
something—'

'So she said. Where's this supposed to have taken place? Here?
Or over there?'

'I don't know. I *do* know that when she told Nanny Campbell,
instead of comforting her, the old witch told her it was her own
fault.'

'How'd she make that out?'

'Said she must have led him on. Tempted him in some way.'

'Sounds like a High Court Judge.'

'Poor Fee.'

'The nanny sounds a bit of a menace.' For a moment Penny
contemplated Nanny Campbell taking the overnight sleeper
down to London to murder her former charge for bad behaviour.
She certainly sounded enough of a fanatic.

'She is. At least the girls don't have to take so much notice of
her now that she's in a wheelchair,' Ewen said.

'Why's that?'

'Arthritis, I think. It's got much worse over the past two or
three years, though.'

Another theory bit the dust. 'What did Dr McIntosh say about
this attack? Rape. Whatever.'

'I doubt if Fiona ever told him. He'd probably have killed
her.' Ewen looked at her gravely, like the high-grade financial
adviser he would one day be. 'Frankly, I never thought the
relationship he had with Fiona was awfully healthy.'

As one theory dies another is born. Could Dr McIntosh be
the murderer? It was something to bear in mind. 'This ring you
gave her,' Penny said, changing the subject. 'What was it like?'
The question sounded both mercenary and inconsequential. In
fact it was neither.

He winced at the memory. 'Expensive.'

'Like, how much?'

He told her. She winced too.

'A ruby surrounded by diamonds,' he said. 'It was a lot more
than I thought we ought to pay, but she wanted it so I . . .
Luckily there's this trust fund set up by my grandmother.' He
looked up at the walls, not seeing them. 'I wonder where that
ring is now,' he said.

One place it was not was in Fiona's jewel-case. Had it been
on her finger when her body was discovered, or had her killer
taken it? It might be worth checking that with the police. And

118

she could ask Chrissie Osman some time whether the girl usually wore a ring and, if so, what it was like. Chrissie's dollar-wise gaze would be able to reckon the value of the stones down to the last cent.

'How d'you mean?' Penny said.

He took his caramel spectacles off and polished them on his shirt. 'Well, you see,' he said, settling them back on his nose, 'she lost it.'

'Jesus.'

'I know. She was in some ladies' loo somewhere. Took it off to wash her hands and forgot it. By the time she'd realised and gone back – about two minutes later – it had gone.'

'Wow.'

'Quite. Thank God I'd had it insured.'

Penny remembered the chequebooks in Fiona's luggage. 'Did Fiona come into a legacy at some time?' she asked.

Ewen frowned. 'Why do you want to know?'

'I just wondered.'

He didn't ask why. Just as well. Even though he'd asked her to look into Fiona's death, prying into other peoples' chequebooks might look over-zealous. 'Not as far as I'm aware,' he said. 'The family was quite poor.'

'I see.'

'Her mother's rolling in it, of course. But that wouldn't affect Fiona. It's Esteban money. Presumably it would eventually go to the sons.'

So where had Fiona got hold of the stuff in her various bank accounts? Had she somehow earned it? And if so, why? What did she want it for?

Stupid question, really. And one that only someone who'd never been without it could ask. Like herself. Like Ewen Hamilton, with his background of titles and trust funds. The family was poor, he said. In whose terms? By whose standards? His own, presumably.

On the other hand, Fiona probably shared them. In which case, 'poor' was something she wouldn't want to be, either in her own eyes or in those of others. Poverty was contagious. Poverty tainted. Blacks belonged to the same undesirable minority. Lots of places, women did too.

It was always possible that Fiona had been driven by some kind of pack-rat mentality. Or a desire to guard against the inevitable rainy day. Perhaps she had a psychological need to

119

make herself safe as a counterbalance to the insecurity caused by her mother's original defection. Paco Esteban had said the two of them had not got on well together. But the banked sum was huge. At her age, it would be impossible for Fiona to have accumulated so much of it from simple pay packets. She hadn't been working long enough. And if Ewen was right, there'd been no legacy.

She realised she was in the process of building a case against Fiona McIntosh herself. Establishing a reason why she might have been killed. Just for-instancing here, suppose you got yourself engaged to half a dozen well-heeled guys, either simultaneously, or in tandem. You let them buy a ring. You pretended to lose the ring, flogged it instead, and banked the proceeds. The only people weeping would be the insurance companies. Barnaby worked on very much the same principle. Theoretically the girl could have kept on going indefinitely, with no more serious charge against her than carelessness in the matter of holding on to valuable property. Unless one of the fiancés caught her out. Was that what had happened? Was it a fiancé who, enraged at the scam, had strangled her?

The fiancé in front of her was standing up. Taking her hands. Saying: 'Please don't stop now.'

'You mean, finding out what I can about Fiona's murder?'

'Of course.'

'What about the police?'

'They still seem to believe she was killed by the man who murdered those other girls.'

'They could believe right.'

'No. They're wrong.' He seemed utterly convinced.

'I don't seem to be doing too good a job so far.'

'I know you'll come up with something.'

Yeah. Sure. A handful of shit. Poking into the privacies that people like to conceal was a garbage way to spend your time. And if you keep digging into garbage, shit's what you find. She wanted to tell him that. Instead, she too stood up. She put an arm round his shoulders. He looked like he needed it. 'Don't know about that,' she said. 'But I'll keep trying.'

When he'd gone, she changed into a sweatshirt and pants. Ask a six-foot sister like herself to spend two days or whatever crouched in a boat built for a gnome and what you came up with wasn't any kind of fun. What you came up with was aching joints and high stress levels. Add a spot of sudden death and whatever way you cooked it, it didn't taste good. She felt like her coat was staring. Stretch her out on a fishmonger's slab, wasn't nobody gonna start singing about how fresh from the sea she looked.

She got a piece of fillet steak from out of the icebox. Squeezed garlic through the little gizmo that was always such a bitch to clean. Rubbed green olive oil into the meat and added salt and fresh-ground pepper. A sprig of rosemary would have been just fine. Trouble was, it grew right by the pond and she couldn't face those frogs right now. She set a beef tomato out on the counter. Pulled an eyeshade down on to her hairline. Then she ran. Hard and long, until the sweat was running down the backs of her thighs and along her ribs. The globe turned under the zigzag soles of her Reeboks and she felt powerful. She felt good. Awful good. Running might not change the world but it certainly changed attitude. Back home, she turned on the grill and went up to shower.

The telephone began ringing while she was still wrapped in a bath sheet. Chrissie Osman calling.

'I've had the police down here,' she said. Her voice was belligerent.

'Don't talk to me, lady.' Penny was no slouch with the belligerence herself, when she wanted to be. 'I didn't kill nobody.'

'I'm not saying you did. What they're really bugged about is that you've got all her stuff and they can't get hold of you.'

'You managed.'

'Just lucky, I guess,' Chrissie said. Real sardonic.

'So what's the beef?'

'Uh – have you by any chance looked through her bags?'

'Why?'

'It's just.'

'Just what?'

Silence. A sigh. Then Chrissie said: 'My fucking husband's just told me he was screwing that goddamned little bitch.'

'Did he s—'

'Says she came on to him like he was Paul Newman or something. I mean, I love my husband and all that crap, but I'm not going to try and hang him in the National Gallery. An oil painting the guy is definitely not. So what did she see in him?'

'What did *you* see in him?'

'Lots of things. Power. Money. Protection, if you like. Somewhere to tie up to. But darn it, I've got fifteen years on that kid. I was ready to drop anchor. She wasn't. She can't have wanted to take him away from me, even if he'd have gone, which he wouldn't.'

'Did he ever give her money?'

The line was quiet. When Chrissie spoke again, her voice was low. 'How'd you know?'

'I didn't. How much?'

'Lots. He paid her every time she – oh Jesus. The miserable little jerk. Why'd he do it?'

There was pain in Chrissie's voice. Penny didn't think it was merely the pain of someone who'd just seen their meal ticket shredded. It sounded too much like the genuine article. 'Was that why you rang?' she asked quietly.

'No. This is so ... There are some ...' She stopped. She started again. 'Zach said he'd written her some letters.'

'And you don't want the cops to find them.'

'Right. So I wondered if you would—'

'Case out her bags?'

'Yes.'

'What makes you think she might have kept them?'

'Come on, Miss Wanawake. She was going to put the heat on him, wasn't she? Or try to.'

'You think she was into *black*mail?'

'You're darn tootin' I do. Or planning to be. No wonder she was always giving Zach's desk the once-over. Probably looking to find more stuff to hit him with, on top of what she'd already organised.'

A familiar excitement slowly squeezed Penny's lungs, making her breathe more quickly. She back-burnered the multiple fiancé caper. Blackmail. Was that the answer she'd been looking for? Or one of them? Was that the way Fiona had filled those three bank accounts?

It was kind of hard to credit. Perhaps she'd read too much classic detective fiction. Blackmailers were loathsome men with too-white skin and something showy in the way of motors. They held long cigarette holders between manicured fingers and wore grey spats. It was difficult to revise the image sufficiently to accommodate a young woman with amazing blue eyes and the ability to accelerate from primness into super-sexuality in a matter of microseconds. Perhaps it was a trait Fiona had discovered in adolescence and decided to put to good use. If you've got it, put it to work for you. After all, it was a skill. No different from being a maths professor or a car mechanic. Not, at least, until you combined it with extortion.

But blackmail necessarily implies both greed and contempt for others. Was that why Fiona now lay refrigerating in some police morgue? If so, presumably her murderer had been one of her victims. As she in turn had become his.

'Would it have worked if she had?' she said.

Hesitation rolled down the line. 'I think not. I can't see Zachary falling for that "Pay-out-or-I'll tell-your-wife" routine. Either he'd've 'fessed up or he'd've . . .'

'Have what?'

'. . . dealt with it some other way,' Chrissie said.

'What does *that* mean?'

'Let's just say he really hates to be pressured.'

Enough to put the frighteners on? Enough to kill? Strangulation wasn't one of the nicer ways to go. Was the little round man with the nervous giggle really capable of choking a girl to death? It wasn't one of those questions you asked. Not if you expected an honest answer.

Penny asked a different question. 'Supposing I find them, you want these letters back?'

'Yes,' Chrissie said. 'Please.' It didn't sound like a word she used a lot.

'While we're talking, there's something I wanted to know,' Penny said. 'Did she wear a ring when she was working for you?'

'Not all the time. Sometimes.'

'What was it like?'

'She had more than one. There was a rather cute opal one – her grandmother's, she told me. And a really fantastic diamond and ruby ring. And sometimes she had this terrific emerald. Must have cost a mint. I mean, Zach's given me some good stuff but that emerald was really something else.'

'Where'd she get it?'

'It was her engagement ring.'

'What was the diamond, then?'

'Some guy gave it her who died in a motorbike accident the week after they'd got engaged. I felt rather sorry for the poor kid, actually.'

Ewen Hamilton might have found the story a little hard to swallow. Penny moved the idea that there was more than one fiancé right back to the front of the stove. She was beginning to admire the erstwhile nanny. Why not both blackmail *and* misrepresentation?

'I kind of assumed she'd got over the guy that died,' Chrissie was saying. 'Which makes it all the weirder that she was giving my husband the treatment. Wouldn't you say?'

'Uh ...' said Penny cautiously. The question required an affirmative answer but agreement would imply criticism of Mr Osman. Mrs Osman might resent it.

'I mean, a guy who can afford an emerald like that? He must be some kind of freak if she's driven to Zachary for sex. Which I'm damn sure she wasn't. God knows he's no superman in the sack or anything. At my age that doesn't matter quite so much, but at hers it damn well ought to.'

'Did the police say anything about either of those rings? I mean, that they were part of the – uh – the scene-of-crime effects?'

'Not to me, they didn't. Come to think of it, they asked me if there was a boyfriend or whether she was engaged. That would kind of suggest there wasn't any ring when she was found, wouldn't it?'

'I guess so.'

'But if she was wearing one when she left the house, I didn't know about it.'

'That was her regular day off, wasn't it?'

'Yeah. Every Wednesday. Plus a half day on Friday.'

'And anyone who knew you would probably know that?'

'Knew me?' Indignation made Chrissie's voice slant upwards. '*My* friends don't go round —'

'Or knew her, obviously,' Penny said, smooth as the linctus Nanny Simpson used to pour down her throat when she had a cough. Probably had quinine in it. Or laudanum. Some habit-forming narcotic of the kind. Standard nanny practice. It was amazing that England had functioned at all in the last hundred years when you considered what the nannies of the ruling classes were dosing their charges with. In fact, the loss of Empire and the slide in industrial output might well be attributable to habits acquired by the managerial classes in the nursery.

Just a thought.

'Take me through it,' she said.

'Through what?'

'That last Friday.'

'I already did this, you know. With the cops. I really don't see where I —'

'Just for me,' Penny said.

After some heavy sighing, Chrissie said: 'First of all, this guy came down to visit her. Her step-brother or something.'

'Really?'

'Yeah. Really.'

'Which one, the older one?'

'He had glasses and white hair. My sort of guy.'

The description fit Paco Esteban like a wet-suit. 'What happened next?' Penny was fairly sure that any guy with Paco's income was Chrissie's sort of guy. She wondered why Paco hadn't mentioned visiting Fiona the morning of her death. Though there was no reason why he should, it was odd that he hadn't.

'She gave him the brush-off, far as I could see. Anyway, he drove away again pretty soon after he'd arrived. Then she came down all gussied up. We exchanged a few words about nothing. Then Shane drove her into town or wherever it was he was taking her.'

'You didn't offer the use of a car?'

'Of course we did. It would've been much more convenient all round. But she didn't drive. We don't have much of a bus service here, and it was part of the deal, we'd get her where she wanted to go on her day off and pay for a taxi home again if she couldn't get a lift.' There was a short pause. 'We didn't have to pay too many cab fares, if you're interested.'

'Right.'

'We weren't expecting her back early. Anyway, we were out ourselves at a dinner party with some local friends. So it wasn't until the next morning, when Junior started raising Cain, that we realised she wasn't around.'

'When did you decide she wasn't coming back?'

'After we had that phone call. I already told you. Some man calling up saying she wouldn't be coming back. Frankly, I didn't give a damn. I was so mad I just called your agency and told them to get me someone else by the beginning of the week and the hell with it. I mean, if she'd showed up that same day, I'd have fired her anyway.'

Behind Chrissie's voice, a baby began yelling. Almost immediately it stopped. 'How're you finding Miss Carrington?' Penny asked quickly.

'Hey, listen. That girl is neat. Joshua likes her. She likes Joshua. We like her. Everybody's happy.'

Funny that the real nanny had seemed vaguely incompetent, while the fake one was so good at the job. 'Even so, I bet you'll be keeping your private papers under lock and key.' It was the best Penny could do in the way of warning without coming right out and shopping Vanessa. She hoped it sounded like a joke.

'Right. My husband, too.' Chrissie pretended it was one.

Throughout the conversation Fiona McIntosh had not been mentioned by name.

With the police on the trail, Penny decided next morning she better get into her Pauline Pry act right this minute. When the telephone rang for a third time, she didn't answer. It might have been the cops.

She found a thin pair of rubber washing-up gloves and put them on. Even though she could have justified rootling round ('One of our gels, officer? Naturally I had to find out all I could, see if there was any clue to her present whereabouts.' The fuzz might not buy it, but there wouldn't be a lot they could do about it) it was best to be discreet.

Her first impression was right. Fiona didn't get a lot of correspondence. Or if she did, she chucked it away. There was nothing much among her papers. Predictable letters from Ewen, boring on about lifelong devotion and the privilege of caring for her. More from Paco Esteban, saying much the same thing in different style. A couple from Katrina, still in their unopened envelopes. Alongside the letters were a few bills, some receipts, a couple of stiff cards warning Fiona of the official engagements of various friends, three or four invitations to parties.

There was something missing. It appeared this was a girl who lived dangerously. Whose inside was everything her outside wasn't. But where was the evidence? So far, there was nothing which said Fiona McIntosh was any different from the thousands of middle-class girls she'd grown up with. Yet Penny knew she was. Knew she had to be. She went through the other pockets of the bag. An old credit card receipt for gas. Three creased tissues. Three cards from different florists. One was plain and white and said: 'I love you. E.' One showed a stylised bouquet and had the words 'Without you I die' written on it with an ultra-fine felt-tip pen. V. romantic. The third was printed with the Interflora logo and had the address of a flower shop somewhere in the City. It had been written in black ink with a thick-nibbed pen and said: 'Always always yours.' Looking at it, Penny shivered. Oh God. Oh no.

Don't think about it. Not now.

There was a diary, too. Only one. Looking at the year stamped on its cover, Penny wondered why. Perhaps it was the only year Fiona had bothered to record the events in her life. Perhaps it had been a memorable year. If so, it was hard to see how. Penny leafed through the pages of schoolgirl handwriting, the nothing-type events. Daddy this. Dymphna that. Went swimming, shooting, to a party. Hate Miss Mather. Met this *fabulous* man, think I'm in LOVE!!!! Caught the 'flu from Emma Cartwright. By the summer hols, Fiona's enthusiasm for diary keeping had waned. The final entry read: 'Off to stay with Mummy tomorrow.'

There was something sad here. Something that made the breath stick in the back of the throat, thinking how soon the schoolgirl had grown into the corpse.

She was about to turn to the photograph album when she stopped.

Hey, sister: this isn't one of those dumb novels about some Sleeping Beauty housewife with three kids and an Ideal Home, waiting for the sensitive drop-out poet to kiss her awake into social awareness and physical fulfilment. This is Penny Wanawake doing her Shamus number. So do it.

She did. The bag had a plastic-wrapped stiffener along the bottom which gave it a base on which to stand and could be raised for easy storage. She raised it. And found a vein of pure gold.

The Osman letters were grouped together inside an elastic band. Six of them. Penny's eyes skittered from paragraph to paragraph. Anyone who could use phrases like 'twin orbs' and 'lissom curves' without blushing, let alone 'wondrous' almost anything, probably deserved whatever he got. Including black-mail. It stuck out a mile that the relationship between Zachary Osman and the nanny was based on nothing more elevated than sex. Elevated being the *mot juste*. Yet in the enlightened eighties, was anyone prepared to fork out ready cash to prevent this kind of thing reaching his wife? Penny thought not. Particularly not when the wife had been around the way Chrissie Osman had. Penny tried to think of circumstances in which such letters might prove to be weapons of leverage. They were few. They did not fit Zachary Osman.

It was much more likely that Chrissie wanted them back in order to apply a little domestic pressure of her own. Thinking that, she also thought about Chrissie. She kept herself in shape. She had the lethal legs and sinewed muscles of a dancer. She was more than capable of pulling a ligature tight for long enough to cause death by strangulation, particularly if the victim was small and taken by surprise. Did she also have a reason to do so? Could she, enraged by finding the lovers in bed or incriminating letters such as these, have decided to knock off the nanny when a suitable opportunity arose? Possibly. Yet from what she'd seen of the woman, Penny'd have laid bets that, whatever damage she might do in the heat of the moment, cold-blooded killing was not her scene. Besides, she had an alibi. Dinner with friends. It was bound to be solid, since by now the police would have checked it out. And anyway, all she had to do was send Fiona packing, with a month's wages in lieu.

But the Osman letters weren't the only ones. There were others, written on flimsy paper in an extravagant hand. For a moment, Penny hesitated. But what the hell. In for a Wanawake, in for a pound. She started reading and felt her cheeks grow hot. This was the sort of stuff a girl wanted to hear. This was passion in its extremest toe-curling form, complete with misquoted lines from the better-known love poems, plus some embarrassing examples of the home-made kind. This was windy sighs, burning tears, longing, despair. Any girl reading these letters would feel loved. She was also liable to be reduced to moist desire within seconds. Judging by various references to letters received, Fiona had been.

Hmmm.

Who'd written them? They were unenveloped, so no clues there. There was no address. No dates, either. The signature was an indecipherable letter that could have been anything except X. There were plenty of those after it and the two didn't jive. Penny took a deep breath and read the pages again. They made her feel old. However much you adored someone, when you'd been living with them for six years, the passion was subsumed in the contentment. Still there, natch. But without the need for flamboyant expression. What could she gather about the guy who'd written them? It *was* a guy. He made that abundantly clear, describing with immodest detail what the thought of Fiona did to him and where he'd like to put the results. Other than that, he didn't give much away. Place, time, family, employment weren't given a look-in. Love excited him to such a degree that he lost control of the language, leaving out most punctuation and often dropping unnecessary words in his haste to convey the really important ones. He spent whole paragraphs cataloguing what he would give Fiona if only he was a millionaire: that didn't mean much. He talked frequently of the miles that separated them: again, this offered little clue. If you were as horny as this guy, five miles could be as great a distance as five thousand. The two of them seemed to meet fairly regularly since he took up a lot of space going through what they'd done when they were together. They'd done quite a lot. They'd done things that Penny hadn't done. Things, when she thought about it, she had no intention of doing. Inventive was probably a good word for them.

She put the letters back where they'd been. Although she'd guessed right about Fiona, it didn't make her feel as good as she'd like.

After that, the photographs were a let-down. The usual collection of family snapshots. She recognised Dymphna, a plump child growing into a fat adolescent. She recognised Paco Esteban, too. His hair startled among exotic Douanier Roussea-type greenery, on the back of a horse, standing formal-suited in front of a cathedral door. In that particular photograph, he was accompanied by an older man, by Katrina and by a slim dark kid in white shirt and striped tie. Guessing, Penny decided that this was an Esteban family group: the cricket-loving playboy, the woman who'd left her children for him, his two sons. She guessed also that the photograph of a man in tweeds and a scowl standing against a background of bare hills was Dr McIntosh. The various ponies didn't need speculation. They were just ponies. There was Fiona herself, in party frock and short white socks, in jodhpurs, in bathing suit beside a palm-fringed pool, in nurse-type uniform holding a baby in her arms. There were several of a younger Ewen Hamilton, some with what might have been his family, in basket chairs before a turreted stone mansion, some alone or with Dymphna. There were school-friends, larking about.

The contrast between Scotland and Brazil must have been something of a culture shock to the two mother-deprived daughters. More than that. A bit of an emotional tug of war. There was no clue as to where Fiona had been happiest, no over-abundance of photographs from one life or another. The dark stepbrothers, the handsome stepfather, appeared as frequently as the dour doctor or the girls from school.

There were two photographs she looked at for some time. In one, Fiona and her sister were dressed in jackets and absurd tweed caps, with guns under their arms and five brace of murdered pheasant at their feet. The other showed Dr McIntosh standing in the porch of what was probably his house. He had one arm around Dymphna, the other round a space that had been cut out of the snap with a pair of nail scissors. Had the space once contained Nanny Campbell?

The police would be here soon. Once they'd taken away Fiona's things, there'd be nothing more for Penny to do. It wasn't her problem. It wasn't her pain. Besides, the days of the amateur sleuth were numbered. The notion that an ordinary citizen with a mortgage to worry about and a job to do should constantly be stumbling across corpses and spotting significances where the fuzz had failed to was outrageous. By now, they would certainly be far down the road to solving the Nanny Murders. It was only Ewen Hamilton who thought that Fiona's murder was anything other than another tragic death in an already tragic series.

She checked the bag again and found something she'd missed before: viz, one short violent note on yellow recycled paper:

> Listen, you bitch [it said]. The answer's NO and always will be. You won't get away with this – there's too much to lose. Just leave us ALONE.

There was no signature.

What was *that* all about? Fiona putting the squeeze on someone who refused to be squeezed: that was obvious. She tossed up about keeping the note but decided she'd better leave it. She took one last look at the florist's cards and put everything back into the bag except the letters from Zachary Osman.

She pushed open the french doors into the garden. Another day of heat. The English weren't used to it. They couldn't handle heat gracefully. Battersea Park would be full to the brim with yoghurt-coloured bodies and boobs in unsuitable tops. There'd be pink noses and ill-shaven armpits. There'd be wimps trying to look macho in shorts. This year the last word in shorts was Bermuda, preferably patterned in Day-Glo geometry. *Not* a style to overwhelm one with a sense of masculine beauty. Only the young could wear Bermudas. Most of them shouldn't.

A chorus of amphibian complaint surged towards her. Coax-ax-ax. Coax-ax-ax. Aristophanes got it dead right. Coax-ax-ax. Darn those frogs. She stepped out into the syringa-flavoured heat with ants' eggs for the goldfish in her hand. I's a-comin', guys. Just hold your horses. She'd like to stay home today. Lift a few weights. Eat some fruit. Maybe do some work in the darkroom. Get on the phone about the BlackAid concert. Take it easy. With Miss Ivory back in harness, she didn't have to do a damn thing she didn't want to.

She wondered if Miss Ivory had organised a cook for Martin Harding. He slid into her mind, thick-haired, thick-lensed. And with him a remembrance, something she'd been aware was eluding her. She grabbed it, held it down, examined it.

Darn it. So much for ease-taking. Now she had a second reason to get down to Wrestebury again, this time not one she'd prefer to shove to one side. But before that, there were a couple of things she better check. It wasn't that she thought she knew more than the cops. Far from it. It was because she was a damned nosy bitch. Because she was a woman. Women didn't like ragged edges or loose ends. And the end she rather thought she'd remembered was, or might be, very loose indeed.

11

Time for another run. On her way out she saw another letter lying on the doormat. She picked it up. Gave it the quick double-o. Tore it open. It was hand-delivered and tissue-lined. The writing was firm and forward-leaning, as though each letter were the prow of a hurrying ship. Her heart sank. She'd seen the hand before. It spelled trouble.

'*Vital you contact me urgently*,' she read.

Something would have to be done. Some time. Only way to handle it was to do a Scarlett O'Hara number. Think about it tomorrow. Or the day after. She pushed it into her pocket. Pulling the front door shut behind her, she set off towards the river. She wore her white jogging suit, a brand new pair of the Reeboks with blue towelling interiors, and a white sweatband low on her forehead. Just to show she was being serious here.

She ran along beside the river. There was a sombre sky above, matching her mood. The granite walls of the Embankment, as unforgiving as the hands of a hangman, hid the water. She settled into a rhythm, calves bunching, unbunching, feet slapping the roadway with the regularity of a heartbeat.

Running provided an opportunity to think. What she thought about was the BlackAid concert. Only three weeks away, and it seemed like nothing at all had been done. They'd had replies from Sade, from Tina Turner, from Belafonte. There were maybes from Terence Trent d'Arby and Aswad.

Meanwhile, she had a decision to take. A personal one. One of the coordinators had asked if she wanted to be in the show herself. A dance routine, he'd said, looking at her legs. Or part of a backing group. Backing what? she'd said. Anything. Country and Western. Heavy metal. Whatever you want, he'd told her. She'd said no to the former. The thought of the latter filled her with a furtive excitement of which she was vaguely ashamed. She wanted to do it. To sing with a mike in her hand, dressed in something skintight. Her voice snaking out over an auditorium full of appreciative ears. Great. And those lovely whining harmonies back of almost any country song you cared to name. When she was at Stanford, she'd kept her car radio permanently tuned to the twenty-four-hour C & W station. Riding the freeways you could sing along for ever, sliding up and down the backing lines, grabbing at notes, soprano here, tenor there, yet still part of the whole. But could she really carry it off? Let's face it, she was lots of things but performance artist wasn't one of them.

Yet.

By Chelsea Bridge, she turned up Lower Sloane Street towards Eaton Square. At one of the big cream-painted houses she stopped. Marking time on the step, she pressed a bell. Her mother's voice grated from the entryphone with the metallic timbre of a cowbell. The front door edged open to let her in.

Lady Helena was checking out the orchids in the conservatory built on to her garden flat. 'You look down,' she said.

'I feel down.' Penny gave her a potted version of the last three days. 'I don't want to believe Ludovic Fairfax is involved in murder.'

'I remember how fond of him you were when you were children.'

'As a child, he was an award-winner. It's as a man he's got me worried,' said Penny. 'He's up to something. And I suspect it's no good.'

Lady Helena cut the stem of a spray of miniature cymbidiums and held it towards Penny. 'Lovely, aren't they? How do you think I can help?'

Penny sniffed desultorily. 'Super. Like I said, he absolutely insisted that I bring him down to the house when you had that dinner party with the Osmans.'

'I remember. He's turned out awfully good-looking, hasn't he?'

'Handsome is as handsome does,' said Penny, tarter than a pickled onion.

'Goodness.' Lady Helena laughed. 'You looked just like Nanny Simpson when you said that.'

If there was one thing Penny could have done without, it was being compared to bloody Nanny Simpson. Tell the truth, the way she felt now, if she never heard the word 'nanny' again in her life, it would suit her just fine. 'That's really made my day,' she said.

133

'Has it?' Lady Helena reached under the slatted wooden staging and brought out a brass spraying-can. 'I must have missed that pot when I watered this morning.' She moistened the potting compound round the roots of a Miltonia and put the can back underneath. 'So what do you want to know?'

'I remember reading something in one of the gossip columns a while back, about Ludo and some girl. Do you know who it was?'

'Let me think. I'm sure Amabel told me something about it....' Baskets of stephanotis and vanilla hung from the cross beams of the greenhouse. Lady Helena pulled a spray down and sniffed it. 'Funny how they still give off a scent, even when there aren't any flowers.'

Life could be like that, too. Still pungent even after death has deflowered it. Penny followed her mother between the banks of plants to the warmer greenhouse.

'Ludovic,' said Lady Helena. 'I don't think it lasted very long. Not with the girl that was in the papers, at any rate. She was a deb or something. Ended up marrying one of the Roxburgh boys.'

'Are you sure?'

'Yes.'

So Penny's hunch was wrong. She'd held it in her mind like a Molotov cocktail waiting to be thrown. If the girl who'd been linked with Ludo in the gossip column photograph had been Fiona McIntosh ... But she hadn't. If there was a link between Fiona and Ludovic, that wasn't it. Penny didn't know whether she felt relieved or let down. She lifted a Brassocattleya stem and bent her nose to its purplish-pink blooms. The scent had the underhand kick of cheap perfume. She sneezed. Twice. Coming out of the second sneeze, she heard her mother saying, '... she didn't like her much.'

'Sorry?'

'I said, Amabel didn't like her much.'

'Who?'

'Amabel Fairfax, dear. Who did you think? Said there was something a bit off-beat about her.'

'About whom?'

'Penelope, do try to concentrate a bit harder. About this girl.' Her mother was walking back through the open french windows into her drawing-room.

Penny followed. 'Which girl?'

'The one I'm telling you about. The one Ludo was besotted with. He met her at a party, I think it was. Or was it that she *was* Portuguese?'

'Are you OK, Mom? Your *sequiturs* are a little *non* this morning.'

'It was something like that. A definite *coup de foudre*, Amabel said. She was rather relieved it didn't last very long since the girl was rather odd.'

'How long ago was that?'

'Four years? Maybe five?'

'What happened to her?'

'The usual thing, I expect.'

'Which is?'

'Ludo dropped her. Or, more likely, she dropped him. Poor Ludo. He really doesn't seem to have much luck with women, does he? I know Amabel's simply dying to have some grandchildren. Though I suppose strictly speaking they'd be step-grandchildren, wouldn't they? But the way Ludo's going, she thinks she'll be dead before he makes her a grandmother.'

'Wrestebury comes first with Ludo. Then Amabel.'

'Perhaps that's why he can't seem to hang on to any of his girlfriends long enough to get married to them.'

'What else could it be? He doesn't do drugs. He doesn't beat them up.'

'You can't be sure.'

'Mother, you're not seriously suggesting that Ludovic Fairfax is violent, are you?'

'No. Merely that one knows nothing about the private lives of one's friends. Ludo could be doing anything to anyone, in the privacy of his own home, but we'll never know about it.'

Like Paul Ford-Harrison. 'If my father hit you, what would you do?' Penny asked.

'I'd hit him right back,' her mother said. 'Only harder.'

'What if he kept on doing it?'

'I presume we're talking theoretically. The idea of Benjamin hitting anything, particularly me, is perfectly ridiculous.'

'Answer the question.'

'I suppose I'd leave him,' Lady Helena said. She thought about it. 'Unless I loved him enough to overlook it. Or liked being hit.'

Were those the reasons why Mary Laurence stuck wtih Paul Ford-Harrison? 'Does anyone?' Penny asked.

'Some people do. And of course, if I was poor, with several children and nowhere to go, no one to help me, I might not have any option.'

What character trait in Ludo caused women to leave him, or him to leave women? The outlines of the Ludo Penny knew shimmered into indistinction. Once she had swum with him, danced with him, kissed him. He was a man who appeared to have everything: brains, charm, background. Now he was melting into a shape she did not recognise. A man locked up in himself, unlucky in love, envious. Unexpectedly, she wanted to weep.

Lady Helena noticed. 'Especially when you consider how fearfully bright he is, too,' she said, pottering and chattering about the room. It was deliberately done, a ploy to give Penny time to regather herself. 'As well as good-looking, I mean. A Double first at Cambridge and President of the Union. Do you remember that quiz show thing he was on? *Brain Teasers* or something? Amabel was so proud of him.'

Click. Like someone flicking on a switch that started the countdown to Red Alert, Penny remembered. For some weeks in his second year at university, Ludo had taken part in one of those TV programmes which test the participants' ability to remember isolated facts. His college team had ended up as champions, by which time their faces had become familiar in homes across the land. Or those, at any rate, which went in for that kind of intellectually élitist stuff. Even in some which didn't. Ludo's good looks had ensured that in households where the finger on the button was female, the ratings shot up on Thursday nights. He had been the only man on his team. The other three were girls. One of them had been something a bit ethnic: Greek perhaps, or Pakistani. One had been blonde.

The third had been stolid and broadbrowed, totally unflappable, never missing an answer.

Just as she was today.

Because, unless Penny was very much mistaken, she had been Vanessa Carrington.

Hoo, boy. Whatever game Ludo was playing, it was dark and deep. She'd realised early on that Vanessa was a plant. She tried to remember. *Brain Teasers* had been question-mastered by an amiable man with not much hair. Each week he gave a potted biog of the contestants. What had Vanessa been? Something non-humanities, she was sure. Maths? Sociology? Economics?

Whichever, it was a fairly sure bet that Vanessa was in the same line of business as Ludo.

Preoccupied, she glanced at a slew of invitations. They lay on a Victorian papier mâché tray inset with thin slabs of mother-of-pearl. Not really seeing them, her mind plugged in to circuits for which she couldn't find the switch. Or else there was a power failure.

'Mother,' she began.

The connections suddenly glowed with juice. She picked out one of the heavily embossed cards and looked at it more closely. There'd been one just like it in the Estebans' hotel room. For, if she wasn't mistaken, the very same occasion.

'Hey, Mother. This invitation. Is it from the guy you had to dinner in the spring? The ambassador or whatever he was?'

'That's right,' Lady Helena said. 'We used to know them when we were in Washington, before your father was appointed to the United Nations. Yes. We were rather surprised to find Carlos had been given the London Embassy, I must say.'

'Why?'

'According to your father, the man is a crook of the worst kind. And totally ruthless. Cocaine, emeralds, white slaves: you name it. And he's never even been in Europe before. Your father says he must have bought this ambassadorship.'

'Greased a few palms, you mean?'

'A lot of them. He needs to add respectability to his image. Make himself more acceptable to the voters.'

'Which voters?'

'The ones he hopes will eventually make him leader of his country.'

'Couldn't he have by-passed London?'

'That's what I thought. Your father says no. No foreign power of any stature is openly going to hobnob with a man like that unless he's earned a modicum of acceptability first.'

Some of them didn't bother. Hadn't seemed to make any difference. The Marcoses. The Duvaliers. All the corrupt ones who bled their poor countries until they were nothing but skin and bone. Penny had seen some of the results. People who'd had everything taken from them. Everything. Even the strength to protest.

'Will you go to the reception?' she asked.

'Most certainly not.' Lady H. pulled a cushion into violent four-squaredness. 'We heard some horrific stories about his

137

activities when we were last in Washington.'

Penny looked at the invitation again. Carlos Ramirez. He was the same nationality as Rodolfo Esteban. Had they known each other?

'Can you think of any reason why Ludo Fairfax should be so keen to meet Zachary Osman?' she said.

'None. As a matter of fact, I was staggered when you wanted to have him invited to our little supper party. I mean, when you consider everything.'

'What sort of everything?'

'All those investments the Brig made just before he died.'

'What about them?' Penny felt her nostrils flex like a dog's.

'He'd put all his money into one of Osman's companies. Thousands and thousands. That's why Amabel's so short of cash all the time. The whole lot went right down the tubes.'

* 12 *

If she'd been hoping that the Estebans' hotel had blown away in the night, she was fresh out of luck. It stood there in the dusty sunshine, breathing money. In, that is. Out, it breathed illusion, fostering the poignant dreams of colonies long since gone independent yet still wistful for lost pomp and circumstance. Trooping the Colour. Changing the Guard. Crown Jewels and ravens and places where real royalty slept. All very well being a brave new world. *Ipso facto*, it wasn't old. Pomp tended to be. So did circumstance.

Out front, a uniformed tub of guts stood guard. A dress coat of black hugged him closer than peel does a banana. It had yellow facings and several vertical rows of gold buttons. There was a gold cockade on his black top hat. If he wanted to audition for *Die Fledermaus*, the outfit was fine. For opening doors and hailing taxis, it was kind of OTT.

Penny grinned at him as she passed. She hoped he was paid extra for wearing the topper. She rode the lift to the second floor. It bulged with the kind of people who have foreign accents and big bank rolls. She could hear the first and feel the second. On the second floor, she popcorned out into the passage. She could breathe again. No doubt about it, money makes the world go around. And most of the world seemed to be in the lift.

She walked down the corridor. She didn't know what she was hoping for by coming here. She didn't know what she'd do with it if whateveritwas turned up. The morning papers had mentioned that a man was helping police with their enquiries regarding the so-called Nanny Murders. The upmarket ones were discreet. As far as the downmarket ones went, the guy was guilty until proved guilty. Yet, like Ewen Hamilton, she was by now fairly sure that there was more to Fiona's killing than random bloodlust.

She'd tried to tell the cops. Several times. They didn't want to listen. They'd arrived that morning to take away Fiona's bags. One of them wanted to know if she'd touched anything. She figured if she denied it they might find out anyway, so she pleaded guilty. He wanted to know why.

'It was a Need-To-Know situation, officer,' she said. She went into her Good Citizen mode. 'One of our girls was missing. As the agency employing her ... well, I'm sure you understand.'

He did. He gave her a visual strip-search and went away.

Outside Room 204, she paused. There were so many questions needing answers. Intimate ones. The kind people tended to resent being asked. Yet the key to Fiona's murder surely lay in her character. And to understand that, she needed to know more than she did already. That rape, for instance. That *possible* rape. Did anyone else know about it, apart from Dymphna and Nanny Campbell, that is? And, of course, the rapist himself? The *alleged* rapist. If he existed, had it been rape simple, if any forced penetration could be so called? Or had it been something worse, the sort of violence hinted at in reports of criminal proceedings, involving objects other than the male sex organ, involving orifices other than the vaginal? These weren't matters she wanted to know much about.

Quietly, she knocked. It was totally tacky to be butting in like this, but what else was she to do? There was a longish pause before the door was opened. Mrs Esteban. The former Mrs McIntosh. She looked dreadful. Sudden grief had destroyed the barriers she had previously erected against age. All her years and a few extra showed in her face. Too many tears had laundered the blue from her eyes. Now they were the colour of jeans gone pale with washing.

'Yes?' she said. She blinked. 'Weren't you here the other day.'

'Mr Esteban asked me to find Dymphna.'

'That's right.' She said nothing more. Her blonde hair hung dully, too young, too bright for the face it surrounded. Like the pearls round her neck, she had lost her lustre.

'Mrs Esteban. I can imagine the shock all this has been to you. I'm terribly sorry about it all.'

There were tears in her voice though her face was dry. 'It's my fault,' she said. 'If I'd stuck it out, none of this would have happened.'

'Stuck what out?'

'My marriage ...'

It didn't sound like a doorstep topic. Penny glanced down the corridor. A young couple stepped out of the lift, hand-in-hand.

Even at a hundred paces, she could tell they were Germans. Behind them crept a palsied old boy sporting a striped apron and several hundredweight of baggage. Both of the young people wore one of those waterproofs that can be folded up to make a bag to hang over the touristic shoulder. It was a duality the purpose of which Penny hadn't yet discovered. It wasn't even the kind of bag you could put stuff into.

'Look,' she said. 'Could I come in?'

Katrina Esteban was drooping like an umbrella whose spokes have wilted. She stood aside. 'If you want. I'm afraid I'm alone at the moment. The boys have taken my daughter for a walk in the park.'

Which boys were those? Paco Esteban? But Paco was hardly a *boy*. Did she mean Paco and his brother? But the brother ought to be somewhere else, not here in London. She followed Mrs Esteban in and closed the door.

Katrina suddenly caught sight of herself in a gilded looking-glass on the wall. 'My Lord,' she said, pushing at her hair. 'I'll be back in a moment. Do sit down.'

Might as well expect a rabbit to stay celibate. The minute the door shut behind her, Penny was glomming the place. It had lost its air of well-being. Newspapers lay ragged on the floor. An open document case leaned against one of the gilt-armed chairs. Crumpled tissues mourned on the sofa. It's not so much the loss of a loved one that makes us grieve, as the unbearability of all the might-have-beens, the if-onlys that death leaves behind.

Penny peered into the document case. Papers, mostly. A couple of paperbacks whose titles she couldn't see. She spread the case wider. Pages of printed stuff. They looked like insurance forms or land contracts. Since they were printed in a language she didn't know, she would never find out. Spanish, was it? After a recent embarrassing episode in a Sevillian pharmacist's, she'd been thinking of taking a night-class in Spanish. Not that it would have helped much right now. This was some other language.

She heard the door handle turning. By the time an improved version of Katrina Esteban had come back into the room, Penny was standing by the windows, looking at the grey skies above the Palace.

'Now. How can I help you?' Mrs Esteban said. She seemed to think Penny had a right to be there. Perhaps she wasn't entirely clear about Penny's role. Penny didn't put her wise.

'I hate to bring up things that I'm sure you'd prefer to forget,' she said. 'But there are one or two matters that need clarifying.' It sounded good. It sounded official.

'Anything,' Katrina said. 'I just want this terrible ...' She shrugged. The movement jerked fresh tears out of her eyes.

'You said just now that this wouldn't have happened if you'd stuck it out. What did you mean?'

'If I'd stayed with Gordon.'

'Gordon?'

'My former husband. The girls' father ... If I'd stood up to him. But you see, by then I was so damned tired of it all. The coldness, the emotional bullying, the way he treated the children, the lack of ...' Another shrug. A sliding away of the eyes. Penny guessed she meant sex. 'When I met Rodolfo and we fell in love, I suddenly realised I couldn't stay another minute with Gordon. I realised I hated him.' Her hands twisted in her lap. 'God, how I hated him.'

This was a different woman from the one Penny had been picturing. 'If you felt like that about him, why did you leave the two girls behind?' she asked.

Katrina stared at her. 'You can't imagine for a moment that I had any choice, can you?' She began to cry again.

'What was to stop you?'

The laugh she gave came straight from hell. 'Gordon.'

'The law doesn't like separating children from their mothers. Particularly such young ones.'

'Don't think I didn't know that. Rodolfo's lawyers said that on the evidence, no court in the world would have awarded custody to Gordon.'

'So what happened?'

'Gordon said he would let me go with Rodolfo, as long as I left the girls behind. I said in that case I'd stay.'

'How'd he take that?'

'He told me he wouldn't have me back.' Katrina drew in a juddering breath. 'He said I was tainted, soiled, an adultress. In front of my little girls he called me filth. He spat at me.'

'He sounds completely nuts.'

'I think he is. I begged him. I actually got down on my knees and pleaded. It was no good. He said he knew I would get custody but he didn't care. Whatever happened to him afterwards, if I tried to take the children away, he would track me down and then he'd – he'd kill them. The girls.'

142

'And you believed him?'

'Oh, yes.' She shuddered. 'Absolutely.'

Penny knew she was listening to the truth. Not just Katrina Esteban's. Gordon McIntosh's too.

'That's why I stayed away from England when Rodolfo was killed,' she went on. 'I didn't dare come back, for the girls' sake. And of course I couldn't tell them the real reason.'

'Why not?'

'They lived with their father. I didn't want them to hate him.'

'They seem to have learned to do some of that anyway.'

'Maybe.' Mrs Esteban sighed. 'I did what I thought best. It led to a certain amount of coolness between my daughters and me. And now it's too late for Fiona to understand.'

More tears. Penny waited. There was something else she wanted to know. If anyone knew the answer. Putting pressure on Katrina Esteban at this juncture was like shooting a kitten between the eyes. She still felt she had to do it. 'Did you know that a few years ago Fiona was – possibly – raped?'

The other woman's chin shot up. Her face went rigid. The tears were still there on her cheeks but they seemed frozen in place. 'What?' Her voice was as hard and as cold as the edge of an ice-skate.

'Apparently. According to Dymphna.'

Her hand twisted the pearl necklace. 'Not Gordon,' she said. 'Please. Not that.'

'I don't know.' Penny gave the pause a count of four, then said: 'Surely you're not accusing your former husband of – of incest, are you?'

'From what I've heard of his behaviour towards Fiona, he's quite capable of it.' The smile she gave would have looked better on a skeleton. 'Funny, really, that someone so eager to see the sin in others was blind to it in himself.'

'Are you surprised that Fiona didn't tell you about it?'

'Of course not. Not after Gordon and that terrible old woman ...'

'Nanny Campbell?'

Katrina nodded. '... were through with the girls, they could barely bring themselves to speak to me. The two of them – Gordon and the Campbell woman – deliberately destroyed my relationship with my children.' She got up and pulled some of the newspapers into a rough pile. Without looking at Penny, she said, 'Are you sure about ... this rape?'

'Not entirely.'

'Oh, my poor child. Men are so vile. And Fee would have thought the whole thing was her own fault. Because she was wearing a dress that clung too tight or a blouse that showed too much.' She stood with her hands full of the mink coat. 'Perhaps I'm being unfair on Gordon. Nanny Campbell's really the one to blame. She made him what he was.'

'How'd she do that?'

Katrina Esteban raised eyebrows as thin and fine as corn-silk. 'She more or less brought him up.'

'I hadn't realised she was your former husband's nanny as well.'

'Oh yes. His father was a Presbyterian minister who'd married above him. The mother was more concerned with the state of her kid gloves than with her son. So the nanny had complete authority. I realised the sort of woman she was the minute I met her. I refused to have anything to do with her, though Gordon tried to insist that we employ her. Quite apart from anything else, I don't believe in paying other people to bring up my children. But as soon as I left, she was installed in the nursery. There was absolutely nothing I could do about it.'

'Was it worth it?' Penny said.

'Leaving Gordon?'

'And your daughters.'

Katrina crimped the edges of her mouth. 'I don't seem to have the knack of choosing men,' she said. 'Rodolfo was a terrible womaniser. But it didn't seem to matter that much. He loved me. In his own way, he needed me. It sounds odd, but he was a man who liked to be married. He would never have asked me to marry him if his first wife had been alive, however much energy he might have spent on persuading me into bed with him. That was a kind of consolation. And I had the boys, to make up for the loss of my girls. And then . . .' she paused, trying to get it right '. . . I carried on loving him in spite of his faults. With Gordon it was the other way round: I learned to hate him because of them.'

'What sort of women did Mr Esteban womanise with?'

'Any and every. Including me. Even though I was his wife.' She laughed fondly.

The infinite accommodations of the heart never failed to amaze Penny. And to cheer her. 'Do you have any idea who killed him?' she said.

'Of course.'

'You do?'

'It was undoubtedly one of his close friends.'

'That's what friends are for.'

'Sounds strange, I know. But it's the truth. Rodolfo had decided he wanted to go into politics. He invited a few highly influential people down from the city to shoot for a couple of days. Diplomat friends, people already in power within the government, that sort of thing. Prominent persons. It was his first step towards what he wanted.' She wrinkled her nose slightly. 'It's what these days they call networking.'

'Did he invite them as a precaution, or as part of his campaign?'

'Precaution? How do you mean?'

'I assume that he must have had enemies who would need sweetening.'

'You're very astute.' Katrina Esteban smiled slightly. 'Two of the men staying with us professed to be friends but in fact disliked him intensely. Or more likely feared him. He was a very rich man, and in a country like his, money buys a lot of power. But that's politics, isn't it?'

'Strange bedfellows, right?'

'Dog eat dog. But I can't believe that politics had anything to do with Rodolfo's death. He was in a bad mood that day. He had left the house early that morning and, by the time the girls and I arrived with lunch, he was still angry. I think he was probably thinking more about the row we'd had and wasn't taking care. Stepped into the line of fire or something. The bullet passed right through his head, so they were never able to say which gun had fired it, but I'm convinced that it was just one of those terrible things that happen. An unlucky accident.'

Although it differed in detail, it was subtantially the same story that Ewen Hamilton had told her.

'Do you still see any of these people?' Penny asked.

'Most of them.' She glanced at her reflection in the glass. 'One of them is in England right now, actually.'

'Would that be the new ambassador?'

Katrina raised her eyebrows, looking puzzled and faintly annoyed.

'I couldn't help noticing an invitation to some embassy function last time I was here,' Penny said quickly. 'My parents were also invited.'

'Really.' Her tone was short. 'I didn't go.'

'Was he one of the people around when your husband was shot?'

'As a matter of fact he was. But that's not why I didn't go.'

'What was?'

She didn't want to answer. For a moment she chewed her lip. Finally, she said: 'I suppose it can't do her much harm now ...'

'Fiona?'

'Yes. There was an ... incident.'

'Sexual, I imagine.'

'You obviously know about my daughter.'

'Or maybe about Ramirez.'

'Sssh.' Katrina looked around as though someone might be behind the sofa. 'That's not the sort of thing you say if you want to stay out of trouble.' Then she laughed. 'But I forgot. I can say what I like. I'm in England.'

'What about this incident?'

'Fiona was always fundamentally innocent, even though I know she'd already had some, well, experience. It was as if she gave off an unconscious message. A musk, like a bitch in heat. But that wasn't until later. The time I'm talking about was a year or two before Rodolfo's accident. Fiona can't have been more than about fifteen. Ramirez tried to get into her bedroom one night. She was terrified. She told me she didn't dare scream for help because she knew he was someone who could help Rodolfo in politics.'

'Isn't it a bit odd that your husband invited him back?'

'I didn't want him to, of course. But he said it was important that he came. Fiona was rather upset when she saw him, I do remember.'

'Mrs Esteban, is it possible that he could have had some reason to want Fiona out of the way?'

The beautiful blue eyes widened. 'Oh no. I absolutely can't believe that. It was years ago now. No, I'm sure you're barking up the wrong tree there.'

'Probably,' Penny said. She ought to be leaving. She should be heading for Norfolk again and the confrontation which awaited her there. Perhaps she lingered because of something Katrina had said. This was a woman who should have been loved and because of a series of unlucky accidents, had not been. 'How did your stepsons handle their father's death?'

'Paco was philosophical about it. He had already left university by then, and viewed his father with a – a kind of cynical affection. Eduardo has never spoken of it from that day to this. At least, not to me. Nor, as far as I know, to his brother.'

'It obviously upset Fiona.'

'She'd been very attracted to Rodolfo, like every other woman he ever met. And he adored little girls. I'd like to have produced a daughter for him myself but it didn't ever happen.'

'She never came out to visit you again, did she?'

'No.'

The door of the suite opened. Dymphna came in. Behind her was Paco. Behind him, presumably, Eduardo. All three of them stopped when they saw Penny. Alarm curled into the room like smoke from an abandoned cigarette. It had been covered over with blandness before she could be certain which of the three was its source.

Paco spoke. 'Miss Wanawake. How nice.' He gave her a look that was a subtly rude blend of surprise and enquiry. If anything, he'd grown even more handsome since she'd last set eyes on him. She'd have been happy to take him home with her. Stick him on the mantelpiece, between the handpainted Rockingham candlesticks. Man as *objet d'art*.

'What's she doing here?' Dymphna asked.

Penny smiled. 'I hope you didn't mind my showing up like this.'

'I do,' said Dymphna.

'Of course not.' Keeping his gaze fixed on her, Paco pulled a wallet from inside his jacket. 'I imagine you've come for the money I owe you.'

As insults go, it was one of the smoothest Penny had ever received. 'That's not why I'm here,' she said. As if he didn't know.

'What is?'

'One or two things I wanted to clear up.'

His brow was suddenly full of wrinkles. Each one brimmed with bewilderment. 'What things can *you* possibly –' She loved the way he leaned on the word 'you'. Like, sure you're part of the human race. That doesn't mean I have to invite you to my party.

'I understand you met with Fiona the day she died.'

Paco glanced briefly at his stepmother, straightening his shoulders as he did so. One hand brushed across the white sheen of his hair. 'Yes,' he said. 'I planned to take her out to lunch, since she told me she was busy that evening. He looked at Katrina again. 'Obviously I wanted to see her. After all, we were ... engaged.'

'Was this a formal engagement?'

'Yes.' He spoke unwillingly.

'With a ring and everything?'

'Yes. Except she'd managed to lose it somewhere.'

Looked like Penny had been right about at least one of Fiona's capers. 'But in the end you didn't manage to spend much time with her, did you?' she said.

'No.'

'You didn't even take her out to lunch.'

'As it happens, no. When I got to the Osman house, she told me she had to meet someone unexpectedly. That it was important. So I came back to London.'

'Were you annoyed?'

'Annoyed enough to hang around all day and then finally, when my rage had come to an explosive boil, to seek her out and kill her? No, Miss Wanawake, I was not. I spent the day instead with Katr – with my stepmother. We went to the Scandinavian exhibition at the Royal Academy, which she'd expressed a desire to see, being of Norwegian extraction.' His handsome face was sardonic. 'Anything else you'd like to know?'

There was, actually. Like, when are you free, dude? But here, in front of his family, she wasn't about to ask. Not that she had much chance. For some reason, he hadn't taken to her.

The man behind him pushed forward. 'Who is this, Paco?' he smiled at Penny, holding out a hand. 'I am Eduardo Esteban.' The accent was that of a mariachi player in a Latin-American combo. So was the smoulder which came with it. The back of his head was shaved to above ear level, except for a glossy little hank which nestled in the nape of his neck. A silver cross hung from one ear. Beautiful. He had none of the looks of his elder brother but three hundred times the charm. And all of it the dimestore variety.

'Hi. I'm Penny Wanawake.' She held out her hand. He took it. His thumb lightly caressed her palm as he folded it against his lips. As tricks went, it was one of the cheapest. She repossessed her fingers so fast she practically broke his front teeth.

He gave her a grin which she didn't bother pretending was infectious. It would have been bearable if he hadn't been wearing a John Travolta-type black sleeveless tank-top tucked into baggy camouflage trousers. She tried to think where, apart from *Saturday Night Fever*, she'd seen him before.

What was he: twenty-four? Twenty-five? At a push, twenty-six. Most of his life lay ahead, yet already he carried an air of failure around with him like an empty wallet. He gave the impression that by making him a younger brother, life had made damn sure he didn't stand a chance. The dice had been loaded against him from the very beginning and there wasn't a thing he could do about it.

Penny guessed that the women went for that sad-little-boy routine in a big way. No question, she liked little boys herself. But she liked big ones a whole lot better.

'I wanted to have just a few words with Dymphna,' she said, looking at Paco. 'Though I realise that it's a bad time for all of you.'

'Dymphna?' Paco turned to the fat girl. 'Do you mind?'

'I just don't see exactly what she has to do with us,' Dymphna said loudly, not meeting Penny's eyes. 'I don't see why we have to answer her questions. She's not the police or anything.'

'She's a private investigator,' Paco said. 'I cannot see that it would do any harm.'

'Nor can I,' said Katrina Esteban. Her voice was tentative, as though she hesitated to exert her maternal authority. 'Anything, anything at all that can help find who ... was responsible for Fiona ...' She turned away, the sentence cut off in its prime.

'All right.' Ungraciously, Dymphna pulled out a chair and dumped herself in it. 'What do you want to know?'

'It'd be easier if we went somewhere else,' Penny said.

'Or *we* did. Come on, boys.' Katrina moved her stepsons to the door and followed them out of the room. Her round hips pushed at the oatmeal of her linen skirt. She was a fine woman. Easy to see why the playboy Rodolfo had stayed with her, despite his sidetrips with other women. Penny recalled the handsome, dissolute face in Fiona's photograph album and realised why Eduardo was familiar. He could have been a younger version of his father.

Dymphna porpoised around in her chair. Her body had a sleek rubbery look under the jeans she wore, the flesh firm and inviting. If she didn't shed it, soon it would all begin to droop and sag, but for the moment she gave off the same feel-me invitation as a ripe avocado. 'I can't imagine what more I can tell you,' she said. There was colour on her cheekbones. And on her lower lip, which she was trying to eat.

'There's only one thing, really,' Penny said. 'About Fiona. I know you were hoping to meet up with her on your river trip.'

'So?' Dymphna looked defensive. Her eyes took on the hard shine of someone prepared to lie their way out of trouble if they had to.

'Did you?'

Dymphna's lips stayed shut.

Penny watched her trying to decide whether or not to tell the truth. That in itself was an answer. 'So you did,' she said. 'When? The same day that she was murdered?'

Dymphna still didn't speak. She stared at Penny. Panic was beginning to erode the lines of her soft round face.

'You might as well tell me,' Penny said. 'Even if you don't, the police will want to know.'

'I won't have to talk to the police, will I?'

'I should think it's very likely. I'm surprised you haven't already. After all, you're the victim's sister. And you were in the area at the time of the murder. Or close, anyway. So. Did you see her?'

'Yes. It was her day off. I rang her the night before and we arranged to meet at a place we knew, about halfway between where we were and that place where she was working.'

'Where was that?'

'A pub. It belongs to the parents of a friend. One of those girls on the boat with me.'

'The Harrison Arms?'

'Yes.'

'This was for lunch, was it?'

'It was for whenever we could get there. Boats don't make for very accurate timekeeping. But lunch was the general idea.'

'When did you get there?'

'About two. She was a bit annoyed. She'd been waiting over an hour.'

'How long did you spend together?'

'A couple of hours.'

'But not the evening?'

'No. We wanted to get on upriver before it got dark. Anyway, Fee had a date. And before you ask, I don't know who with.'

'Look. I know the two of you had been kind of on the outs recently. Because of Ewen Hamilton.'

Dymphna's truculent gaze reminded Penny of Paul Ford-

Harrison's remarks about the girl's temper. She said fiercely: 'I wouldn't have minded so much if she hadn't already got someone of her own.'

'Paco, do you mean?'

'Heavens, no. That was some stupid idea cooked up by the two of *them*.' She jerked her head towards the door behind which the others were doing whatever they were doing. 'Fee only pretended to be going along with it to keep them quiet.'

'So who was the someone she had, then?'

'Someone she'd been in love with for absolute yonks. I don't know who. She never talked about him. She said it had to be kept secret.'

'Was it reciprocated?'

'Must have been. Nobody stays madly in love for – what? Six, seven years? – if the other half's not reciprocating. Unless it's a film star or something. Someone she knew she couldn't ever have.'

'In spite of her pinching your boyfriend, you'd made it up, had you?'

'Obviously. Otherwise we wouldn't have arranged to meet, would we?'

Penny ignored the girl's challenging tones. Given that she had no right to be here, to be asking questions, stirring things up, she'd have been rude herself. 'How did your sister get there?'

'She said she'd been dropped off by someone called Shane. He worked at the same place.'

'How was she going to get home?'

'Um . . .' Dymphna thought back. 'I don't think she said.'

'You're quite sure?'

'We didn't discuss it. Since she had a date with someone after seeing us she must have made arrangements to get back.'

'Didn't she give you any indication of who she was going to see?'

'No. She seemed rather pleased with life, I do remember that. But whether it was to do with her date or not . . .'

'In what way pleased?'

'You know. Kind of sleek. Smiling for no real reason. She told me everything was going right for her at last.'

'What did she mean?'

'I presumed she meant she liked the job. And that she was glad to be seeing whoever it was later.'

'About whom you didn't ask?'

'No, I bloody well didn't.' Getting up, Dymphna strode over to one of the baskets of fruit. She took a green apple and sank her teeth into it. Through the mouthful, she said: 'If it was Ewen, I didn't want to know.'

'And she didn't say anything more specific?'

Dymphna folded her arms across her own plumpness. It was a gesture designed to stop secrets leaking out. If she wasn't too late. 'Look. I honestly don't remember, OK?' She stuck out her chin. Her voice wobbled. 'I didn't know she was going to get murdered that night, otherwise I might have paid more attention.'

'All right.' Penny stood up. 'One last thing. How often does your father get down to London?'

The reaction to the question was startling. Dymphna suddenly slammed her apple down and dropped her face into her hands. She began gasping. The gasps were full of words. 'Oh, God,' Penny heard. 'Daddy. Please. No. Oh God.'

'Hey, kid.' Penny hunkered down beside the girl's chair. 'What's going on?'

It took some unlovely weeping and several tissues from the box wedged into the sofa before she could make out what was terrifying Dymphna. Dr McIntosh, it seemed, had been in London the very weekend that Fiona had died. Dymphna had somehow convinced herself that her father could have been responsible.

'Why?' Penny said. Gently, as though Dymphna were a baby, she wiped the girl's nose.

'You don't know him.' Dymphna shuddered. 'He can get so raging mad over absolutely nothing. And he and Fiona ...' She pressed her fingers against her mouth to stop its frightened twist.

'Could it have been him she was meeting that evening?'

'Maybe. Oh, God, I hope not. But I suppose it could have been.'

'I certainly wouldn't assume *my* father was a murderer on the sort of evidence you've given me. So far it adds up to absolute zip.'

'Really?'

'Really. There's nothing to suggest that she even met your father that weekend, let alone that he could have killed her.'

What Penny was saying didn't amount to spit. There was nothing to suggest that Dr McIntosh *hadn't* killed Fiona, either. But it seemed to comfort Dymphna. Penny looked at her watch.

152

'Any chance of saying goodbye to your mother?'

Dymphna called out. Katrina Esteban came back from wherever she had been. Her bedroom, probably, since she'd put on a little more make-up and brushed her hair up into a knot at the back of her head. Behind her came Paco. He was wearing glasses, rimless and scholastic. Penny saw that he was older than she'd thought.

'I'm sorry to have intruded,' she said. 'I just hoped I might be able to help.'

'You have already, my dear,' Katrina sounded warm. 'Thank you so much for finding Dymphna for us.'

'Yes.' Paco held out his hand. 'Thank you.'

'And Eduardo,' Penny said. 'Tell him goodbye from me.'

'Eduardo,' Katrina called. She said to Penny: 'He can tell you himself. He's just getting his bag packed. He's got a train to catch.'

It was one of four possible responses that Penny had been hoping for. She tried not to look too much like someone who just hit the coconut and won the kewpie doll. 'Can I drop him off somewhere?' she said. 'My car's in the hotel parking space.'

Katrina and Paco consulted. 'Well . . .'

'What station does he . . .?'

'That's very kind of you . . .'

'I'm sure he'd be . . .'

'I'm actually driving down to see friends in Norfolk,' Penny said guilelessly. Her sweet round mouth laughed ha ha ho. 'If that's any good to anyone.' She knew damn well it was. One of the names on Martin Harding's list of adult participants had been E. Esteban.

'Norfolk?' frowned Paco. 'Where in Norfolk?' He stared at her with suspicion. She was really hurt by his lack of trust. It just about matched her own. Why hadn't he told her – until she asked – about visiting Fiona at the Osman house the very day she died? Why had he lied about taking Katrina to the Scandinavian exhibition?

Before she could get launched on it, Katrina was exclaiming. 'What a coincidence,' she said. 'Eduardo's going to Norfolk too.'

'Really?' Penny said politely.

'He's doing a course in intensive English at a place called Wrestebury Park.'

'But that's exactly where I'm going. How extraordinary. The

153

place belongs to some friends of mine.'

Paco's expression was as easy to read as an autocue. He knew she was scamming him. 'That is rather a coincidence, is it not?' he demanded.

'They do happen in real life, as well as fiction,' Penny said. She spread her hands continentally. 'I'd be glad to drive your brother down there. If he wants to come.'

He did.

Paco and Katrina walked them to the lift. Penny had revised her opinion of Fiona's mother some time ago. She was revising something else, too. Not an opinion exactly. More an estimate. When Paco stood beside his stepmother, she could see that the age gap between them was so small as to be insignificant. As the lift doors closed, he put his hand on Katrina's shoulder, comforting, and she glanced back at him. Penny blinked a couple of times. She needed her sunglasses. This was love, no doubt about it. Love, resplendent and assured, bright as a volcano. My true love hath my heart and I have his. But in that case, she wondered, as the lift jerked downwards, why had my true love been planning to marry my daughter?

It didn't make sense.

Nor did the fact that under the love, mixed up and entangled in it, had been something that was unmistakably fear.

As they stepped out into the hotel lobby, two broad-should-ered men in grey suits got into the lift. Their neat, self-contained faces might have belonged to bank managers or salesmen, even to professional cricketers. But it was the blow-dried hair which gave them away.

Cops.

* 13 *

She'd had to be manipulative in order to get Eduardo into her passenger seat. Now he was there, she wondered quite what she had hoped to achieve. A chance to talk about Fiona, maybe learn something more about the girl, was the most she could expect. There couldn't be much else to learn, could there? It was already crystal clear Fiona had used sex to get what she wanted. Which must have been approval first, Penny guessed, as much as love. It would only have been as she failed to find it that her self-image became low enough for her to try to use sex for control as well. Trouble is, there's no place to go when the self-image hits the ground. There'd been a girl called Norma Jean once, who found that out the hard way.

Eduardo whistled appreciatively as she unlocked the door of her car.

'Latest model. You must be very rich,' he said. He made it sound like it mattered. His eyes slid slyly towards her left hand and back up again.

She didn't bother telling him her four-year-old Porsche had recently lost a right of way dispute with a truckload of lettuces. Terminally. The Porsche had been parked outside her house. The lettuces had been shortcutting through Chelsea. The Mercedes was a replacement gift from her maternal grandfather, Lord Drumnadrochet, who'd bought it at the Motor Show, characteristically forgetting that he was unable to drive because his licence had been revoked. Rogers, his valet, had flatly refused to step inside such a flashy vehicle, deeming it inconsistent with his own image, never mind that of his employer. 'After all,' as he'd frequently had occasion to remark to Penny, 'your grandfather's not going to last for ever and I have to be thinking of my next position. A nice Rolls, now. Or a Daimler ...' His long face had been wistful.

The smile Penny gave Eduardo was the sort usually called quizzical. 'You too,' she said. 'From what I hear.'

155

'Me?' Pulling down the seatbelt, he grimaced. 'No. My brother. Not me. Not yet.'

She launched them both into the traffic. It wasn't until they were on the motorway that she said: 'This is your first trip to England, I understand.'

He nodded.

'I'm sorry it should have been so tragic an occasion.'

'Yes.' His tone was perfunctory. He stared straight ahead through the windscreen. Glancing at him, she got the full benefit of a profile sharp enough to slice salami.

'You must have been very fond of your stepsister,' she said.

It took him a while to come up with an answer. Then he said: 'I would have to say no.'

'Any particular reason?' Though why, when you got right down to it, should he be? Apart from Ewen, no one seemed to have liked the girl much. And, presumably, Paco. What had Dymphna meant when she said the engagement had been dreamed up by Katrina and him?

'She was . . . strange,' Eduardo said.

'How?'

'She didn't —' He struggled for the right word. 'She didn't react to women. Not at all. Only to men.'

'Sounds like most men I know, only vice versa.'

'In my country, this is very odd. Only whores behave like this. Yet Fiona was a well-brought-up young girl.'

'How did you respond to her?'

His hands spread. 'I am an ordinary guy.' He laughed in a way that made her feel she was about to choke to death on machismo. 'I gave her what she seemed to want.'

I'll bet you did, asshole. 'And Paco?'

'He is different. Perhaps a better person than I am.' Another little laugh. 'Though I don't think Fiona would say so.'

'He's engaged to her, right?'

Eduardo laughed. 'It was one way of dealing with the problem.'

'Problem?'

'Fiona.'

'Is that how you thought of her?' No wonder the girl had been all kinds of mixed up. One half of her family saw her as a sex-crazed nympho. The other as a problem.

'Well.' He spread his hands again. 'It is obvious that my brother did not love her.'

'Why did he want to marry her, then?'

'He did not. But he thought that if he could take her back with him to South America, he would be able to watch her. Keep her out of mischief – is that right?'

'Could be.' Penny digested this information. Of all the darned crummy ideas. Unless Paco was the one Fiona had been in love with. She thought about it. Couldn't be. Hadn't Dymphna said her sister had met the man at a party? Anyway, there would be no reason for them to keep the thing secret. 'How did she get on with your father?' she asked.

For some reason he was bothered by the question. 'I know nothing of that,' he said, his voice unwilling.

'But you must do,' she said. 'Surely. I mean, she spent the summer vacations with her mother, didn't she?'

'Yes,' he said grudgingly. 'But I did not take any notice.'

'You trying to make me believe you were, quote, giving her what she wanted, unquote, but you weren't taking any notice of her?'

'That's not what I mean.'

'What *do* you mean?'

Silence. Plus something heavy. Resentment, was it? Or fear? Would it be more productive to keep pressing him or to stay silent herself? Whichever, she was glad he had, even if only temporarily, abandoned the lady-killer routine. Without it, he seemed reduced, vulnerable, like a snail torn from its shell. There were two things that posers never seemed to grasp. One was that most poses were transparently obvious. The other was that the average citizen, confronted by a transparent pose, takes an immediate dislike to it and an even stronger one to its perpetrator. Which rather defeats the whole object.

There didn't seem to be any percentage in explaining this to him. Instead, she tried to work out what made him tick. The kid's mother dies when he's quite young. He turns to his father, but his father turns to a new woman who tries to take over his mother's role. A couple of cute stepsisters show up. His father goes all out for them, neglects him. His elegant nose is put very much out of joint. Then the father dies and he's left sucking hind tit. And hating the girls? The surrogate mother? The dead father?

Which reminded her. 'They still haven't discovered who killed your father, have they?' she said.

'No. They never will now.'

'I suppose not. It's been six years, hasn't it?'

'Four years last week.'

'Ah.'

'You are detective, yes?'

'Yes.' And right now, I'm trying to detect the significance in what you just said. *They never will now*. If there was any.

'If you had been there, perhaps you would find out who was responsible,' he said.

'Perhaps.'

Perhaps not.

She tried to slot Eduardo into the murderer's place. That involved setting up a map of Norfolk on her internal projector screen. Geography was not her strong point but, even so, once she started thinking about it she came up with something she hadn't hitherto noticed in any but the most peripheral sense. Wrestebury, the Harrison Arms, the good ship *Ecstasy* and the Osman place were all within relatively easy reach of each other. Not only that, she could confidently place Dymphna, Paco, Zachary Osman, Ford-Harrison and Ludovic more or less on the spot, more or less motived and opportunitied, during Fiona's final day. Which did not take account of others, not known, or whose motives were still semi-obscure, who could easily have got there.

Like Ewen Hamilton. So what, if he professed to be crazy about the girl? He certainly had motive enough to kill her. Fiona's promiscuity. The way she'd cheated him over the ring – if that was what had happened. Maybe even a simple desire to surf down the tempestuous waves of passion back into the calm well of habituated love, as represented by Dymphna. It wouldn't be the first time a murderer had tried to divert suspicion from himself by calling in someone to look into a crime he himself had committed. Double bluff. You had to be very sure you'd covered your tracks before you did that. Yet his despair at the loss of Fiona had been genuine, she was sure of that. Nor could she imagine him, even in anger, getting violent enough to kill.

Even so, it would be easy enough to build a case against him. Less so against Eduardo. Yet posit the theory that he – just for example – had been the one to send the fatal and unfound bullet crashing into his father's brain, for whatever motive. Posit too, the fact of Fiona making financial hay from it until he eventually got the opportunity to organise Fiona's final dissolution. It would square with the girl's refusal to go back to her stepfather's

158

house, wouldn't it? If she was blackmailing him, she'd have known she was in danger. Only problem was, Eduardo seemed to be fairly short of ready – or even unready – cash. Could he really have paid up all these years?

OK. So take Dr McIntosh. Maybe Dymphna had it on the nose. Maybe the old brute had come down from Scotland and discovered his daughter in a position close to compromising. Had given her the benefit of his opinion on that and on her character generally. Had received, instead of daughterly compliance, some lip. Had been so enraged that he'd lashed out and inadvertently killed her.

Nice scenario, kid. But unlikely when you remembered that Fiona had been strangled with one of her own stockings. An inadvertent lash was one thing. Removing your daughter's intimate garments to use them as a murder weapon was quite another. Though there was the well-known attitude that doctors had towards their patients. Not so much people as pieces of fly-blown meat. Would that carry over to his own flesh and blood? Possible but improbable.

Trouble was, with a lively imagination, you could pin almost anything on almost anyone. Briefly, she tried to work out how to pin it on President Bush. But perhaps that was going a little too far. Dan Quayle ... ?

'I was in love with her once,' Eduardo said suddenly. 'Or I thought so, anyway.'

'Yes?'

'I wrote to her all the time. My stepmother said I was – uh – besotted.'

Which probably explained all those letters in the bottom of Fiona's bag. Why had she kept them? Just in case they might one day prove useful? They were hardly the stuff of blackmail. 'Uh-huh,' she said. It was one of the most useful sounds in her vocabulary.

'For her it was only – ' Eduardo snapped his fingers suddenly. The noise sounded like a pistol shot in the car ' – only an exercise.'

'In what?'

'Manipulation: you can say that?'

'You certainly can.'

'Yes. Manipulation. To see if she could do it. Do you understand me?'

'I think so.' Even more, she understood Fiona. Or thought

159

she did. Another bastion breached. Another notch on the trigger. Another search for love or approval that was ultimately unfulfilled. 'Why did you stop being in love with her?'

'An association based on sex cannot go very far.' He sounded serious, like his elder brother. It was the first resemblance she had noticed. 'There was nothing between us. Besides, a girl like that ...' She felt rather than saw the contemptuous twist of his lips. The double standard is alive and well and living in any Latin American country you care to name. I, a man, can sleep with any woman I choose and it merely enhances my macho image. You, a woman, can sleep around and you become a slut.'

'Did you resent her?'

'Resent? What is that?'

'Were you upset when she and her mother and sister became part of your family?'

'No. I was glad. We needed to have women in our house.'

Sexist jerk. Penny checked her watch. 'What say we have a drink somewhere?' she said.

'That would be good.'

'Or even lunch. I know a place on the river.'

'Good.'

With only a couple of false turns, Penny got them to the Harrison Arms. Approached by road, it was more imposing, its former origins as a gentleman's residence clearer than when seen from the river. Dark grey stone. Virginia creeper. A fine front door. Still debating the theory that Eduardo could have murdered Fiona after meeting her here, Penny watched him as they walked from the parking lot to the business part of the premises, but he showed no change of expression. Nor any when she ordered a bottle of good Chablis and some smoked salmon sandwiches. The bullying Paul was not in evidence. His semi-wife, as oppressed by his absence as his presence, seemed pleased to see Penny again. Not ecstatic, though.

They sat outside, close to the river. The wine was cool, dryish, perfect under the sun which had emerged from the heavy cloud cover and was now shining strongly. Penny sussed out pretty soon that Eduardo was not a man used to alcohol. By the time he was draining his second glass, he was giggling, hands loose at the end of arms which moved about with abandon.

There were other people lunching in the garden. Families with dogs and children. A couple of elderly yachting pairs, white-haired and navy-clothed. When Mary Laurence brought their

160

sandwiches out to them, Eduardo leaned towards her and put a hand on her arm. 'This is famous detective,' he said. He waved a finger about in roughly Penny's direction. 'Señorita Sherlock Holmes.'

Ms Laurence frowned. 'Sorry?'

'This lady is detective. You must not tell her your secrets.'

'I haven't got any.' The woman set down a platter of granary-bread sandwiches garnished with crisp lettuce and cherry tomatoes. She looked at Penny. 'Are you really a detective?'

'Sort of.'

'I hadn't realised.'

'My brother pays her,' Eduardo said, laughing. 'She will find out who kills my stepsister.'

'This is Fiona McIntosh's stepbrother,' Penny said. 'Her mother married his father.'

Mary Laurence nodded. 'Would you be Paco? Or Eduardo?'

'Eduardo.'

'I've heard about you, from Dymphna.' She turned back to Penny. 'If it's not a rude question, what exactly is your role in this? I mean, the police are investigating the murder, aren't they? They've been here already.'

'Of course. It's just, someone asked me to keep an eye out.'

'And have you done so?'

'You bet.'

'What have you seen?'

'Quite a lot,' said Penny.

For a moment the woman stared at her without speaking. She turned the tray she was carrying so it lay across her body like a shield. 'Poor Fiona,' she said. 'Poor disturbed creature. It was bound to end like this.' She smiled vaguely. Penny watched her as she walked away from them, back into the house.

'That is a sad lady,' Eduardo said. One hand played with the back of his head where the miniature tail of hair hung down over the neck of his tank-top. His eyes gleamed between thickets of black eyelash. 'Like Fiona was sad.' He gave her a touch of the Latin lover. 'I help to make this lady happy, yes? Like I did with Fiona?'

'For heaven's sake ...' Penny was bored by Eduardo. Simplistic views. Shallow imperatives. She told herself to stay cool. Non-judgemental. How could the guy be otherwise when his grasp of English was close to rudimentary? In his own language he was probably as witty as Dorothy Parker, as subtle as Wittgenstein. Oh yeah? And P. W. Botha wants to marry Winnie Mandela.

She wished she'd kept her mouth shut about stopping on the way. She had to get back to London this evening for a BlackAid meeting that was likely to drag on most of the night. She could have done without this. But it was too late now. She bit into a sandwich. Mmm. Good. The bread had been spread with something faintly citrus. Not lemon. Lime, perhaps. Fresh curls of parsley bulged between bread and salmon. The tomatoes were sweet.

A spaniel the colour of mature marmalade suddenly ran across the lawn, starting up the half-dozen ducks who were dozing at the water's edge. They squawked indignantly across the water to the opposite bank and, as they went Eduardo, laughing, aimed an imaginary gun at them. 'Pop, pop.' He lounged across the table at her. His lips were wet. 'I go like Fiona,' he said.

For a moment, Penny could not imagine what he meant. Then she remembered the photograph she had seen earlier. 'Fiona liked to shoot, didn't she?' she said.

'Not just ducks.' Eduardo tapped the side of his head with his finger.

'What else?'

'Men.'

'What are you talking about?' *You drunken bum.*

'My father.'

'Whaaat?'

'Yes.'

'You actually saw Fiona McIntosh shoot your father?'

'No, no.' His smooth-skinned face seemed alarmed. 'I did not mean this.'

'What *did* you mean?'

Obviously he wished he hadn't started it in the first place. Wine trembled against the side of the glass he was holding.

'C'mon, Eduardo. Don't hold out on me. What did you see?'

'Not me,' he muttered. The skin round his eyes had paled so much that he looked like an albino racoon.

'Who? Fiona?'

'Yes.'

'Fiona saw someone shoot your father?'

'Yes.' The sound squeezed from him as though being forced out under pressure. 'I think so. But maybe she tells lies about it.'

'Why didn't she tell the police?'

'What good would be done?' Eduardo lifted his narrow shoulders. 'He was dead.'

'Back up a little,' Penny said. Had she been right? Had there been some connection all along between Fiona's death and this other six-year-old murder, so casually introduced? Was Eduardo as laid back about it as he made out? *Could* he be? 'Are you telling me that Fiona watched someone pull a gun on your old man and she didn't tell anyone about it?'

'Yes. Except a little bit, to me.'

'Why you?' But there was no need to answer that. Whatever relationship the two of them had once had must have been still on-going at the time. Seeing Mary Laurence at the door of the hotel, staring in their direction, she beckoned her over and asked for the bill. Barely glancing at it, she paid up and turned back to Eduardo. 'Did she tell you who it was?'

'No. But . . .'

'But what? Spill it, man. Tell me.'

'I . . .' He looked across the river at the reeds, the flat landscape, the broadly hanging sky. '. . . maybe I might have guessed.'

'Are you going to tell me?'

He shook his head, moving it slowly from side to side. 'I have nothing to tell.'

'Why didn't you go to the cops at the time?'

Eduardo seemed confused. 'The way Fiona told me, it was more sensible not to.'

'Sensible?'

'There might have been many scandals. Very bad for my family. For my stepmother.' He drank rapidly, filling his mouth with wine and gulping it down.

'Come on, Ed. The guy was your own father.'

His mouth was sulky as he said: 'He did not like me. He always liked Paco better. And Fiona said we need not tell anyone. We could punish him ourselves.'

Fiona still at her tricks. And Eduardo cut in on the deal. Was it money again?

Whether it made any difference was hard to figure. If it were even true. They spoke of other things. Of nothing. Penny was doing double overtime, feeding in the new info, computing it. The print-outs were mostly blank. She wanted to know more about the person Fiona said she had seen shooting Rodolfo

Esteban. Eduardo didn't want to tell her. In the end, she decided that he didn't know. He'd said what he'd said to impress rather than to inform.

Another visit to Katrina Esteban seemed on the cards.

They drove away from the pub. It was not until they were turning in at the gates of Wrestebury that Penny asked, 'What's the English course like?' not deeply interested.

Eduardo shrugged. 'It's OK.'

'I suppose they lay on plenty of activities for you. Theatre trips? Discos?'

'Discos?' he said gloomily. 'You are joking. I am the youngest there. The others are all old people. I don't think they are liking Led Zeppelin, things like that.'

'What did you do last Friday, for instance?' she said. *Sooo* casual. He was probably too dumb to take in the fact that she was checking his alibi.

'On Friday we had a big treat. We played a stupid game of words and then some people came in with pipes.'

'Plumbers, do you mean?'

'For dancing.'

'*Bag*pipes?'

'Pipes and drums and a guitar. Then we must dance.'

'Gathering Peascods sort of thing? Sounds like fun.'

'Folk dancing is not fun,' Eduardo said flatly. He brushed his fingers under his chin several times, indicating near nausea.

'Did you dance the entire evening?' Penny asked.

'Oh no. We finished with best treat of all,' he said, heavily sarcastic.

'A medley of English folk songs, I'll bet. And you all got to join in the chorus.'

'A video.'

'Which one?'

'*A Dish Called Fonda*. Something like that. I did not understand anything of it.'

'What do you think of Wrestebury, otherwise?'

'It is not ... luxurious. The house is big, with many ancient pictures and furnitures. But it is without comfort.'

'It costs a lot of money just to keep it going. Let alone making it comfortable.'

'Obviously. Otherwise I should not be learning English there. The man who owns it – your friend? – is very anxious, I think.'

'I think so, too.'

'Is it about money?'

'I hope that's all.' Penny felt depressed. But at least she'd established that Eduardo could hardly have been out strangling Fiona McIntosh if he was unwillingly stepping through antic hays in the former ballroom of Wrestebury. She wished she could laugh at the thought. It ought to have been funny.

Ludo was in the maze. She found him by following the trail of orange flex which snaked between walls of neglected yew until it reached an electric hedge-trimmer. Seeing her, he unplugged the gadget and stuck it into the thick overgrowth.

'I expected you'd be back,' he said.

'Yes.'

He turned away from her, pushing between the hedges towards the heart of the maze. Although they had not been cut for some time, she could tell that someone had been this way recently. She followed him. Once there had been a white bench, a rickety gazebo, a mediocre statue of a nymph. Now the crowding hedges had reduced the little space, as though they had taken a step nearer the middle. What had once been a patch of smooth turf was wild grass, straggled with dandelions, knee-high except for a flattened patch. Most of the gazebo had collapsed in on itself. The nymph had departed. Penny brushed an accumulation of twigs and leaves from the seat and sat down. An empty wine bottle stood underneath the rotting slats. 'It's years since I was last here,' she said.

Ludo stood in front of her. 'This house,' he said. 'This bloody house.'

'What about it?'

'All my life it's been there, dominating everything, eating up the money. I dream about it sometimes. It's like the jaws of hell, swallowing me up, damning me for eternity. I can never get away from it. Never ever.' He stared at the unkempt walls of green which surrounded them. 'We used to come here,' he said.

'You and Fiona?'

'You guessed.'

'I had some help.'

'She was with me here last week.'

'Last Friday?'

'Yes.'

'You picked her up from the Harrison Arms?'

'Yes. After Dymphna had gone.'

'Anyone see you?'

'Probably not. She waited for me along the lane.' He stood looking down at the unkempt grass. She guessed they'd brought a blanket here. Made love. Drunk wine. 'I loved her,' he said.

'Or merely lusted after?'

'That too. God, yes. But it was love first. She was so helpless.' Ludo picked up a twig greened with damp and hurled it into the hedges looming above them.

'Is that why you've never married?'

'Of course.' He groaned. 'How could I? I adored her. I couldn't let her go. But I couldn't marry her. She was sick. Mentally, I mean. She needed some kind of help. I wanted to give it to her. I wanted to give her anything she could ever have wished for. But I had to consider Wrestebury. It couldn't have worked.'

'Why not?'

'It wasn't just the money,' he said. He started to sob. The sound was terrible, a dry painful wrenching of his chest.

'Ludo . . .'

'Why was I born who I was?' he said. His lips had drawn back from his teeth. 'Why do I have to be the one to carry on, to keep it going? I'm never free of it. Never for a moment. I can't ever be at rest. I'm stuck with it all until I die. And after that, my children. If I ever have any.'

'About Fiona . . .'

'When I met Fee, it was like . . . like falling into bed and going to sleep. Someone brought her to a party one Easter at the flat. They were laughing about her, saying you only had to be nice to her and she'd give you everything. I thought that was terribly sad. She was only sixteen then, and when I actually talked to her . . . She was so sad, you know, Pen. So terribly sad. I thought at first she'd stop being, if I could convince her that I loved her enough.'

'You'd never have been able to,' Penny said. 'There wasn't enough love in the world to do that.'

Ludo's face contorted. 'I realised that, after a while. I realised it was all hopeless. All doomed.'

'Why?'

'My – the family position. My father never stopped talking about my ancestors, about the people who built this place, about the family history. The Fairfaxes of Wrestebury.' He spat the words at the shaggy green walls around them.

'And Fiona wouldn't have fitted in?'

'Think about it.'

'Her family was good enough. Nice, upper middle-class girl, same sort of background, same expectations.'

'But . . . unstable. It would only have taken a cross word from me, or a day when she felt depressed and she'd have been in the arms of the nearest available man, looking for approval or affection or whatever it was she hoped she'd find. The milkman, maybe. The vet. What would Amabel have felt?'

'Perhaps less than you think.'

'And there was the money. Always the fucking money. When I get married, it'll have to be to someone with lots of the stuff. Jesus, it's like the Middle Ages. I've got to make an economically sound alliance. It's the only way I can retrieve the family fortunes.' Snuffling, he wiped the back of his hand across his upper lip. 'Funny thing is, she told me just recently that something had happened which meant she'd be coming into quite a bit of money.'

'A legacy, do you mean?'

'I don't think so. More like some means of earning it.'

'But nothing about how?'

'No.'

Penny thought of Fiona's bank books. There was money there. But not enough for Ludo's purposes. She felt suddenly sickened. Was that what the girl had been trying to do, to earn enough to make herself financially viable as a Fairfax wife? Was that why she had cheated and lied and caused so much chaos in so many lives? Was it for love of Ludo that she had consistently sold herself short? Penny shook her head. To thine own self be true. Otherwise thine own self is liable to get totally thrashed. 'It wasn't you who killed her,' she said.

'Oh God. As if I could have. I already told you that.'

'She loved you,' Penny said.

'I hoped so.'

'Yes,' Penny said. She felt around in her bag. She handed him the square of pasteboard she found. 'Here.'

'What's that?'

'Something I think you'd be glad to have.'

He looked down at it. 'Where's this from?'

'She kept it,' Penny said.

'*Always always yours*,' Ludo said. He turned the florist's card around in his fingers. 'It's true, too.' His face creased up with

167

pain. 'I remember sending them. I hardly ever wrote to her, or sent her things. I never took her out much in public. We liked being alone together.'

'And you didn't want to be seen with her, either.'

'A bit of that.' Dropping his head, Ludo breathed through his nose, trying for calm. When he spoke again, his voice sounded high, ready to break. 'She was so ... touching. I hated telling her we had to keep it secret.'

'She went along with it?'

'Yes.' He slammed his hand down on the back of the bench. 'It was the money, really. If I could only have got that bastard Osman somehow, made him liable for my father's losses, it might have been all right.'

No, Penny wanted to say. Just as Fiona could never have been loved enough, so there would never be enough money for Ludo to restore his heritage to a standard that would satisfy. Just as Fiona had been ruined by her father, so the Brigadier had made a burden of his son's life. Ludo was fighting a losing battle, struggling to maintain an outmoded way of living that depended on an outdated social structure. She wasn't even sure you could admire him for his struggle to fulfil ambitions that were so limited. Was it foolhardiness? Was it gallant? All she knew was that because of them he had rejected a girl he loved and maybe thereby caused her death.

She felt drained by the intensity of other peoples' emotions. She wanted out of this situation where values had given place to non-values. Love of money was supposed to be the root of all evil. In this case, it was the need of money that was causing the problem.

'You organised Fiona into the Osman household, didn't you? All that stuff about laundering money through travel agents was a blind, wasn't it?'

'More or less.'

'It was personal, from the start?'

'I'm going to get Zachary Osman,' Ludo said through his teeth. 'I'm going to make him pay, somehow, if it's the last thing I do.'

Perhaps he would, eventually. What he didn't seem to realise was that it wouldn't help him. Not one little bit.

'Oh, Ludo.' Penny stood up. 'And once you'd taken Fiona back to the Harrison Arms, you never saw her again?'

For a moment, even his yellow hair seemed to pale. 'That's right.' He was almost inaudible.

She had an important question still to ask. 'What time did the two of you leave here?'

'I dropped her at the restaurant at about eight. She was meeting someone there.'

'Did she say who?'

'No. She said things were going to work out for us and I wasn't to worry. So I didn't ask who she was meeting. I didn't want to know.'

She watched him still trying to absorb the enormity of death. How long would it take before he appreciated his own part in it? She said nothing. After a while, she turned towards the ragged gap which had once been an archway.

'But, Pen,' he called after her, coming up behind her, touching her shoulder. 'It wasn't the Harrison Arms I took her back to. It was the Owl and the Pussycat.'

* 14 *

'MAN CHARGED WITH FOUR MURDERS', a discreet headline said the following morning. No mention now of nannies. Nor of Fiona McIntosh. Did that mean the police thought someone else was responsible? Or merely that they hadn't yet gotten around to charging the guy with those killings as well?

Penny was beginning to see how the whole thing had gone down. Sitting in post-luncheon sunlight beside the pool in the Chelsea garden, she watched a pair of dragonflies dart like oil-slicks above the wary frogs. With a couple more pieces of information, she might even be able to prove it. She longed to know how much the police had talked to the Estebans. How far they'd got on the McIntosh murder. She didn't have the kind of clout with the local police department that fictional detectives seemed to. She'd never been a cop herself. Never been kicked out of the force for insubordination but maintained a bitter-sweet relationship with the local lieutenant. Never taken over a private investigation agency when its owner dropped dead, nor been a journalist with a guaranteed tap into the nearest cop shop. Never even been a monocled aristocrat with a convenient Chief Inspector as a brother-in-law. Face it. PI-wise, she was a wash-out.

Not that this was 'her' case. She was in it merely because she'd promised Ewen Hamilton. And for the personal satisfaction. For all she knew, the police were already clapping the bracelets on the guilty party. Even so, she intended to stick with it to the end. Whatever that might be.

The only resource she had to rely on was Lady Helena Hurley. Lady H knew everyone, went everywhere, heard everything. She was gossip first, wife second, mother occasionally. And only rarely a lady. If anyone could find out what she wanted to know, it'd be her.

Frogs breathed quietly at the edge of the pond, mottled skins pumping, nervous fingers splayed, prepared for instant getaway should the need arise. If Haricot got his way, it would. He lay elongated on the garden wall, his tail twitching with frustration, inhibited by her presence. For a moment Penny contemplated. She yawned. As she'd expected, she hadn't got to bed until past four that morning. Now it was almost two o'clock in the afternoon. Clouds were pushing across the sky. The weather seemed like it was about to break. Picking up her portable telephone, she dialled her mother's number.

'I want you to find out the whereabouts of someone last Friday evening,' she said.

'Why?'

'It's this new charity I've founded,' Penny said. 'OTO.'

'What's that mean?'

'Occupy the Old. See, it's based on the theory that elderly people live longer if they're kept busy.'

'How sweet you are to think of me.'

'You were the first on my list.'

'And whose whereabouts do you want?'

'Carlos Ramirez.'

There was short wait. 'The new ambassador,' Penny said helpfully. 'Whose reception you didn't go to.'

'What does he have to do with anything?' Lady Helena finally said. Her voice was far from warm.

'Maybe nothing. Call me back, Ma.'

Penny dialled another number. The tones which answered were honey-sweet and female. 'Dr McIntosh's surgery?'

'Good morning to you,' Penny said briskly. 'I'm the Secretary of the Northumberland Area Health Authority.' She had no idea whether such a body existed. The receptionist probably didn't either. 'I've been trying to get hold of Dr McIntosh.'

'He can't speak to you now. He's out on calls.'

Just as well. Penny had nothing to ask him. Merely something to find out. 'I called him last weekend,' she said. 'On the off-chance.'

The voice didn't want to know the off-chance of what. 'Och wail,' it said, 'he'd have been away tae his conference.'

'That explains it. I tried all Friday evening.'

'No wonder ye didna gait him. He'd have been talking tae his colleagues down in London. Or at the Gala Dinner. He was the guest of honourr, no less. Did ye know he's a expairt on women's problems?'

Yeah. I've met a couple of them, Penny thought. 'I'm sorry I missed him.'

The voice sighed. 'The puir man.'

'Why?'

'His daughter was murrdurred last weekend.'

'How dreadful.'

The voice had the scandalised excitement that violence to the person usually brings. At least, when the person is someone else. 'I know. Doctorr had tae identify the body. She was strrangled. Was it something urrgent you wanted?'

'Not really.' Penny was settling into the role now. Grey hairs sprouted. She felt her eyes change colour, her teeth lengthen, her body grow spinsterish. 'I don't want to disturb him at such a time.'

'He's handling it verra wail, considering.'

'Just as a matter of interest, where was the conference held?'

'One of those big hotels they have down there in England, near Hyde Park. He goes every year. He likes that sort of thing. He says it's the best way tae exchange information.' The voice drew another commiserating breath. 'Puir, puir man.'

'I'm really sorry to hear about it,' Penny said. 'I'll ring back some other time.'

She'd learned what she wished to know. If Gordon McIntosh was guest of honour at a Gala Dinner, there was no way he could have got away without being missed. It wouldn't take long to verify his presence. It hardly seemed worth the trouble. If he was going to off his daughter, even by mistake, Friday night would have been the worst possible time for him to do it.

Which left her one other lead. She looked at her watch. Hurry up, Lady H. The newspaper blew about a bit as a breeze caught it. A cold breeze. Autumnal. Summer was ending, no question. She picked up the scattered sheets and folded them. Her eye skimmed the reviews. The *Batman* movie. A ballet company from Madrid. New plays on the South Bank. There was a quarter page ad for the BlackAid spectacular.

Penny stretched. There was so much still to do on it. She faced an imaginary audience and gave them everything she'd got.

' "Layin' in the arms of a steel-drivin' gitah-pickin' man," ' she belted, giving the frogs a start. Then, changing mood, voice breaking: ' "I'm so lonesome now you've left me, gotta heart that's up for grabs." ' Boy, they'd love her. Sequins.

Western-style boots. A green stetson. She might even get to be a star.

Sure she would. Like, how many black C & W singers have *you* ever seen?

There was always heavy metal. Or rap. She could grow herself some dread-locks. Buy a Rasta hair-catcher. But it wasn't the same. If she was going to sing, it had to be those corny sour-sweet songs which mourned lost loves and broken hearts, rooted in some non-existent hicksville full of cheatin' women and gun-totin' men. White ones. Not for her. Sad, really. I may be black, but O! my neck is red. Anyway, that wasn't what the BlackAid thing was all about.

She went slowly into the house. At the end of the hall, a white envelope lay on the mat. She saw it with a downward sink of the spirits. God. She'd have to do something. Get the writer off her back.

'*Call me immediately*,' it said.

Yes. She would. Promise. Soon, anyway.

She stared at the telephone sitting importantly on the leather-topped desk. Also silently. She picked it up and shook it. It rattled. Didn't ring.

Ring, damn you.

In a while she would have to leave again for Norfolk. She wanted her mother's information before she set off. Just to be sure. It occurred to her that she'd never looked further into the voice which had telephoned the Harrison Arms and left a message for Dymphna. It also occurred to her that Dymphna probably knew more about almost everything than either she or Penny had realised. Was it worth calling her? No. By now the cops had picked her up and squeezed her dry.

The telephone rang. 'Yes?' She had it pressed to her ear before the first vibrations had finished.

'Miss Wanawake?'

'Speaking.'

'My name's Sarah Jones and I'm ringing you in connection with the special discount terms that the Easiglide Double Glazing Company is offering to new custom –'

Penny slammed the receiver down before Sarah Jones could even mention the free prize or the unique time-share offer. Dammit. That sort of thing could really piss a person off. Talk about invasion of privacy. If she wanted double-glazing she'd go down to the double-glazing shop, thanks. Not hang about at home on the off-chance someone would call her up to offer a deal.

In front of her, the BlackAid files were open. Instead of getting on with them, she wrote down the suspects she'd come up with in the McIntosh case. Possibilities. Then scored them through.

The names stared up at her. Ewen Hamilton. Dr McIntosh. Katrina Esteban. Dymphna. Ludovic Fairfax. Paul Ford-Harrison. Eduardo Esteban. Theoretically they could all have motives. But they couldn't all have done it. Some had alibis. One or two she just couldn't see in the role of murderer. Which didn't entirely knock them out. Playing hunches was a mug's game. Instinct never had it over fact. Even so, going through the list again she wasn't inclined to readjust it.

Which still left Paco Esteban as a remote, though unlikely possibility. But where would be his motive? The notion that he was prepared to marry Fiona in order to be able to keep her under control, away from other men who might exploit or ill-treat her, had a quixotic gallantry about it that was almost believable. Yet this was the late 1980s. Would any man seriously try to exert such pressure, even in a Central American country? Would any girl submit to it? Why would Fiona go along with such a scheme, especially when she was in love with another man?

For an emerald ring? Which by now was probably taking up space on the shelf of some high-class pawnshop. Money. That's what it came down to. Ludo wanting it. Fiona trying to supply it the only way she knew how. What had she meant by saying that everything was going to come right for her? Dymphna thought she was talking about the job with the Osmans. Penny tapped her teeth with her pen. Much more likely was that she had found the ultimate mark. The patsy who was going to make her eligible in Ludo's eyes at last. The sucker who rather than be hamstrung for the rest of his life had chosen to take hers.

Sad, really. Even if she'd suddenly become heir to the Rockefeller fortunes, Ludo would still never have married her. His position wouldn't have allowed it.

She looked at her suspects again. There was one more good reason to keep Paco on the list. He'd lied about the Scandinavian exhibition. It hadn't opened until the Monday, three days later than he'd said.

She stared again at the phone. Come *on*. She needed to hear what her mother had to say. If her latest hunch was wrong, Paco Esteban was all she had and she didn't really like him for it. Unless both she and Ewen were mistaken. Perhaps Fiona had simply been the victim of the dark impulses which sometimes seize solitary men, sexual in content but rooted deeper. In power, in control, in the pleasure of giving pain.

The telephone chittered. She snatched it up.

'Mother?'

'Yes.'

'Did you get it?'

'Yes.'

'So tell me.'

'Nobody seems to know what he was doing that night. However, his wife is eight months pregnant.'

'And?'

'The aide I spoke to hinted that a man like Carlos has needs. The kind that heavily pregnant women are reluctant to supply.'

'That's gross.'

'Exactly what I hinted back to the aide. I think the poor fellow was rather dismayed. Anyway, the suggestion was that Carlos had gone searching for relief and if everyone knew which side their diplomatic bread was buttered, they wouldn't be asking any questions when he came back.'

'Do we know when that was?'

'Late on Friday night. The aide happened to know because he not only saw him parking his car but had occasion to speak to him about something.'

'So Carlos has no alibi.'

'Not really. Unless he can produce some floozy to say he was with her.'

'Which no doubt he could if he had to. You can buy anything if the price is right.'

'Are you trying to pin something on him?'

'You bet I am.'

'Something serious?'

'Very.'

'You'll be the first who's managed to do so.'

'Good.'

'And even then, he'll probably manage to wriggle out of it.'

'That's not really my business. I just like to establish the truth. Insofar as a concept like truth exists.'

'Penelope, for God's sake be careful. The man is ruthless. I wouldn't be surprised if he carries some kind of weapon.'

'Have you ever seen me doing karate?'

'No.'

'Believe me, Ma. Strong men become as little children when threatened with one of my chops.'

'Have you ever thought of taking a cordon bleu course, dear?'

'Very droll.'

'Seriously, Penny. Take care.'

'Seriously, Mother. I will.'

It was hanging together. All she had to do now was place Carlos Ramirez on the spot and he was nailed. Driving yet again towards the Broads under a rain-spitting sky, she wondered if it would make any difference to him at all. Her mother was right. Carlos probably already had his ass covered. He only had to plead diplomatic immunity and get himself sent home. Chances were, in his own country nobody would even know what he'd done. Thing to do was to keep an eye on developments. As soon as his name came up in the newspaper reports of world events, give his opponent the tip-off. It could be done. Benjamin had connections. And it might prevent yet another self-server getting into power on the bowed backs of his countrymen.

Maybe.

Trouble was, for every tyrant in power, there were fifty wanna-bees standing in line.

Place names whizzed past. Cambridge. Newmarket. Turn-offs to places that, if she took them, would be as full of action and intrigue as any other. People working, dreaming, planning. People isolated, people lonely, people in love. Estate agents, computer technicians, housewives, vicars. All involved in the infinite variety of activities that man dreams up to combat his fear of the dark. Climbing, gardening, smoking, singing, teaching, cooking, making plans.

Mildenhall. Thetford. Subsumed in the names were the individuals who made up the corporate whole. Their busyness. Their lives. Wymondham. Norwich. She passed the turn for the Osmans' house. Further on, the one for Wrestebury. The road not taken, she thought. The one less travelled by. Sooner or later, Ludo would have to give in. Face up to the fact that if you wanted to live in the past, you had to come to terms with the present. Wrestebury had to become self-supporting if he was to hang on to it. And these days there were any number of ways to do it, without turning the place into a zoo. Flower-arranging seminars. Stencilling workshops. Handcrafted furniture. Dried flowers and chutney.

Circling Norwich, she took the road towards the stretch of river she was after. The Owl and the Pussycat was buried deep in the countryside. But not so deep an ace tin-star like P. Wanawake couldn't find it. She hoped. Another thing she hoped was that the guys would have time to get down and bat the breeze a little.

She knew exactly what she hoped for. A positive ID that would put Ramirez across the candles from Fiona last Saturday night. That's all. Anything further would be a bonus. Evidence of harsh words passing between them, for instance. Table banging. Frowns. Or Fiona getting into his car. Diplomatic plates would be great but too much to rely on getting.

The scenario leading up to this final confrontation jerked like a magic lantern through her mind. It would have started when Fiona first realised the effect she had on men. Theoretically, she could do anything with that power if she wanted. Then came the reality. The man coming into her bedroom at night. Taking off his bathrobe. Climbing into her bed with a hard-on. Terrifying her. And the well-brought-up adolescent, not wanting to make a fuss, not knowing what to do except that she mustn't scream if she wasn't to ruin her stepdaddy's prospects. Perhaps he even threatened her. Said he'd kill her if she told anyone. Standard male ploy.

Was this the rape, or near-rape, she'd hinted to her sister about? Or had that been later, on another occasion, with Rodolfo Esteban still looking for political favours? Fiona's own character would have developed by then, distorted by the combined poisons of Nanny Campbell and Dr McIntosh. The earlier incident might even have confirmed Nanny's assessment of her in her own eyes. So that when he tried again, turned on by the sexuality poor Fee couldn't handle, she submitted, feeling she had no option, feeling she was merely acting the way they expected her to, agreeing with them. Slut. Whore. Easy lay. Piece of dirt.

Two years passing. Time to think about what had happened. Time to grow up a little. To harden. Meeting Ludo, perhaps. Falling in love. Then one last holiday in her mother's house. The breakfast-time row, stepdaddy flinging out of the house, the political friends arriving, the shoot.

177

Penny changed down into first gear. Fairly rapidly. A piece of yellow farm equipment driven by a beardless youth had moved out in front of her from an open gate. Behind it came a flat-bed truck piled with steaming manure. On either side spread Norfolk, flat as a mattress. The road was too narrow for her to overtake. She hoped there weren't too many miles to go at this speed.

Yes. The shoot. Accustomed to such things, Fiona would have been there. Dymphna too. They'd have spread out, separated, individuals alone among the trees, watching, listening. Perhaps she'd have been able to see Rodolfo below her, his green hat with the cord band and little feather conspicuous. Still angry, not speaking to his family. Better make that his *black* hat. Green would have been lost among the leaves. And then, coming down a path, rounding a thicket, stepping out from behind a boulder or scrambling up from some dried stream-bed, she'd have seen Carlos Ramirez, and hidden herself where she could keep an eye on him till he went away. She'd have heard the click of a gun being readied for firing, seen her tormentor raise his weapon to his shoulder, followed the direction of his fire, seen the green – *black* – hat jerk, fall, disappear.

Or maybe she hadn't realised until later that he had been aiming at her stepfather. Either way, she'd have remained hidden, probably, breath jerking with terror as the man in the expensive leather boots and imported English tweeds had gone on his way. If he'd seen her, he might have killed her too. As it was, she waited, picked up the ejected cartridge, perhaps, not knowing why, or perhaps already formulating the basis of the blackmail she would use against him.

It had worked, too. For five or six years. Until he'd managed to get himself a posting to England and come looking for her. Had she realised he was out to kill her? Or had she assumed that things would go on as they had been? Maybe she'd even tried to swing one last payola, telling him she'd let him off the hook, promised to give him back the incriminating cartridge in return for a final preemptive payment.

Not bad. One or two holes. Like the gun. Would he have kept the gun all these years? It would have been like a time-bomb, ticking away, ready to explode on him. Unless Fiona had never told him exactly what proof she had to pin the murder on him. He might be rich, but so were the Estebans. Katrina wouldn't easily let a murderer off the hook, especially if he was a rapist as well.

Slowly – far too slowly – she and the manure truck came up to a signpost. She had plenty of time to read it. The farmer's boy ahead was doing about half a mile per hour. Dritton 2 miles, it said. On impulse, she turned. Dritton was where the Harrison Arms was. Maybe she could get roundabout directions to the Owl and the Pussycat from there. It hadn't been very far. At least, not by the river route. The lane was narrow. Trees overhung it, making it into a green tunnel. Behind the hedgerows were fields of corn, a muted gold bloodied with occasional damp poppies.

When she reached it, the parking area for the Harrison Arms was almost empty. She hoped she could get Mary Laurence on her own. With Paul looming, it would be difficult. How the woman stood him ... but what did she know? Just because the guy looked like a bruiser didn't mean he was one. Maybe he was good in bed. Maybe he loved Mary in his own way. Or, more important, needed her. There were all sorts of reasons why a couple might stick together. She didn't have any proof at all that the two of them weren't just as chirpy as a nestful of fledglings.

The Ramirez theory was such a beaut, she'd overlooked Paul's possibilities as a suspect. He had opportunity, after all. And with an active brain like hers, she could easily come up with a motive, if she wanted. She didn't. Not for the moment. Not until she'd checked out Carlos. She went into the hotel and found the bar. Through broad windows she could see the lawns lying passive under the patting rain. It wasn't pouring down yet, but there was a feeling it would any minute now.

Mary Laurence was standing behind the bar, listlessly washing glasses. When she saw Penny she stopped.

'Yes?' she said.

'I wondered if you could give me directions to the Owl and the Pussycat,' Penny said. 'I need to get there as soon as possible.'

The woman put down her tea-towel. 'It's at least forty minutes from here by road. Probably more. They're harvesting now, which means lots of farm traffic clogging up the lanes.'

'Tell me about it,' Penny said, feelingly. 'I was hoping you could give me a short cut or something.'

The woman tore a piece of paper off a yellow pad under the bar and began to write. 'Turn left ... go straight on ... follow the road round,' she murmured. When she had finished, she

179

gave it to Penny, at the same time saying: 'The quickest way is by boat, of course.'

'I'm sure you're right. Just don't happen to have one on me.'

'It'd only take you twenty minutes by river. If you're in a hurry, I suppose you could take one of ours.'

'Could I really?' Penny quickly adopted her St Francis expression, the one that made her look trustworthy and responsible, as though passing birds wouldn't have the slightest hesitation in stopping for a quick spot of R and R on her shoulders.

'I don't see why not. We more or less know you now. And you know Dymphna.'

'Absolutely.'

'When would you bring it back?'

'As soon as I can. I have to get back to London tonight.' It occurred to Penny that she'd been a little hasty here. She could just as easily have rung the Owl and the Pussycat up, heard what they'd got to say in the comfort of her own home, instead of trekking all the way out here. Still, it was too late now.

Ms Laurence took a key from the glittering shelf of booze behind her and came round the bar. 'You can take *Charlotte*,' she said. 'I'll show you. It's in the boathouse.'

'Just a minute.'

Penny went outside to her car. Standing in the carpark, she changed from her jeans into a white track suit. It was wet, the rain persistent. She zipped up her white waterproof and pulled the hood over her head.

Mary Laurence was waiting for her back in the house. The two women walked across the wet grass to a creosoted wooden structure standing astride a cut at right angles to the main channel. The boathouse was full of water-chuckles and darkness. At one end, doors opened on to the river. Mary walked ahead of her along the concrete edging, a black shape against the lighter sky showing through cracks in the wooden siding. As Penny's eyes grew accustomed to the dim light she could make out stuff piled haphazardly: life-jackets, spare outboard motors, oars, water-skis. Canoes hung from the ceiling. A rowboat lay on its side, out of the water. Two motor cruisers rocked on the water, side by side with a small sailing dinghy.

'You're obviously into boating,' Penny said. She tried to conceal her own dislike of it.

'Very much so. We also keep an ocean-going yacht on the East Coast. Not that we do so much, now the girls have grown and gone.' She stooped. 'You shouldn't have any trouble. You do know how to start an outboard motor, do you? And to steer with a tiller?'

'Unfortunately, yes.'

Mary gave Penny the key. 'Here. I'll open the doors for you.'

'Listen. I really appreciate this.'

'Not at all. I imagine you're still looking into that awful business of Fiona.'

'Yes, actually.'

'Getting anywhere?'

Penny nodded. 'I think I've cracked it.'

'Good. That poor girl. Have you told the police what you've found out? Or are you working with them?'

'I'm not. And I haven't told them, not yet. One more piece of information, and I shall, though.'

'Good. It'll be a relief for Fiona's family.' Mary's mouth turned down at the corners. She looked woeful, as though life had dealt her unexpected blows of a cruelty she could not have foreseen. Penny felt sorry for her. She patted her arm.

'It's all right,' she said softly. 'I do know.'

Mary nodded. 'I thought so.' Her voice was equally soft.

Penny stepped down into the little fibreglass craft, a single-cabin river cruiser and very basic. Mary stood on the edge above her. 'Go carefully,' she said. 'The Broads aren't dangerous in any way but it's treacherous weather. You wouldn't want to run aground. I'll open the doors for you.'

Rain had darkened her hair, flattening it against her skull. She wore a green summer skirt with a white blouse tucked into it. Once she had been an attractive woman. She tugged open the river doors and watched as Penny pulled on the starter. The outboard burst into noise. Penny pushed the throttle just beyond neutral, feeling the little boat respond.

'I'll be fine,' she said.

'Say hello for me to Greg and Jeff.'

'Who?'

'The boys at the restaurant.'

'Oh. Sure.'

Waving, Penny swung out into midstream. The wind, not particularly strong, nonetheless caught her amidships and blew the little boat across to the opposite shore. Before she knew what had happened she was nose first into a reed bed. Darn it. She felt an idiot. Carefully she reversed out, swung round, took the wind and headed up-river. Twenty minutes to get there.

It took twenty-nine. The wind was against her. The wind was a pain in the butt, as a matter of fact. It was blowing quite hard. Not only was it blowing straight into a person's eyes, it was also playing merry hell with a person's complexion. Just because a person belonged to a racial minority didn't mean their cheeks didn't chap. She had to steer the whole way through a blur of wind tears. The cold air caught the thin paper nylon of her windcheater and billowed it out so that she looked like an over-inflated balloon.

Tying up at the smooth frontage to the Owl and the Pussycat restaurant, she reflected, not for the first time, how much she disliked boats. She looked at her watch. With any luck, the boys would be gently bitching the time away between the early and the late sitting. Not that Thursday night was usually heavy. But this was holiday time. And they had a reputation.

She found the two of them letting down their hair in a small room behind the bar. Owl put his up again when he saw her. 'Excuse me,' he said, 'this part of the restaurant is strictly private.' Today his glasses were square and lime green. Unless she was mistaken, there was a touch of diamanté at one corner.

Pussycat was more friendly. 'Oh. It's you again. The lady detective.' He waved a glass at her. Gin and tonic, she thought.

Owl seemed affronted. 'Detective? I thought you said she was in the trade.'

'I did. But she's not, are you, dear?'

'Depends what trade you're talking –'

'Anyway, Mary Laurence told us she's a private investigator. Isn't that right?'

'Hundred per cent. And what I'm privately investigating right now is whether you saw this girl here last Friday.' Penny showed them the photograph of Fiona.

'I don't take much notice of girls, personally.' Owl turned to Pussycat. 'Did we see her, or not?'

Pussycat held the photograph at arm's length. 'You tell me, dear. Looks familiar, but you know me.' He glanced at Penny. 'All look like Kylie Minogue, these days. I suppose it's a step up from when they all looked like Princess Di. Couldn't move for royalty in those days, could we, Jeff? Not that I can tell one from another.'

'I've told you before and I'll tell you again,' Owl said, 'You shouldn't go round without your glasses on.'

'So ageing . . .'

'Sooner or later you're going to have a nasty accident.'

'I should be so lucky.' Pussycat gave a titter and a pout. 'Anyway, my nose is too short for specs.'

'Contact lenses . . .'

'All that fiddling about. Worse than diaphragms.'

'What would *you* know about them?'

'You'd be surprised, dear.'

'Boys, please.' Penny tapped the photograph. 'Yes, no or don't know?'

'Last Friday?'

'Yup.'

'I have a feeling she was here,' Owl said. He looked at his partner. 'Wasn't she the one we put at Table Twelve?'

Pussycat frowned, head on one side. 'I do believe she was.' He smoothed his cheek as though rubbing in cold cream. 'Yes. Pretty, too, if you like that sort of thing.'

'Personally, I don't,' said Owl. 'If memory serves, she ordered asparagus, filet mignon, fresh vegetables.'

'*Très* boring,' his partner said.

'I don't want to know what she ate. I want to know who she was with.' Penny wondered whether they knew that the girl in the photograph was dead. No reason why they should. No point telling them.

The two of them looked at each other. 'With?' Pussycat said.

'Yeah.'

'Oh no, dear. You've got it wrong. She wasn't *with* anyone.'

'That's why we remember her. You don't often get girls eating out on their own.'

'How come she was? Stood up, was she?'

'She'd booked a table for one. Some Scots name, if I remember rightly. We don't often have single tables on a Friday night. As a matter of fact, we squeezed in an extra cover for her. See, we normally lay forty-four covers. A singleton costs us money, you know. So what we did was, we brought in a spare table from the –'

'She booked for one?' Penny could hardly believe it. She'd been so certain. Matter of fact, she'd been ready to slip the noose right round Carlos Ramirez' neck and open the trapdoor. 'But she told people she was meeting someone for dinner.'

'*After* dinner,' corrected Owl.

'Clever you, Jeff,' said Pussycat, 'remembering.' He registered pique, provocatively, pushing his lower lip out at his friend and tilting his head on one side.

'How do you know?' Penny said.

'She told me,' said Owl. 'When I brought the bill. Asked me the time because she was meeting someone.'

Darn it. Penny wanted to throw a temper tantrum. Every time she got close to a solution, it slipped away from her. She'd been assuming that Fiona was meeting someone for dinner but thinking back, no one had actually said so. 'And of course you have no idea who?'

'Sorry, dear. Too busy tidying up.'

'What *was* the time?' Pussycat said.

'Just after ten-thirty.' Owl considered. 'Last orders at nine-fifteen, you ought to be through in the dining-room by ten-thirty, ten-forty-five at the latest.'

'We keep country hours down here,' Pussycat said. 'Not like you Lunnon volk.' He seemed to think this witticism memorable. So did his friend. Both of them laughed uproariously.

'The place is like a morgue by eleven, even on Saturday nights,' Owl said finally. His face was still squinched with laughter.

'A morgue.' Fiona might have appreciated the irony of that. 'And you didn't see who she went off with?'

'Sorry, dear. I wrote out the bill, she paid, she went into the hall and waited.'

'Where?'

'By the front door, because I saw her there a few minutes later when I was getting someone's key from the desk.'

'My. We *were* keeping our eyes peeled, weren't we?' Pussycat camped it up a bit, twisting his upper body about.

Penny ignored him. 'What was she doing?'

'Standing there, looking out.'

'Waiting for someone?'

'That's what it looked like to me.'

'We're definitely talking about the same girl here?'

'Yes. That one.' Pussycat's hand touched the photograph. 'She was wearing a rather nice two-piece number. Something silky, a peplum jacket with a belt, over a straight skirt. A splashy design of red and navy flowers on a white background, with touches of green here and there.'

'Plus navy-blue stockings and shoes,' added Owl.

'Don't miss a trick, dear, do you. You're making me quite

jealous,' Pussycat said. 'How do you know they weren't tights?'

'Because, ducky, she was hitching them up as I came through the hall.' Owl arched a plucked eyebrow at Penny. 'You know the way women do. Check their suspenders when they don't realise anyone's watching them.'

Penny did. Fiona McIntosh had been a melody in a minor key. The vignette of her tugging at suspenders was another of the poignant grace-notes that, for Penny, had given her life despite her violent death. Like the blue bear. Like the well-washed panty-girdle. Like the photographs. One of the clichés of murder were the comments after the fact on the ordinariness of the perpetrator. 'Ever so quiet, he was.' 'Didn't look as if he'd hurt a fly.' 'Wouldn't have picked him out in a crowd.' Until some cataclysmic irremediable event occurs, everyone is ordinary. It's the blood on the hands that sets a man apart. It was harder to remember that victims are ordinary people too, right up to the moment when violence occurs.

'Thanks, guys,' Penny said.

The depression of it all was getting to her. Time to jack it all in. She would call Ewen Hamilton in the morning. Give him what she'd got. It was up to him what he did with it. He could pass it on to the police, if he wanted. If *they* wanted. Not that there was much to pass, except some eliminating of suspects. The proof she'd hoped for concerning Ramirez had failed to materialise. Basically, she'd done nothing. Got nowhere. Wasted a week of her life. Next time someone asked her to look into something, she'd simply hang up on them. They wanted a private dick, they could go to the professionals. Personally, she'd had a bellyful. No more. Never again.

She meant it. Definitely.

15

It was cold out here on the water. And dark. At least, not so much dark as lightless. And rapidly getting more so. Grey river, reflecting grey skies. Trees in the rain, leached of colour. Flat fields, flat water. A lack of differentiation between earth and air.

Penny nudged forward, away from the Owl and the Pussycat's narrow wooden jetty. She let the boat float to midstream, put the throttle into gear, pressed the starter button. The outboard kicked into life first time. Was that a good omen? Behind her the river had a bend in it. Ahead, it stretched away undisturbed by any sign of human life. Not surprising, considering the lateness of the hour and the shittiness of the weather. Penny started downstream, keeping her speed ecologically low. It was too dark to see much beyond the fields flattening away on either side into the evening. Summer was on the turn, tamping itself down towards autumn.

She strained into the gloom. Rain fell. Wind blew. Things passed her in the water. Was it weed or fish or floating hair? Probably not. More like an empty beer can, not yet swamped. Or a supermarket carrier, lying just below the surface of the river like an opaque jellyfish. In the heavy dampness, the sound of her motor magnified, almost loud enough to be two instead of one. So much so that she turned and looked over her shoulder. It *was* two instead of one. Another boat had come up behind her. It was larger than hers. She didn't know if they could see her, but she waved anyway. Reach out and touch someone. Boat people were friendly folk. And there were only the two of them on the river. Everyone else was either tied up waiting for the storm to clear, or in the nearest pub. Pubs were bright. Pubs were warm and cheerful. Not like her. There were goosepimples on her arm. Even more of them on her spirits. She'd have given a case of Jack Daniels to be out of there.

She glanced over her shoulder. The other boat was moving

up on her fast. Probably felt about the same as she did. It wasn't a day for river cruising and the sooner they got where they were going, the better. She couldn't see clearly who was at the wheel. In this kind of light the eyes hallucinated. Saw things that weren't there. Missed things that were. She could see yellow oilies, the hood blue-lined and pulled up over a pale face, no individual features.

She moved over. If the guy wanted to overtake, fine. Except he didn't. He stuck to her stern, tailgating. Why would he want to do that? She speeded up. So did he. The river stayed empty. Just the two of them pushing through the choppy water. Little waves slapped harshly at the boat's shell. The wind was trying to work itself up to a howl. Slap. Slap. Howl. Slap. Crack. Slap.

Jesus.

It was difficult to be sure but that sounded exactly like a gun shot. She looked over her shoulder again. Nothing much had changed. The boat behind. The empty sky. The yellow shape at the tiller. It waved at her. Had she imagined the shot? Must have. Because there wasn't anywhere else it could have come from except behind. Yet here the guy was waving at her. She hunched her shoulders a bit. Jerked the boat around. No sense giving him an easy target.

She booted her brain into problem-solving. Suppose she was right. Suppose the guy behind had just taken a shot at her. Who could it be? And why? Paco? Ludovic? Ewen Hamilton? Who knew she was coming here today, apart from Lady Helena? Was it possible that her mother had let something slip to the embassy aide who'd then passed it on to Ramirez? And because he was guilty, Ramirez had jumped into a car and come after her? In that case, where would he have got hold of a boat? Not that that was a big problem up here on the Broads.

Osman. The name jumped at her. She hadn't fully considered him. Not recently. Perhaps she should have. Suppose Fiona, snooping through his papers on Ludo's behalf, had actually stumbled across something incriminating. Had confronted him with it. Had suggested he meet her so they could talk about it. And knowing her, the way she'd let him sleep with her for money, he'd have known she meant blackmail, even if she hadn't said so. His own wife had said he was ruthless. Suppose he'd arrived at the rendezvous with murder in mind, had pretended to go along with it, agreed to her terms. Then, taking her back to the house, had strangled her, made it look as close to a sex crime as he could. Dumped the body near the railway. It was certainly one way to handle the problem.

It was possible. Except that she'd have gone for all the marbles that Osman's ruthlessness was the sort which operated from behind a desk, or at the end of a telephone. To find him out in a small boat on an evening like this simply didn't compute. Besides, how could he have known where she was? Unless he'd followed her from London. She tried to visualise the river in relation to its surroundings. He could, of course, easily have come downstream from his own riverside home, where he might equally easily keep a boat.

So could Ludo, for that matter.

Could either of them possibly have known she was here? What about one of the gays? Mutt and Jeff. *Greg* and Jeff. But why? What in the world could either of them have to do with Fiona? The rain was coming down more heavily, driving right into her eyes so that she had to steer with them screwed up. Visibility was down to a couple of yards. Her wet hands slipped on the tiller and the little craft veered suddenly sideways. As it did so, something hit the water ahead of her, sending up a little plume of spray. She heard another cracking sound. No question that time. Goddammit. The guy behind was actually firing at her.

All the vertebrae in her back shrank. She could feel them, rattling together like dice, reducing her six feet to as near two as was possible. The instinct to take up the smallest amount of space she could made her bend her knees. Her arms tucked themselves against the front of her body. Her head dropped between her shoulders.

In spite of the chill, she was sweating. Fear ran through her limbs, fizzed at wrist and knee, warming her. Whoever the son-of-a-bitch was, he meant business. The kind you didn't want. The kind you turned away from your door. No hawkers or circulars. The phrase jerked through her head like ticker-tape. No hawkers. No circulars. On either side of her the reeds crouched against the wind. Ahead, the river stretched into grey darkness, whipped by rain into a miniature ocean. Thin whitecaps ran across the surface, to peter out against the reed beds. On shore she could see occasional houses with lights on in them. Where the river widened, moored craft bobbed about, clashing against wooden jetties. Halyards snapped at aluminium masts. On either side, the yellowing reeds rustled, encroaching on the water, pushing back the land. She couldn't even nose into the side, leap on shore, make a run for it. She was alone out here. Except for a homicidal maniac.

As she thought this, she saw from the corner of her eye the other boat coming alongside. The figure in the cockpit had the drawstring of its oilskin hood pulled tight so that only a small circle of its face was visible. It took one hand from the wheel and pointed a gun at her. Something short and dark. And lethal. She almost felt the air part as a bullet sped into her head, smashing the bone, scoring its way through delicate brain tissues, causing irreversible damage.

No, she thought. Not yet. What about the BlackAid Gala? What about the photographic exhibition?

Instinctively she dropped to her knees. Not so instinctively, though, that she let go of the tiller. If she landed up in the reed beds, she'd be a sitting duck.

She tried to think why anyone would want to kill her. A body with a hole in it was bound to make the cops start scratching their heads. And bullets could be matched up to the weapons which fired them. It was asking for trouble.

Dragging on the tiller so her boat zigzagged across the river, she felt cold sweat break out at the base of her spine. Fighting to keep away from both the reeds and the other boat, she realised what he was trying to do. Not pierce her. Pierce the fuel tank. With a petrol leak, there'd be inflammable vapour. Another bullet could easily ignite it.

She twisted the wooden tiller sharply to one side. Then back again. The channel was wider here. Plenty of room to manoeuvre. To see that the smallest possible area of the stern was presented as a target. It was a hopeless gesture. The maniac with the gun didn't need to be precise. Sooner or later one of his bullets was going to puncture the tank. Which would mean the end of the line for Wanawake. The big sleep. The long goodbye, The final curtain.

The hell with that. She hadn't even reached the finale of the first act. And everyone knows the opera isn't over until the fat lady sings. So the fat lady better open her mouth and get singing. She jerked back and forth across the water with savage wrenches at the wheel, sending up sprays of water which collapsed into the cockpit on top of her. With the acute physical sensitivity that ODing on adrenalin brings, she was aware of her sodden topsiders, her clammy tracksuit, the cold creep of wetness inside her windcheater, the fear-sweat under her breasts. She could smell mud, varnish, the faint reek of the Elsan, cut grass, motor fuel, a reek of something bitter. In the galley, all hell was breaking loose. Glasses clattered, crockery racketed about in its teak casing, the doors hiding the Calor-gas cylinder under the tiny sink crashed open, slammed shut, opened again. She caught a glimpse of cushions sliding to the floor, the gas container lurching, the heave of the spherical compass, the little gas lamp dancing madly on its hook above the table.

But hang on here. She was losing her mind. The boat had an outboard. *Ergo*, it had no fuel tanks. *Ergo*, the lunatic couldn't be trying to ignite them. So what the hell *was* he doing? She swung the *Charlotte* towards the other boat instead of away. It took the figure in the cockpit by surprise. He turned sharply towards the bank, only at the last minute straightening out and zooming ahead in a frantic effort to escape smashing into the shore. Penny smiled. The fat lady'd come out with an arpeggio or two there, all right. Her own craft rocked in the swell from the other. She thought of turning round. Making for the safe haven of the Owl and the Pussycat like a bat out of hell. Pointless, really. The other boat was much speedier than this one. And if she carried on downstream, she'd have to come to civilisation eventually.

She wondered if she dared take one of the side turnings while the boat ahead went on down the main channel. Decided not to. If it came after her, she could end up running out of river. Something was nagging at her. Apart from the man with the gun, she was aware that she'd seen something else horribly wrong. She kept right behind the boat in front of her, so close that its helmsman couldn't take a pot shot at her. Pot shots.

Memories of the dreadful time she'd crewed for her mother in the Fastnet Race came back to her. Great. Nightmares were just what she needed at this time of personal crisis. On the other hand, the recall had a point to it. She remembered her mother firing off a flare, the coloured light blazing out into the pitch-black night, landing on the raging sea, lighting up the sky.

Though it was obvious the guy had a gun of some kind, the one he was now pointing at her was not a gun at all. At last, not a firearm. Not in the strictest sense of the word. It was a Very pistol. She looked ahead at the back of his yellow oilskin hood. It was hopeless to try and deduce who was under it. She simply didn't have enough data.

Just as well, really. Not making deductions meant she was concentrating on steering. Otherwise she would have smashed into the back of the boat in front when it suddenly stopped as dead as a floating vehicle on a moving body of water can stop. The wrench Penny gave the tiller to avoid an aquatic pile-up nearly dragged her arm out of its socket. The *Charlotte* took the turn sluggishly, catching the wind on its bow, almost not making it. Straddled across the river, it presented a perfect target. The bones in Penny's shoulders felt as though they were made of butter.

Miraculously, he didn't fire at her. The gusting wind had caught the other boat too. It needed both hands on the tiller to avoid being swept into the reeds. Now they were both facing upstream again. With Penny in front. She pushed at the tiller, trying for a 180 degrees turn that would bring them bow to bow. As she came broadside on, the guy lifted the flare pistol and took careful aim into the cockpit. And even as she frantically twisted the boat back, she realised what it was she had noticed without taking in its significance. The wheel on the Calor-gas cylinder was screwed to its highest level. In other words, it was full on. Gas had been leaking the entire time they'd been on this nightmare journey. And Calor gas doesn't disperse like other gases. Being heavier than air, it sinks down to the deck floor and winds up in the bilges, where it builds up in lethal concentrations. All it needs is the tiniest of sparks to ignite. Nobody in their right mind could call a Very flare a tiny spark. The nutter on the other boat was after the loose gas. Like Snow White waiting for Prince Charming, the gas waited for the fiery kiss that would bring it awake.

Oh Jesus. She could practically feel the heat of the blast, the unimaginable pain. The scent of singed hair filled her nose. It would be a quick death, she told herself. Unless the blast merely took off a leg or two and she was left to flop back into the grey water, bleeding, her life's blood making the grey one red. At least there were no sharks. Be thankful for small mercies. No hawkers, either. Desperately she tried to fling the boat around, away from the nozzle of that lethal pistol, far more dangerous to her than any gun could possibly be. Slowly, clumsily, the little craft turned, stopped, carried on. Once again the two boats were bow to bow. If the *Charlotte* had been a speedboat, she might have tried using it like a dodgem car, planing along the surface, nipping between the bank and the other boat to get

191

ahead and out of sight. But it wasn't. She wondered how long this could go on, the two of them slowly circling each other in the darkness. No circulars, she thought. She knew she couldn't keep this up indefinitely. Sooner or later, the flare would find its mark. She could hear a grating sound and something hammering, like a pile-driver. It was her own breath, her own heart.

Above her, slate-coloured clouds feathered heavily across the huge expanse of air. Behind them, she could see the steely sky, dark as ash to port, growing silvery to starboard, towards the open sea. The drumming of rain on her shoulders was already less insistent than ten minutes ago. The clouds were shifting, breaking up. The wind had lessened. The storm was ending.

So was her life. The obvious thing to do was jump overboard and swim for it. But where to? It would be just as easy for him to kill her, using, say, the boathook. Holding her under until she drowned. Or simply to come alongside and let the propellor mangle her. Oh man. Looked like she had a choice between being fried, marinaded or finely chopped. She'd never be able to eat hamburger again.

He must have waited for her. Must have gone aboard while she was inside the Owl and the Pussycat, loosened the tap on the Calor-gas thing, and – of *course* – spilled petrol about, just to make sure. If she'd been a smoker ... Or had lit the little oil lamp ... Jeez. Don't think about it.

She poked her head over the far side and looked over her shoulder, downstream. Only yards away, she could see the lights of the Harrison Arms. If only she could get down there, could scream for help. She wanted Mary Laurence to come running so badly she could almost taste it. Even Paul Harrison-Ford would do. Ahead of her, she could make out something dark in the gloom. A white riding light hung high above the reeds like a star. My God. Someone else was on the river. Someone coming downstream towards them. Above the rain she could hear voices. *A voice.*

'For Christ's sake pull your ruddy finger out, will you? How many times do I have to tell you the boat goes in the opposite direction to the tiller?'

Thank God. A yacht. Fellow humans. Witnesses. With someone around to see what was going on, it looked like she'd been reprieved. If she could survive the next ninety seconds she'd be safe.

Her would-be killer was sliding alongside her now. Any

second now, both cockpits would be parallel. She saw him glance sideways at her, point the Very gun towards her again, look back over his shoulder at the on-coming yacht to make sure it hadn't yet rounded the bend. Without a second look at his victim, still staring backwards downstream, his finger tightened on the trigger. Before it had even found its target he was whipping his boat round and making off downstream towards the oncoming vessel, full speed ahead.

The crimson flare lit up the sky as it arced towards the *Charlotte*, followed by a grey tail of smoke. It landed in the cockpit. There was no sound at first beyond the faint fizz as it burned fiercely against the dark sky, turning the landscape into a watery hell. Then she heard a slow rumble that became a roar and developed instantly into a full-blooded kerr-umph. A fireball leaped from the cabin out into the cockpit. The portholes exploded outwards, allowing more fire to escape and roll upwards over the already rising cabin roof. More fire appeared at the bow, red clouds of it edged in black. The little boat erupted. Pieces of shattered fibreglass were hurled upwards on a fountain of roiling black smoke and spark-littered flame. The cabin roof split in two, the larger piece flying upwards, the smaller smashing into the scarlet-stained reeds. There was a secondary roar as the outboard overheated and the fuel inside it ignited and exploded. Wooden planks, fenders, a blackened fork, half a plastic bucket flung towards the sky, hung suspended against the grey, descended again. A roll of bog paper slowly unfurled in the air, turning to black ash and blowing away downstream as it did so.

The river was suddenly full of debris. The nearby rushes caught fire, flared briefly, were extinguished. On the bow of the yacht, the man with the aquiline nose watched in disbelief, his lips silently forming the words: *Jesus Christ!*, hands clutching a length of rope. In the cockpit, his blond son held both hands to his hair, as though protecting it from the blast. The other boat bobbed alongside, the helmsman staring back. The three of them watched as what remained of the *Charlotte* spun on the surface of the water, burning fiercely despite the rain. Voices drifted towards the charred rubbish.

'What the *hell* happened, Dad?'

'Looks like a gas explosion.'

'Bloody hell.'

'I'd just overtaken ...'

'Gas leak: happens all the time.'

'Dad.'

'What?'

'Where's the crew? I mean, any chance he could still be . . .?'

'Not much.' The tall man turned to the boy. Shock had accentuated the likeness between them. His face was white, the mouth shaking. He looked across at the crew of the other boat, whose face reflected his own horror at what had happened. 'Get out the oars, son. We'd better see what's what. If there's anyone we can help. But don't look at anything too closely, understand?'

The two boats moved slowly towards the flaming litter. The air above it was hot and ashy. 'Can't see anything that looks like . . .' said the father. He didn't want to articulate the word 'body'.

'Wouldn't it be at the bottom of the river?' the other adult said.

'Or in among the reeds,' the boy said. His voice shook.

'Maybe. God. This is awful.'

'It just went off like a bomb.'

'Just like a . . . I can't believe I saw it.'

'Nor me.'

'Better tell someone. The police, I suppose.'

'Yes.'

'You do that,' the aquiline man said. 'We'll hang around till someone comes.' The reeds shivered violently as though a wind had ploughed through them. Churning concentric circles still hurried towards the banks, splashing against the stems. A few birds – mallard, seagulls – had flown up. A heron blundered through the air above their heads. The silence after the roar was unhealthy. They looked at each other again, then the little motor cruiser turned and headed downriver once more.

* 16 *

'Will I still be beautiful when they take off the bandages?' moaned the figure beneath the covers. One hand reached feebly towards the man by the window.

'*Jee*-sus,' he said.

'Give it to me straight.' The figure writhed a bit.

'That's the third time you've asked,' the man said. He didn't sound like he cared a lot. He looked down at the book he was holding. *Anna Karenina*.

'Maybe because I want to know the answer, dummy.'

'For god's sake. You've only got one bandage to take off and that's round your *knee*.'

'Oh right. I remember now.'

'Can't you cut it out? Trying to keep track of these Russian patronymics is making my head ache, without you interrupting all the time.'

The figure in the bed raised itself on one elbow. 'You want headaches? I'll give you headaches. Take a look at this.' It pointed to a criss-cross of plaster on the side of its temple.

The Tolstoy reader groaned loudly. 'No.'

'Why not?'

'Because I looked at it just a couple of minutes ago, that's why. I didn't learn much then and I don't suppose I'd learn anything more if I looked now.'

'All right, then. How about you peel me a grape?'

'How about you feign dead?'

'C'mon, Barnaby. I've never had a grape peeled for me in my entire life.'

Barnaby shut his book. There was a bowl of fruit beside the bed. He pulled a grape off a bunch of them and peeled it. 'This does *not* constitute a precedent.'

'Except if I'm ill again,'

'If you're ever ill again, I shall emigrate to Siberia. You're the lousiest invalid I've ever had to sit by. *Anyone's* ever had to sit by.' Barnaby handed Penny a grape shorn of its skin.

She inspected it. 'Did you take the pips out?'

'I took the goddammed pips out, all right? Now will you please shut up?'

She did. For a while. Then she said: 'I wonder how I'd feel if you killed for me.'

'Never happen. I used to think you were worth swinging for but not any more. Not after five days of non-stop sickroom duty.'

'Get outa here. What about my mom? She's taken her turn.'

'You don't bug her the way you bug me.'

'That's only 'cos I loves you, honeybunch.'

'If you really loved me you'd dry up for five minutes.'

'OK.'

There was another pause. As Penny opened her mouth, Barnaby lifted a hand. 'That was only three minutes. Still got two to go.'

'You think you're pretty cute, don't you?'

He didn't answer.

'Hey, Barnaby,' she said, two minutes later.

'What?'

'You got to admit, huh? Clever stuff, huh?'

'What was?'

'Working out who it was.'

'It'd've been a lot cleverer if you'd worked it out sooner. Like before you got on that damned boat instead of after you'd been blown up.'

'But better late than never, huh?'

'With some people, never is a lot better than late.'

'You're just saying that.' Penny lay back on her pillows and closed her eyes. Her head felt like a water-melon. Same size. Same colour. She wanted to sleep for a month or two. The doctor had talked about concussion in a breezy sort of way. Funny how many doctors seemed to have come straight off the rugger pitch . . .

She'd had two or three seconds – maybe less – to slip over the side of the boat furthest from her assailant before the Very light landed. By the time the boat burst apart, she was only a yard or two away from it. She heard the roar of the rolling flames and felt their heat. The reeds around her exploded into flame as again she ducked below the surface of the river, pushing

196

against their strong roots while struggling deeper in among them. Although she had kept almost entirely submerged, the force of the blast had caught her like a punch in the back. She had been half flung further into the reed bed. Pieces of burning fibreglass fell around her as she burrowed her way into the pale protecting stems. Something hard caught her on the side of the head. A chunk of debris whirled past her and sank hissing underwater. The lurid light from the flare reddened the rustling reed thickets. After a while the huge noise died away and all she could hear was the crackle of flames. People were talking, their voices awed into a graveside monotone.

'Dad,' she heard. 'What in the hell happened?'

She recognised it. The vegetarian teenager with the blond hair. She was safe. Paddling like a dog, she turned in the water towards the sound. People. Rescue. They would take her home. And out of the sky came a splintered piece of wood, flame edging its outlines against the darkness as it fell towards her. She ducked. Too late. One corner smashed against her head. She fell backwards, feeling her eyes turn up and an enveloping black obliterate the scene.

When she came to, the river was silent. She lay half in, half out of the water, buoyed up by the reed stems. She pushed slowly towards the clear channel of the river, terrified in case her movement sounded like what it was: one scared spitless black girl trying to get out of a nasty mess. She couldn't be sure who was out there on the river, floating in the darkness, waiting to finish her off. But the river seemed empty. She could see clearly up and down the waterway, even hear distant voices. She launched herself into the water and swam carefully across to the other side. She followed the line of the bank until the reeds thinned out and gave way to wooden pilings, solid earth. She pulled herself on shore. She was shivering now, shaking uncontrollably, her head aching, her knee throbbing with pain. She touched it and felt the raw flesh where something had burned away her skin. She was in a field. Beyond it, she could see fencing, another field, the indistinct blur of sheep.

It took her ten minutes to find the road. Each time she stumbled over an unevenness in the ground, her knee jarred. The pain in her head was blinding, so severe that twice she vomited. Jagged lines of light danced in front of her eyes. Her whole body was cold. She felt as though she'd been stored in a deep-freeze for several months. Once she'd climbed the fence into the road, she leaned against it, eyes closed, swaying a little. No death had ever seemed as close as the one she had just escaped. She felt in the inside pocket attached to the waistband of her track suit. Her car keys were still there. Tears of relief fell weakly down her cheeks. She wanted to lie down. She wanted to go to sleep and not have to wake up again. She thought of Fiona. She was no nearer a solution to her death than when she started out. So many shoulds. She should have talked to the police. She should have smelled the gas, or guessed what the guy planned. She should never have gotten involved. Never would again. Never. Ever.

By river, the Harrison Arms had been no more than a couple of minutes from where the explosion had taken place. By road, it seemed more like a couple of hundred miles. She could see the tiny diamonds on her watch glinting the hour as she turned into the parking area of the Harrison Arms. 9.30 p.m. Was that all? Decades seemed to have passed since she set off from the Owl and the Pussycat. She opened the door of her car and fished out the jeans and BlackAid sweat-shirt she'd been wearing earlier in the evening. She took off the wet track suit, her sopping panties, bundled them up and threw them into the back of the car.

She couldn't remember when clothes had felt so good, though the struggle to get into them exhausted her. She leaned against the Merc, her heart racing. She pressed both hands to her head, trying to contain the pain inside it. What should she do now? There were half a dozen other cars in the lot. At this stage, she was unlikely to come to harm. Yet some reluctance kept her from running through the doors into the brightness of the hotel lights. Why? She didn't believe in intuition. There had to be a reason. Something half recalled, briefly glimpsed.

If only she could remember. She reached into the back seat and pulled out the tartan rug which lay there. Somewhere in the corner there was a nametape: 'CEDRIC HURLEY 5491'. Her grandfather had taken this same rug off to prep school the year after the Great War. She wrapped it round her, hoping it would warm her. Maybe she'd never be warm again. She thought she was probably in shock. She should be drinking hot sweet tea, shouldn't she? Or lying down with her legs higher than her head. Or something.

Poor Penny. The weak tears started again. She felt in the

pocket of her jeans for a tissue. There weren't any. Only the paper with the directions to the Owl and the Pussycat which Mary Laurence had given her. That recycled paper was too stiff and coarse to use as a tear-blotter. She wiped her face with the back of her hand.

Inside her skull her brain buzzed, like a tired wasp. Recycled what? Recycled *paper*? It set bells ringing somewhere. If she'd gone by road, none of this would have happened. In the light from the lamp over the front door of the hotel she looked at the directions written out for her years and years ago.

And looked again.

Oh, my Lord. Oh Jesus. What had she done? What had she overlooked in her eagerness to produce low-grade fiction about Fiona and the person who had strangled her? She really ought to take up romantic suspense, instead of pretending to be a gumshoe. She'd seen it all so clearly. Elaborated so many theories. Scenes of all her ludicrous theories came back to her. The South American shooting party. The uncontrolled lash of a father's hand. Ludo. Paco. The knuckleless fingers of Paul Harrison-Ford holding a navy-blue stocking.

'*I do know,*' she had said. Idiot. Nerd. And the woman nodding, had answered, '*I thought so.*'

'*I only need one more piece of information before I go to the police,*' she'd said. Thus setting herself up to be the murderer's second victim. Common sense might have indicated that she wouldn't have said that to a person she suspected of being responsible for or even implicated in Fiona's murder. But to the guilty party, common sense probably didn't mean much.

Oh shitaroni. She had held the paper in front of her eyes again. Rain drops spattered, blotching a 'b' here, an 'l' there. She should have looked before. She should have noticed that Mary Laurence's writing exactly matched that on the note she'd found in Fiona's bags.

And then she should have drawn some conclusions.

Driving dangerously back to London, she'd tried to decide what the motivation could have been. That it was Mary Laurence who had wanted to blow her up she had absolutely no doubt. Proving it was something else. She wondered if she was suffering from thickening of the brain cells. It should have been perfectly obvious who the assailant in the other boat was. No one else but Mary could have known she'd be on the river at that time.

The woman must have followed her up-stream and simply waited around the bend until she left the restaurant, first taking the opportunity to sneak aboard the *Charlotte* and unscrew the tap on the gas cylinder.

But why?

Was it on her own account? Or on Paul's? If the latter, what could Fiona possibly know that was worth killing to hide?

Through the pain in her head she went back to her original scenario. The one where Paul forces Fiona to have sex with him and then murders her when she threatens to tell. Remembering those hands, Penny thought it could easily have happened. OK. So the guy comes home. And what? He confesses to his wife – his *would*-be wife? It didn't seem likely. Especially given the way he treats her. All right. Somehow Mary guesses what's happened and being the kind of woman she is, instead of turning him in, she goes all out to protect him. Perhaps helps him to conceal the body.

And then along comes this big black girl, shouting all over the place about being a private detective and then actually saying she only has one more item of info to find out before she gives the lot to the police.

OK. Possible. Plausible even. Except for the fact that Fiona's murderer picked her up from the Owl and the Pussycat. And from all accounts, Fiona was expecting something good to happen when he – or she – did. Something good in Fiona's terms tended to mean money. Sticking with Paul for the minute, that would mean, wouldn't it, that she had something on him. Something blackmailable. But not sex, either forced or under-age. Because the further you got in time from the offender in question, the less clout it had. It might tarnish a reputation but unless it could be proved, it would do little more than that. Was it a killing matter?

Penny wrinkled her nose. It didn't sound right. In the end, it would come down to Fiona's word against his. And reputations. Fiona's wasn't one you'd write home to Mother about. But locally, Paul's was pretty lousy, too.

On the other hand, Dymphna had said he was besotted with Fiona. So how about bringing in the multiple fiancé theory again?

Boy, had she ever been dumb. Lying there in bed, Penny groaned. Immediately Barnaby was standing over her. Not exactly smoothing her brow but definitely in the attitude of one who would smooth should the need arise.

'Are you OK, sweetheart?' he said.

Penny nodded bravely. 'I guess,' she said weakly. 'But . . .'

'What?'

'Would you peel me another grape?'

'Honestl –'

'And take the pips out.'

'Don't push me too far, Pen.'

Peeled grapes sucked. They felt like peeled eyeballs would. Holding the thing in her mouth, Penny thought about Mary Laurence some more. Given the fiancé caper, if the woman had killed Fiona on her own account, her motivation was obvious.

Mary Laurence wants to be Mrs Ford-Harrison. For years she's worked with that object in mind, been a partner in Paul's restaurant, mothered his children, put up with his bullying. Then along comes this chit of a girl, makes eyes at Paul and suddenly the ring from Cartiers is being slipped over *her* finger, not Mary's.

It was all too easy to imagine. Fiona, standing in the hall of the Owl and the Pussycat, waiting for Paul to pick her up and drive her back to the Osmans, as he'd probably done before. Perhaps they had sex together, perhaps he paid her for it, the same way Zachary Osman had. Only this time, when the car pulls up, it's Mary Laurence, with murder in her heart. She'd have seen Fiona earlier in the day, noticed the navy stockings, brought one along with her. It would be a simple matter to remove one of Fiona's after the deed was done, replace the ligature round the by-now-dead girl's neck with her own stocking, take the murder weapon away with her.

Poor Mary, desperate for the spurious security of a married name. Poor Fiona, compulsively whoring in order to live up to the expectations of her. And both of them driven by love for men who weren't worth it.

But who is? Penny looked at Barnaby's red head. Perhaps it was envy she should be feeling, not pity. Certainly she lacked the fine passion that could lead to such cataclysmic events. She had no desire to be Mrs Midas. And though she loved Barnaby, certainly she couldn't imagine circumstances in which she would sell herself to anyone who offered, in order to subsidise his income.

Downstairs the doorbell rang. Barnaby sighed. He put *Anna Karenina* face down on the bed and got up.

Penny's eyes felt as if they needed crowbars to lever up the lids. She decided to leave them shut. 'If that's Miss Ivory,' she said, 'for God's sake don't —'

But she must have dozed off in the middle of the sentence because the next thing she knew, Antonia was sitting beside her, holding her hand.

'I've been trying to get hold of you for days,' she said.

'I know.'

'Didn't you find my notes?'

'Uh —'

'You've been avoiding me, haven't you?'

'How'd you guess?' Briefly Penny debated asking her to peel a grape but decided against it.

'Look here, Penelope. Nobody could call me prejudiced —'

'I could.'

'What?'

'Well, you are.'

'That's absolute nonsense. It's simply that girls of the right calibre from the — uh — ethnic groups never seem to apply to us.'

'Crap.'

'What did you say?'

'You heard.' Penny struggled upwards and forced her eyes open. 'Girls from the — uh — ethnic groups know it would be pointless trying to get into the R.H. Agency. You know as well as I do that you've been operating a one-woman apartheid system for years.'

'Really, Penelope.'

'It's true. And now I've breached it.'

'You don't know what —'

'The Managing Director of UniChem told my mother that those two kids cooked like angels. Best lunches they'd ever had, he said.'

'Really?'

'Yes. They loved all that Afro-Caribbean food. He's bought a whole block of tickets for the BlackAid concert at Wembley and he's taking them along with the entire board of Directors.'

'Amazing,' Antonia said feebly.

'Yeeah.' Penny smiled. She could vaguely hear the frogs in the garden, calling gently to each other. 'The latter half of the twentieth century, Antonia. Gotta log in or drop out.'

She fell asleep.